ALL MEN ARE WORSHIPPERS

STORY OF A WOMAN WHO WAS NO DEITY

DINESH PRASAD

Readomania

Readomania
An imprint of Kurious Kind Media Private Limited
readomania.com
Email: contact@readomania.com
Facebook: facebook.com/iamreadomania
Twitter: twitter.com/iamreadomania
Instagram: iamreadomania

First Published in 2023 by Readomania

Edited by Indrani Ganguly (Managing Editor, Readomania)

ISBN: 978-93-91800-46-8

Typeset in Palatino Linotype by Shine Graphics
Printed in Delhi

For Deepti

…when words made of air tremble, may they find home on paper

…when time made of moments flies, may it catch the sunlight and turn golden

PROLOGUE: 1917
YOU REFUSED TO BE BORN

You knew that if you let the world open on you, you would only have an endless hope to contend with. Frieda, you were the second child. You had refused to be born.

'Frieda refused to be born.' Everyone said. You stubbornly resisted the pressure of the uterus. When her water broke, the Mother was inundated with a powerful tsunami of pain that hit her in tides. She was walking by the river with the foetus clung to the roots of her womb. An unbearable pain was tearing her apart down the middle. She fell into the river debilitated by the pain. She swallowed so much water that it got into your cavities, Frieda. Even today if you stand against the sun, you become translucent, with endless water coursing your organs.

The Gypsy, who was searching for his lost lover with a sunburst on her breast, was on the banks of this river called Narmada. He, of bronze skin and taut muscles, saw the Mother's agony and jumped in. He floated the Mother with his powerful left arm under her lower back and put his right hand inside her vagina and pulled the baby by her hair. Despite all the resistance, you came floating to the surface.

Tenaciously you clenched your soft pink puckered lips and buoyed up easily, refusing to breathe, turning blue. He lifted you, still connected to the Mother through a vascular pink cord and slapped your round, dimpled bottoms. You screamed indignantly as the blood rushed under the surface of the skin on the bottoms marking his finger. The waters rose in the river to lift you up while the Mother drowned.

He then dived to bring the Mother up. He put you on the Mother's breasts and pulled both the tired mother and child to the shore.

The Mother decided she cannot love you. She almost died twice giving birth. A belief, that you will be the cause of her death, made its home in the Mother's heart. And the Mother never did love you, Frieda, for the rest of her life. Every mischief of yours as a child affirmed the Mother's belief and your every submission confirmed the Mother's suspicion.

Your mother was an Anglo-Indian with a British father and an Indian mother, and your father was a Hindu orphan converted to Christianity by the priests in the orphanage. They had met at the bishop's estate where she worked as a housekeeper; and he supervised the gardeners. The Mother had seven daughters: Hannah, Frieda, Sarah, Mara, Tamara, Anna, Noa...all biblical names except yours, Frieda. Each time a child had been born in the family, the English priest would come and randomly open a page in the Bible and announce the name. The parents accepted it gracefully as a blessing. For the second daughter, he had already visited the house three times and you had refused to be born, stuck inside the Mother's cavities like a tumour. When he visited the fourth time, he was without a Bible and so he named you Frieda after his German grandmother, whom he remembered as stubborn, proud, and strict. It was also the first name that came to his mind when he saw you.

Hannah was the eldest and had been the source of your mother's strength. She was four years older than you, Frieda. And the Mother would abandon you in Hannah's care most of the time as she looked after the home, cooking, cleaning, and taking care of a husband, who though docile, demanded her complete attention when he was home. The Mother was pregnant again when you were just three months old. And then came a slew of more babies in the next seven years, all girls.

Frieda, you grew close to Hannah since those early days and this special bond lasted your entire lives even after the arrival of all the other sisters.

The seven sisters were all beautiful, each more than the other. However, Frieda, you had always been different, beginning with your name. Unloved by the Mother, you had grown up to be strong willed and iron hearted.

NOTHING EXCEPT A THOUSAND SILENCES

I, Mahesh, the one who loves you, sit here and tell you stories. It's been weeks. Sometimes I get tired of speaking, but I carry on. Sometimes I wish Alfie was alive. But he never spoke much. Lying here in the casket, you look beautiful. You look translucent. It seems time is turning back on your body. Your hair has started turning back to pepper and salt. Your skin seems fresher. You seem younger.

Every day I put together words like a bouquet and present to you. I hope you get the fragrance of it all. I bring sentences of coloured petals, words connected with long slender stems, pain and joy reduced to the beautiful blooms. Sometimes my sentences become long like the summer days and sometimes my silences are long like beams of light that make patterns of dancing dust particles. Sometimes I am lost in the labyrinth of words engrossed in unravelling memories. I listen to your breathing, and I hear roses. I hold your hands and I feel the power of the Earth. I remember your voice, and mirrors open. Our dreams are held together by the flowers you planted in the garden. You should see, they are in bloom out of season and intense in colour, more than ever.

I, Mahesh, who is water and bones, sit by your casket, and narrate the story written in our lives. I observe the damp cocoon of white silk fabric that holds you and embellish it with words. Only I see the flowers growing from under your body and spilling out of the casket with an ode that only I can hear. They lurk and sway in the twisted loops of my words.

I, Mahesh, who is muscle and diaphragm, hold my breath. I want to know if you can feel my presence. I suffocate holding my breath, but the fragrance of the flowers forces its way in and inflates my lungs. There are butterflies everywhere and they change colour when they sit on your body. They glow like little islands of light.

I, Mahesh, who is cochlea and larynx, sing you the songs that are suffused with the sun, but my voice perhaps does not reach the edge of the slopes of the other world that you are walking into. Your breath is that one flower in my bouquet that if pulled, will undo, and break apart the entire arrangement. Sometimes I kiss words on your lips and push memories in your mouth, but you do not reply. I wait for you to say my name. But nothing. Nothing except thousands of silences, nothing except the tubes that run in and out of you. Nothing but silent drops of the saline fluid being pushed in your veins with a hypnotic rhythm. The room is empty except for your casket, and it comes alive with you in it. All the fables and the fiction that we have become come alive here. Nothing happens except that this story runs around like little dust devils. They have become so entangled that now I do not know real from the imagined. I give you only words, words are all that I can give you now as the beacon to hold on to.

I, Mahesh, who is dermis and epidermis, have carried a strange enduring warmth on my skin since the first time we made love. These days you lie in the casket in the room flooded with sunlight as you had wished. There is fragrance of roses blooming wildly outside your window. Your beauty is boundless. As you lie there, your long thick hair with wanton curls surround your face like clouds surround the sun. It will be like gilded snakes when you will braid them. And if you will make a flat circular bun, it will be like a halo. Then you must decorate it with yellow marigolds and frangipani to make it like something venerable. Smooth, luminous skin that shines as if there is light coursing under it rather than blood in your arteries. When you will open your eyes, they will be bright and scintillating with the spark that glows in your spirit. Your spirit has the power to entice and devour, the spirit that is generous and beautiful. You will look at me like lovers do with a velvety surprise and with shyness full of anticipation. You will smile with the slightly broken tooth in the front that adds relief to your smooth beauty. Your teeth are a string of pearls, perfectly aligned to allure.

You are beautiful.

You will open your lips that are like sublime embers. They scald me to the core when you place them on mine. I, Mahesh Babu, will smoke and singe with those embers till we both burst into flames, flames that will rise to the heavens. Your neck is a porcelain carving, and my fingers will slide down its kind smoothness. It will make the hair on my arms and neck stand up with exhilaration and magic. When I place my cheeks against your breasts, I feel like this life is worth it and brings peace to my soul.

You are beautiful.

The softness of your skin is China silk that ensconces me and fold me in the depths of desire and warmth. Like you did so many times many years ago. The softness of your core still makes me want to fathom the mystery that you are, but which I can never do. When I see the cluster of three light brown moles inside your right thigh, I want to trace my fingers from one to the other and the third. You will resist when I reach the one nearest to your core. I like the feel of your trembling fingers holding my hands. Your feet are like marble, lustrous and white and when you put the red dye in them, my blood races in a tizzy.

You are beautiful.

Frieda, I have always admired the strength of your spirit wrapped in such delicate tendons and sinews. Your strength is like a rock steadfast under the liquid surface of the river. I wonder where you get that from. Maybe the providence that made that rock under the water also made that strength beneath your softness.

You are beautiful.

Even after looks are destroyed by age, desire and lust still lurk behind the creased curtains of skin. I admire the beauty of your peach and olive colour skin. It is still taut, and the rushing blood vessels still flush my desire and write the tome of my longing. I see your clavicle and remember running my fingers on the ridge of the bone. I remember encircling your nipples on the little bumps of the areolas. I remember tracing your midriff from between your breasts to between your legs. I remember the feather touch of my fingertips on your thighs causing a tight squeeze of your toes. I remember that I have been here and here and here as I look at your body. I have left my fingerprints all over your body and your flesh has taken the imprint of mine and has become my flesh. Our desires now live in our memories that refuse to die. They don't disintegrate like flesh and bones. They just remain there. To squat in the synapses of cerebellum and cerebrum. I evaluate the loss and pain we have endured. The truth is, my commitment did not let me tear myself from you. The truth is that the blood of our seven sons kept me bound to you. The truth is that your predicaments continued to create a space for me to be there for you.

I keep talking. You never reply. You lie here swathed in brightness and fragrance with silence around you. In this white room, as the morning sun pours in, you look like an angel swathed in brilliance. It does not matter whether you reply or not. You and I are tied together in our spirit. The world judges us for sin but all we have is the truth. You are full of sorrow and regret at the hand life has played you and this is your revolt against the living. My stories will revive you as they did when we first met. My lips are coloured with them. A kiss on your forehead or a caress on your arm or touch on your cheeks will impale them on your brow. I will tell you the stories that I have not told you yet. I will recount stories where you and I are the protagonists or not. I will tell you of my memories or lack of them as stories. I will tell you of our lives or of the silences that it contained as stories. I will tell you of our lives of what I heard and observed.

So much has happened in the decades that we have been together. Seven sons were born, each special in his own way. Their brides have started coming into the family. Alfie has died trying to save his myna. Badi Bai has died in his grief. Only the Gypsy and I remain. The Gypsy sits outside playing his ektara[1]. Let us talk about our sons, these lights that are our creation.

---

[1] One-string instrument.

THE FIRST BORN

That year the red roses had heart shaped petals. As the Gypsy had predicted. And you said, the roses smell so good, just like jasmine. Badi Bai had understood.

Alfie started putting roses in your room every morning. You would tuck a few roses in your hair. Their fragrance lingered the entire day. The next day when you would put it in the vase by your bedside, Alfie would bring a fresh bunch.

We had stopped meeting. You had decided to stop it. Despite that I went to Sheila Aunty's garden every afternoon. She told me gently to not wait for you. I distracted myself with the session of the Congress that happened in our town. That year was 1939. Our town was buzzing with political activity. The Indian National Congress had its session here to appoint its President. Subhas Chandra Bose was appointed the Congress President despite Gandhi's objections in March. He had won against Sitaramayya, Gandhi's nominee. There was mudslinging in the press, difference in ideologies and the working committee resigned. Bose was the leader without the working committee. He then resigned in April. I was in the audience in the conclaves and meetings those days. It was interesting to see how political work happened and I had started thinking of becoming a primary Congress member.

When the Gypsy visited you, he gave you the herbs and asked you to cook them with your food. You did as he told you. Badi Bai would shadow you incessantly, after all you were pregnant after four years of marriage. Badi Bai dedicated herself completely to you. She would go to the rose bushes and predict the number of new roses that would bloom the next day. And she was always correct.

Hannah visited you every day. She would tell you about the Mother and the Father, about Sarah and her daughters, two of them then. The Mother had not visited you even once after your marriage.

That day, when you asked all the roses to be cut and put in your room, Badi Bai knew. The Gypsy turned up like a premonition. He sat outside and played his ektara. He seemed as if he was on a pilgrimage and had reached a place where his worship will be accepted. You liked to listen to him play and sing. Badi Bai prepared for the day well. Alfie was home and sat in the veranda smoking his pipe and listened to the recently released Shostakovich string Quartet No 1 on his HMV turntable gramophone as it played loudly.

When Badi Bai carried the hot water in, the Gypsy said, 'It's a boy.' And when she came back for the towels and razor-blade, he said, 'I know it's a boy.'

It was April when our first son was born in the room full of red roses as Alfie sat listening to the gramophone. The boy never cried. Badi Bai slapped him on his rosy bottoms and he just squirmed his dimpled bottoms and squished his face, but he did not cry. You got up after giving birth and held him. You cried, and you knew. You took the baby and put him in Alfie's lap and said, 'This light, our firstborn, has come to save our souls!' Alfie felt blessed because the offspring to carry his name forward had arrived.

The first son was so quiet that his presence was hardly registered. He would take his feed and sleep. He would play quietly throwing his arms and legs in the air looking at the ceiling. As he grew up, he became close to Alfie and every time I came, he would go and hide behind him. I had moved in the annexe after his birth. I used to stand and watch them play in the courtyard often.

His big brown eyes did all the talking but I was not the one to decipher that. Alfie did. He was close to him. He did not say a word till he was nine. His first words were for the sixth born.

Remember, when the First Born had grown a fuzz on his chin and wanted to shave at fifteen, Alfie gave him his shaving set. The First Born waited for a few days for me to get him the blades. When he came to the dining table for breakfast, he smelled of pine and cedar. You recognised the smell. 'You smell like daddy used to when we were married.'

The First Born smiled, 'Yes, daddy gave me his aftershave.'

'I didn't know he still had it,' you said, remembering that this was the only thing that you liked about Alfie in those days. The warm smell of cedar and pine, like a forest.

'There used to be a European perfumer in Sadar Bazaar. Daddy used to get it from there. I wonder if the shop still exists,' you had reflected. This was 1954 and in seven years after independence a lot of Europeans had closed shops and moved back to Europe.

That same year, the First Born took up a job at the cinema theatre as an usher. He wanted to add to the family income. He would take the boys to watch the movies whenever a new movie was released. Without tickets. The sons became fans of the movies. There would be Laurel and Hardy, or Charlie Chaplin on Saturday mornings and they would all go well dressed, with whatever money they had to enjoy Coca Cola and popcorn during the movie. The eldest promised to take care of them and he paired them up, the second and the seventh, the third and the sixth and fourth and fifth together. The house would be eerily silent then. Those years, one Sunday a month, you and I went to the cinema. We watched *Aar-Paar, Taxi Driver, Mirza Ghalib, Boot Polish,* and others that I forget. I remember you liked Shyama and Nimmi those years...and you were a fan of Dev Anand.

One day, when he was seventeen, the men who worked with him at the movie theatre took him to a two-story house behind the tamarind trees. The house had a turmeric yellow door. The Narmada flowed through the precipice behind the house. When they knocked on the door, a woman not old and not young, opened the door. They all went in leaving him behind. The woman was beautiful with fair skin and slender frame. 'What do you want?' she asked when she saw him rooted outside. The First Born, not given to speaking much, stood and looked at her.

'Don't stare!' she said. When he could not stop staring, she added, 'You are a strange one!'

When he did not reply, she moved to close the door. 'May I come in?' he stammered.

'Young man, how old are you?' The First Born did not say anything. Then she asked, 'Who is your father? I will tell him about your adventures.' When he said, 'Alfie', she stopped stunned. Then invited him in. 'I am called Your-Highness. I knew your father a long time back. We were close then.' She spoke warmly now.

It was a brothel, which had opened recently.

Nobody had seen the prostitutes behind the turmeric yellow door of that house. Your-Highness had kept them hidden. 'These diamonds are not for public display.' She would say, 'Have you ever seen the Kohinoor?'

Gradually, the First Born became the darling of the prostitutes. When he turned eighteen, he would disappear into that house at night. The First Born did not have any money. He had told you he had found a night job and took your permission. The truth was slightly different, which none of us knew about in the beginning.

Your-Highness would allow him in only because he did not speak much, and he ran errands for her. His access was restricted to the ground floor that had the kitchen and the entertainment room. The bedrooms were upstairs. He had not seen any of the prostitutes, even after having been visiting the brothel for almost two years.

One day, when Your-Highness was busy managing an important client who was excessively inebriated, the First Born had slipped up to the first floor. He entered the room at the far end and sat quietly and watched the commercial art of making love. The prostitute noticed him mid-act and her eyes enlarged, but she continued as she had to focus on her business. She was the oldest one around and was a little more than four years older than the First Born. The man on top of her continued to derive his pleasure. When he came, he howled like a wolf. Even the prostitute went into a spasm like an epileptic. The man left. All this while the First Born sat on the chair in the corner behind her saree. He had had the end of the saree in his hand, and his eyes fixated on the prostitute.

That man spread the word of his ecstasy with the prostitute who went into spasms as she came. It was something that had not happened before. The men of the town flocked to dip in the pool of that salvation. Your-Highness was cunning, and she passed on her other 'daughters' who learnt to fake the epileptic spasm. The business improved tremendously for the house with the yellow door so much so that there would be a long line outside it through the night.

The eldest son would never partake. He would only sit and watch this one particular girl. His presence erupted her passions, and the men experienced divine fiery visions of being pulled back from afterlife. She would lock her eyes to his as she fornicated and the sensations that passed through her were supercharged, accelerated and unabating. It became their secret.

She was beautiful with long wavy hair, large languid eyes filled with visions of the world, pencil thin eyebrows like an archer's bow, thin, slender nose and a mouth that could speak a thousand languages without saying a word. It was this language with no words that became common between them. Whenever she was with a man in passion, her body emitted a milky grey light like moonlight filtered through the thin sheet of clouds. Every curve and every angle became mesmerising and just a kiss would pull a string of stars from the sky and bedazzle the men. They would become astronomers floating in space. It was exhilarating and something much more pleasurable and exhausting than an orgasm. It was an excursion that left them weightless and worn out.

The First Born had fallen in love with the prostitute. She was called Urja.

When he brought her home one morning, you refused to let her enter the house. You could see blemishes of dried semen on her crisp cotton saree in different pastel shades of cream and pink. You knew. She sat outside the door for seven days. The First Born sat with her. You relented when the Gypsy materialised and said she is good for you. She will relieve you one day. You believed him. You were angry and upset but still you agreed. On the condition that she cook and eat separately. Urja agreed. And your First Born said, 'I will cook and eat with her.'

Your home that you so cherished had started dividing. This was our first daughter in law…

THE SECOND SON

When he was conceived a year after the First Son was born, you smelled limestone and chalk all the time. The house had a limestone wash and Badi Bai said, it's the breath of the walls that you smell. His birth was difficult.

When the baby was due, Badi Bai called for the midwife. Hannah had been with you for the past few days. As you shrieked in pain, Alfie sat, holding your hands. I was away for a political rally called by the Congress. It was late in the night amidst the August rains when the midwife came, you said, 'Enough. I cannot push anymore. Let the baby remain inside.' She spoke to you affectionately as she massaged your head. Your pain was searing. She asked you for just one more push. You gritted your teeth and pushed one last time so hard that the capillaries under the skin of your face burst into tiny dots. The midwife dug her hands into you and unscrewed the baby like a bottle cap from your cervix and he came out in one urgent gush. She dipped the linen thread in rum and tied it with a double knot and then cut the cord.

Parents cannot fathom the life of their children when they are born. This was our unfortunate one. Hannah helped the midwife clean him and then put him to your chest.

He grew to be a healthy chatty child, dissolving the silences of the First Born with his chatter. The two played together and were both close to Alfie. They would hop around him in their little feet with 'Daddy this', and 'Daddy that'. It was heart-warming to see such happiness in our house. But it wrenched my heart because I could not call them my own.

Those days, you and I spent the afternoon in your room. We would get only a little more than an hour of togetherness. That was enough for us. One afternoon you woke up drenched in sweat. Startled, you said, 'It was the dream.' In the dream you had seen that as the Second Born was playing with his blocks, a black horse jumped over him and galloped away. You decided it was a bad omen. You were shaking with fear.

That day, at the age of six, the Second Born stopped speaking. Alfie noticed it only the next day and checked if he had a fever or if anything was wrong. You were frantic and asked Alfie to take him to the doctor. There were two younger ones now to look after and you could not go with them. When they were leaving, I decided to go along, and all hell broke loose. He threw a tantrum fit like we had never seen before. He did not want me to accompany them. When Alfie realised that, he said, 'You stay here. I will take him.'

'There is nothing wrong with him physically,' the doctor declared, 'give him time and he will be fine.' You said the black horse of your dream had galloped away with his voice.

So, we had a few years when both the First Born and the Second Born did not speak. The house used to be quiet unlike homes with children. Our home was a scene of quietness with turmoil lurking in shadows. Money was short or non-existent soon after. Alfie had the beginning of his troubles. I was unemployed and anxious. You were my only strength; it was your presence that calmed me. Between Badi Bai and the Gypsy, the older two sons were taken care of. The second son went through a phase of designing holes. It was strange but endearing. The world called him weird. The other children were still young, and we were still stuffing their mouths with language and food and their minds with ideas.

Our second son learned the art of expression from the First Born who taught him by moving his iris, by showing his sclera, by moving his eyeballs, by opening and closing the curtains of his long lashes. Solid words floated from his eyes. He had stopped smiling.

I remember one day after he had stopped speaking, while at the dining table, the second son poked his finger up his nose and hooked a piece of snot. He pulled out the creamishyellow ball. You held his hand as he tried to put it in his mouth and then cleaned his fingers with the napkin. The son looked defiant. He pushed the back of his tongue into the throat and snorted. The snot and mucous filled his mouth and he looked defiantly. He smiled unapologetically challenging you.

Then he would find holes in the house and spend hours looking at different shades of darkness in them. He would look at them from different angles and different expressions of fascination. He beckoned to others to come and see what he had just seen. They would sit with him to unravel the wisdom he saw in those dark deep circular structures. Initially, you would sit with him and say, 'That's enough!' And he would get up and walk away. He reminded you of the time when you had given the box to Hannah for safekeeping, and you had dug holes all over in desperation. You remembered your manic phase and you wanted to help. You wondered about what was causing such desperation.

He then picked a piece of chalk, and the house was full of circles of chalk surrounding the smallest to the largest hole. You cleaned it every day. The next day the chalk circles would be back again like marked open graves. When the box of white chalk finished, he started with the coloured ones. After some time, you stopped cleaning. You were tired all the time with the pregnancy of the fourth son and the care of the third little child. Those days, the house was a piece of art with circles of different colours all over the place, on the floor, on the walls, on the ceilings, on doors and windows, on furniture and cupboards. There was no place left untouched. He had enlisted the support of his other siblings who would scrutinise for the holes and thereafter point them to him to circle it. He worked silently while the other chirped around.

I noticed his dislike for me shrouded in layers of sadness. He would avoid my presence and put his hands over his ears when I spoke. When not circling the holes, he would sit with Alfie or sleep, sometimes his one hand would be on Alfie's, sometimes a leg on his lap, sometimes his head jutted on Alfie's side and sometimes he would sleep over Alfie's chest.

He had only learned the alphabets when he stopped speaking. He refused to go to school. He preferred the room he shared with his two brothers. You had tried many things to break his spell. You were firm that it was a spell. You spoke to the pastors and the fakirs and the soothsayers and the astrologers and everyone and anyone who could help. He would hide when he saw any of those around the house. Not because he was scared. But because he simply did not want to speak.

That time, Alfie was in a bad state and went walking all over the town. He had taken up the responsibility of looking after Alfie. He would hold his hand and take him to the bath. He would pour water on him and lather him with soap and wash him. He would wipe him and help him put on clean clothes. The bond between the two older sons and Alfie made me jealous sometimes. But what could I do?

I cannot forget the faces of the eldest and the second one, when one evening in the kitchen you were telling them, 'Both of you are now big and handsome. You don't need milk anymore.' We had a large window in the kitchen that opened into the courtyard. I was passing there to go up to my room. I stopped.

'I like milk,' the second one, now two and a half, said innocently. While the eldest looked at your face with big eyes not saying anything.

'I am grown up. Do I drink milk? Only small babies do.' You said.

'But he is a little boy…see, he is only this tall.' The first one, who was just a little over four, said. The second son just looked at your teary eyes with his hands at his back and feet squirming. Then the First Born put his right arm around the shoulders of the second son and dug in the pockets of his loose half pants to pull out marbles. He flicked the marbles in his hands. The second son's eyes brightened at this, '*Kancha*[1]!' he said. The eldest took him away to play.

I saw you stand up and wipe your tears. You were drinking water from the *surahi*[2] when I knocked at the kitchen door.

'Why can't the children have milk?' I asked.

'I had to stop getting the milk.' You informed.

'Why? Let me speak to milk man. Can't we increase the quantity?' I said, not understanding the situation.

'Where is the money, Mahesh Babu?' You seemed exasperated.

'We will manage. I will find a way.' I said.

'I don't want to run credit. The boys will be fine.' You said with a finality.

I took your two fingers in my hand and stood there. Some moments passed. Then you offered me water and we were back in the real world.

We were testing time as to how bad it could become.

I did not tell you, but I mortgaged my trucks that I had as a contractor to the army. They were being rented out to other contractors, after I had stopped supplying to the army. The money from renting them was not enough but mortgaging them brought in money immediately. It helped run the household for a few months and then I lost them entirely as I could not pay the creditors. We had already sold the car just before the second son was delivered. Then other things went. It was always either the Gypsy or Badi Bai who were sent to the pawn brokers.

Those were immensely sad days. But we had each other. And the children. And Alfie and Badi Bai.

---

[1] Marble.

[2] Thin-necked clay pot to store water.

The two elder sons would take Alfie for a walk. The Second Born would keep his eyes to the ground and he would be anxious and disturbed by all the holes he saw. He would circle them with a stick, or his toe and their walk would become a walk for the discovery of holes. You had instructed the First Born to take care of the Second Born when they took Alfie out. You said he needed fresh air and company. Children in the neighbourhood would not play with them due to the spectacle Alfie created. They would make fun of the three.

She made friends with him when he was ten years old. Her name was Jamuna and she was a year older than the Second Born. She came on the pretext of playing with the fifth son who was a toddler then. She was a petite, bright-eyed girl, who had moved into the neighbourhood, in the house that had a Jamun tree. Jamuna was one of five siblings and I am not sure where she stood in the order of those five. Her father worked in the State Bank. She liked the art that our house had become, and she enjoyed circling the holes with him. She also took upon herself to teach him. She would come and bring her books and do her homework with him. She would read him stories and poetry. And he would sit and listen to her. There was no girl in our house, and he seemed fascinated by her.

She learnt his language after some time. They would sit quietly and communicate the world of thoughts and ideas without speaking. She would burst into laughter sometimes and that was the only sign of their existence, else they had camouflaged themselves in the silence that he manufactured so eloquently.

One day, she had eaten a lot of jamuns. When she came her lips and mouth were coloured with the juices of jamun. It unsettled him. All he could see was the dark, plum coloured hole of her mouth. He was distracted while she was there. When it was time for her to leave, he held her face by the chin, and drew a circle around her mouth with his index finger. She felt sensations that consequently scared her. He was strong at fifteen and she slipped and ran away from under his hands. I saw her running and went to see what had happened. He went into a rage when he saw me. I had not anticipated such a reaction from him. I extended my arms to hold him, and he pushed me and shouted, 'Get out!'

'Calm down!' I said. He looked at me with fire in his eyes. And I realised that he had spoken.

I smiled and said, 'It is good to hear your voice! You can speak.'

And then he told me, 'It's better not to speak in this house. You have been betraying my father. I have seen you and Mummy.' I was stunned that I was the reason for his malaise. I could not explain my relationship with you to him and that he was my blood. I stood there helpless and speechless.

'I stopped speaking the first time I saw you both in her bedroom naked,' he said, eyes full of tears and body shivering with fury. I walked away embarrassed.

In the meantime, Jamuna did not come for some time and yet he would go and sit and read by the door. Absorbed as he seemed, he was waiting for her. Many days passed.

The boys were growing with summers in their blood and warmth in their loins. And when that happens sometimes, it goes to their head. A memory is seared in my mind. The spoken words were frequently lacking in our lives then. It was during teatime. The elder boys had grown to have tea while just the two younger ones were still served milk. As everyone was seated in their places, I sat at the head of the table. 'That's daddy's place,' the second son, who was about sixteen then, said firmly, with a straight face. Alfie confined himself to his room in those days.

'You can sit in my place, and I will get another chair.' The youngest one said. He loved me the most. You did not say anything. I just complied. I sat on last son's chair and held him in my lap.

Soon after that, one night when the second son was late, you stood outside waiting for him. When he came past midnight, you smelled alcohol on his breath. You let him in and did not say anything because you were collecting the pieces of your broken heart. The next day was a normal day. In the evening, Badi Bai realised that you hadn't eaten. When she served you dinner after everyone had eaten, you went to your room and closed the door. But you did check if all the sons were home. The next day also the household was normal, but you did not eat. The third day it started showing on your face. Badi Bai came and told me. You were sad, but you did not say anything when I asked what was wrong. The sixth son said, she is sad. The third son said, she is on satyagraha. The seventh son, who was six then, ran around the house announcing, 'Mummy is on satyagraha. Mummy is on satyagraha.' When Badi Bai told Alfie, he came and pulled a chair and sat beside you, quiet and stoic, looking at his hands.

It was a giddy house in the evening after running and burning through the day. The boys playing and laughing or doing their own things. Alfie was quiet as always. I was as always trying to be resourceful financially and being a bit successful with it now. After the ruckus of the seventh son's announcement, your satyagraha had acquired a gravitas, and brittle tension had settled in the house.

And it needed to be calmed.

When Badi Bai served you dinner the third day, everyone gathered around. When you started walking away, the second son said, 'Mummy, I am sorry.'

You looked at him with fire in your eyes. 'That better be the last time.' And then you turned to the rest of the boys, 'If ever anyone of you touch alcohol in your life, I will kill myself and make you regret it for the rest of your lives. I nearly lost my husband to it and I am not willing to lose you.'

Badi Bai intervened and said, 'All of you, go kiss Mummy and promise her that you will not drink alcohol in your life.'

The First Born kissed you and hugged you and said, 'I promise only if you eat your dinner,' and you melted. Then each of them said the same thing one after the other. You gathered them all and hugged them while Badi Bai, Alfie and I stood and watched.

Your 'Mummy Satyagraha' was good. It was the first episode. But you would use it many times, sometimes to get them to agree, other times to discipline them and yet other times to show disagreement.

When Jamuna came back one afternoon soon after, her mouth was smeared with jamun again. He was agitated and he lifted his hand. She did not sit but beckoned him to follow and sat under the tamarind tree at the back of the house. She held his hand as he stood towering over her anxious and shaking. She pulled his face and kissed him on the lips. Then she laughed. He smiled for the first time in ten years. She looked like a monkey with jamun-stained teeth. Still towering over her, he tentatively traced the circle around her mouth with the index finger of his right hand.

I saw them.

Jamuna had become a part of our home. She enjoyed spending time with you in the kitchen, Frieda, and I saw affection in your interactions. She was respectful towards Alfie and towards me. Badi Bai doted on her and said, 'You are the daughter of this house. You were born in a wrong home.' And Jamuna would smile and hug her. 'Badi Aunty, you are right. I will pack my bags and move here for forever.' The Second Born would broaden his smile at that.

She came into our home two years later.

Her parents decided to get her married. The Second Born was broken and devasted when she came to tell him that. Her parents would not marry her to a depressive mute who was a magnet for dark holes. He could not change that. He said, 'I will desist from circling the holes, if you marry me. Your parents will have no reason to complain then.'

The day she turned nineteen, she packed one bag and came and said to Badi Bai, 'I am keeping my promise to you.' So Badi Bai took them to the temple and got them married. Then she hid her in her room while her parents searched for her. There was a police complaint too. They came to our house and did not find Jamuna because she was locked in a rattan box in Badi Bai's room. Police came to question us every day. In the meantime, I got their marriage registered. I knew people in my role as an elected municipal councillor. Then we presented the evidence and legality of his marriage, and the police dropped the case. Jamuna's parents moved out from the neighbourhood after they found out that she had married the Second Born without their consent. They did not want to see their humiliation rubbed in their faces everyday by staying there.

Jamuna loved you and our family.

THE THIRD SON

What do I say about the third born? He was born two years after the Second Son. Frieda, he was the most sensitive one and now he is with a book in his hand always. He was a congenial child. When he was in your womb, you fed fennel to the caterpillars, and you smelled fennel in roses. Sweet, aromatic, earthy.

He loved you the most. He spent time with you in the kitchen and you would give him a dough ball to roll while you and Badi Bai made chapatis or parathas for the family. Badi Bai would upturn a brass thali and give him a rolling pin. He would make shapes and seek your approval and both you and Badi Bai gave him appreciation and stories. This one looks like a bear…and the story of three little bears would be narrated. This one looks like a map of India and the story of Rani of Jhansi would be narrated. This one looks like a monkey and the story Hanuman would be narrated.

He would help you with your bouquet making. He would sit and watch you pick, cut, and arrange the flowers. He would give his opinion like put the red one there or make one with all the pink carnations and you would listen to him. When small he would walk around like a cherub decked in flowers helping the second one draw circles.

When it was December, you took Alfie's shirts and trousers to be refitted into children's clothes for Christmas. The third son had been born and was three months old. You went to the American Charity after dark to get clothes for the children. There were never clothes that matched or fitted perfectly. Badi Bai and you would painstakingly work on those to fit them. I made balls out of rags and cuttings and rolled them up tightly together for them to play cricket. I made the slings from the V-branches of the guava tree. When the eldest had outgrown his shoes, we couldn't buy new ones for some time. You cut your cotton sarees to make diapers for the newborn.

Sometimes in the evenings I would get unsold bread from the bakery. I knew the baker from my early days as the contractor of army supply. Times were bad for us, and this helped sometimes. Most of the times the bread was good, and you would steam it and we would eat it with soup made from vegetables from the garden and eggs from the chickens we kept. Sometimes, the bread would be mouldy, especially in the monsoons. There would be black veins that Badi Bai would pinch out and heat it to crisp on the pan before serving with a pâté made at home. Once as the children sat, the third son noticed some mould vein and asked, 'What is this?'

'Don't eat that. That thing will grow inside you if you eat. Take another one,' Badi Bai said.

'Like a watermelon seed does if you eat it,' the First Born, then twelve, added.

Do you remember, Frieda, we had to speak with him so many times to quell his worries? In the morning he came over and showed you his blue vein and said, the mould is growing inside me. And you asked, why do you think that? He said, because I ate a mouldy bread yesterday and now it has grown inside my intestines. See, you can see it under my skin. It will burst open anytime. He was very worried.

You said, 'Let us see.' And then you showed him your blue veins and said, 'But I did not eat any mouldy bread. I wonder why it is blue under my skin.' I was passing by the veranda where you two sat, you called out to me and asked, 'Uncle, show us your arms. Do you have anything blue under your skin?' Even I had the blue veins. And then we saw all in the family who had blue veins and who did not. Only the Gypsy did not have blue veins. His skin was too burnt by the sun to show anything under it.

The third son waited for many days for one of us with blue veins to burst open with all the mould pouring out. When no one burst open, he forgot about it.

As he grew up, and other children came, he would help you change the diapers and help with small activities around the house. And Badi Bai would squat and gather him in a hug close to her bosom and he would disappear in the folds of her saree. 'Alfie never gave me the pleasure of a hug when I brought him up. You are a darling.' She would say. He would come out of the smothering hugs flushed and feeling good.

Alfie's condition had worsened after the third son. My political work yielded no income. You sold what little gold you had and got two rooms put up on the terrace. Because there were three children, you had started taking boarders in the rooms on the terrace. That brought us some money. The rest of the income came from your flower art. When the weddings happened, we had some money but when the wedding season was over, we were back to the hand-to-mouth existence.

The Third Born read a lot and told stories to all his brothers at the dinner table. After he had recovered from alcoholism,, Alfie would sit and listen quietly. The day Alfie asked for an additional chapati or more rice, you knew that he was enjoying the story and prolonging his stay at the table. You would look at Badi Bai and it was a communication she understood well. She would go and take time to make the additional chapati so that Alfie could stay longer with his sons. I brought him a couple of books from the public library. He would say, 'Uncle, I have finished this one. Can you get me Dostoevsky's *The Idiot* next time? Or Premchand's *Godaan* or Nehru's *Discovery of India*?' And I borrowed books for him.

The books absorbed his gaze. Little did we know that it was his way of hiding from the strangeness of his family.

Now that you rest in this room, Frieda, let me read from the pages I found in his room. This is him speaking through his words to you, to me and to everyone.

'These are the writings of a young man, who is neither an adult nor a child. There is no fixed date and no fixed place of writing this. I am everywhere and nowhere, careless about things I should care about, careful about things I should not care about. Aimless, troubled, and full of passion. My heart is prey to a strange waywardness that furthermore defies norms and rules. Even my mother's. Or my own.

When the evening sun casts last benevolence on the first dead leaves and last of the roses, the strangeness of the world sets my heart afire. A single desire gets caught in the web of my brain like clouds in the branches.

It is the same house that belongs to Mummy. Like everything else here, like all the men here. All the men are worshippers here. Only Badi Bai does not belong to her. She had a world of her own before my mother arrived and that world has enveloped my mother's, and their worlds exist in harmony simultaneously and never collide. I have made friends with the men upstairs, who are studying for priesthood at the theological college. They live in the two rooms Mummy has rented to them. I know their bedrooms of ochre and purple and magenta and yellow colours with ocean blue window frames and their Bibles pickled in sunshine. They know my agonising dire situation. I remember their very dark rooms full of religious books behind the summer shuttered windows. There was a servant girl in a floral saree dusting the books. Pure, noble, and charming. She pinched my arm.

I rolled the skin of her abdomen in my fingers. Her mouth battered mine like high-tide waves hammering away at the shore. My fingers clawing at her soft flesh to find a grip. I was drowning but I remember her dark red panties under the petticoat. Then utter despair. The walls melted and absorbed her, and warm June breeze slapped my face while the yellow moon looked at me sadly.

What the body does, the mind justifies and what the soul does, the body magnifies. I want glances that heat up my shoulders. The recognition of the beginning was when Badi Bai gathered me in her arms, my cheeks pressed to her soft warm bosoms and the pulses of soft beating of her heart gently caressing my face.

One of the young priests-to-be, had a visitor who came to seek his teachings. I went up and she was all alone. I saw her sitting on the bed naked. There were no lights on. Only a rectangle of yellow light from the streetlight fell on the bed and climbed up her buttocks and illuminated the dimples of her lower back. She offered herself completely with a husky voice and bald pate. I could not see her face. An anguish engulfed me as I tried to recollect her face. A deep melancholic anguish when I touched her on her chest. I pressed my lips to her shoulders and slipped across her body to the terracotta floor. As my cheeks touched the cool floor, the young woman disappeared. I began to cry. I extended my hands and touched the dust under the bed. I was exhausted and yet the tears continued.

When the rhythm of the day normalised, I went to the priest-to-be and asked him, "Where has she gone?" He replied, "To yesterday." This was a benediction that never won. And I suffer and cry when I remember the yellow patch of light washing her lower back.

Then came the one with her handbag full of dreams. She came like a black curve on a white canvas, projecting beneath the silk of unknown meaning, the arsenals of beautiful, strange breasts. She looked from behind the lattice of eyelashes with eyes that sparkled like diamonds. Feathers grew on my genitals. She ushered me to the Chevrolet Deluxe upholstered with roses, white and veined like the sclera of her eyes. In the night, tuned like a piano, she held my hand. We arched our necks and split the weight of the light that fell from the streetlamp. Its bright light illuminated my right and a deep dark night on my left. She removed her fur with the colour of sparks. Clinging to the gossamer thread of desire, I loved her like the first man loved the first woman. The veins of the roses had turned red with our blood. And then the woman sketched herself backwards till she disappeared. My lungs had turned to coral and tears flooded my eyes. The time was suspended in the swing between my eyes.

Between the sinusoidal steep ascent and descent of desire, the endless curve of wanting was a celestial score inscribed disharmoniously across the lines of my veins.

Must I think that beauty is bitter and man vulnerable or that beauty is a necessity and man's desire uncouth?

I cruise each day with hope driving my heart into the flesh of a beloved. With the stealth of a beast, I leap at happiness only to lose it. The autumn infuses lead in the heart. I think my blood has rusted and my soul is charred. I have inherited brown-black eyes, more brown than black, but I know not where I get them from. Daddy's are blue like the sky and Mummy's are black like the night. Mahesh Uncle has light brown eyes like the colour of dried leaves in autumn. From where do I get this sacrilege of love, this lust? My lust is honest as it runs under my skin like a beggar's poverty runs over his skin and it distresses and disgusts me. Who made my mind so hallucinatory? I am willing to pay with the warmth of my body to know the way. I remember the history of my family from what Mummy has ever told us. I know there is more. Like thousand profane enchantments at Christ's body in Simon of Cyrene's grave. Like what people say in whispers when they see us.

I have a pagan spirit and I have made my folklore my religion. Pastors, teachers, priests-to-be, masters will not instil in me a sense of faith. Not even Mummy. I will never be Christian enough though I am baptised. I am an animal who seeks the warmth and fellowship of women but finds none. It's a burning. Dance, dance, dance of the flames. A burning. I have done no wrong. Yet.

What if this perdition is everlasting? I do not believe in God's twin, Satan too. But I am willing to lean on strong spells and illusionary charms, false *itrs* and perfumed oils, shlokas and nursery rhymes to clean this hellfire that runs in my body. My skin is drying up and becoming almost like a desert. I am thirsty for flesh. The phantoms of desire are real. It's the story of my life.'

This is one of the notes from his notebook that he carried then and is now abandoned. I have kept it and I read from it sometimes like I am reading to you now.

When the third son turned nineteen, he decided to take a job as a teacher outside town. He announced, 'I am taking a job in Bombay. I will continue my studies while teaching.' You told him that the older two were working in our own town with the Army production units. Why can't you do the same? And he said, 'Mummy, I don't want to become an industrial labourer.' And you said that your brothers will become foremen and managers one day and that is good. He was adamant and went when the wind and the rains played their furious monsoon games.

The day he left; you stopped eating again. This time you did not eat for seven days and when you were admitted to the hospital with a saline drip, the third son came back. He held your hands and said, 'Mummy, give up your hunger strike. I am back.' And I thought that was another successful satyagraha.

When you were better, you called all your sons to the hospital. You said, 'I have decided that you will all stay together. Promise me. Come what may, whether I live or die, you will all live together. That will be your strength and defence against the world!' None of them challenged you and when you were discharged from the hospital, you started planning how you would organise that.

The past cannot be rescued, and future cannot be fathomed! All you hold and look at is now! And with time, the past seems to shrink but the future seems magnanimous. When our days of happiness are over, we wish from the bottom of our hearts that our children be happy...more than we have ever been.

We wish they have perfect love and an accomplished life. We wish the hand of God upon them, and we want to hide and wrestle the devil away from them. But is that possible...the devil mutates, and so does God, and thereafter lives of children adapt to these mutations...only we are left as spectators and wishing...just wishing happiness. Forever. For them.

Frieda, do you remember the 1965 war and the night curfews? We had to shutter the windows for the evenings and nights when the sirens went off. It was late August, and the rain was falling like lances, stabbing every soul. He was twenty, with shoulder length curly unkempt hair, bespectacled with a calm intelligent demeanour, and it was then that the widow arrived smelling of white lilies.

He used to go for walks in the night when the heat would rise in his loins. It was midnight when she emerged from the darkness. Her name was Maya. She began to speak of her widowhood and that her husband had died in the riots of 1962 and those wars made her claustrophobic in the house and that she walked in the darkness when the curfew starts. She was wearing black. Her skin was dark, and she blended in the night. She was attracted to the third son and the darkness and the sirens and the silence that followed filled her with a certainty. She folded her black umbrella. She removed her clothes, the cotton blouse and a chiffon saree. With one hand she pulled the cord of her petticoat and her black brassiere. These were the remnants of her mourning. He heard her sighs and her measured pauses and each of her gestures imagined in the darkness excited him. Finally, she removed the black panties and stood with her naked glistening body and giddy excitement. She then undressed him which was not much since he was only wearing a t-shirt and shorts. And without the vulgarity of remorse, she disintegrated the inexperience of the third son action by action, till they came together with a guttural moan in the rain as they sat one over the other on the stone floor. Then she left. Only she left behind no proof. And our son wrote about it animatedly and profusely, which went on for months. He would wait outside, observing every night of the curfew for signs of her to return. She returned intermittently after having given up her black attire of mourning.

It is all there in his diaries.

And so, many years passed, reading, writing, and waiting. He had many encounters with imaginary flesh, and he remained feverish with desire and yet inadequate in his soul. He is still the same. No woman can rise to the allure of his imaginary women. He remains unattached and unmarried.

THE FOURTH SON

You continuously smelled the fragrance of water.

The middle one was born in September during the festivities for the ending of World War II. It was also the time when Alfie's situation had deteriorated. I had come home only for a short while as I was organising the festivities as a member of the Congress party. You discovered his anomaly on the third day when you took him to the sunlight. He was the colour of light shade of bronze. When the sunlight fell on him, his penis shone golden, and it was a fish, hanging by its tail attached to his pelvis. You sat looking at it in wonder.

He grew up to be a good swimmer. He had come to be known in the town as the boy with a fish for a penis. His Hindi teacher at school called him Matsya Lingam. You called him *Awaara.*

Frieda, you were fond of the milk skins. When the sons were served milk after school, they would wait for you to come and scoop the skins with your spoon one after the other and make it disappear in your mouth. They would then gulp down their milk.

One day, at the dining table after school, with their cups of milk in front of them, you heard the fourth son ask sotto voce, 'Has Daddy got a heart?' Then he asked the others, 'What do you think?' You had heard this as you were coming from the kitchen to the dining room with a spoon to skim their cups and you stopped behind the door. You waited there. When none answered his strange question, he persisted, 'I can't imagine a heart under his ribs.' So, when you came to the dining table, they were all silent and looked at you with large eyes like they had committed a mistake. 'I think he has a big heart. One that fills his ribs entirely.' You said smiling. He was adamant, 'It is empty.' Now it was a challenge and the other sons waited to see how it would end. 'I know because I have seen his heart under his smooth skin,' you said. 'You lie,' he countered. Then you told them, 'When I was to marry, my groom was lost. Your daddy came with his heart on his palms and asked me to marry him. That's when I saw it and that's why we were married.' The second son, now ten, squirmed when you said that. He shook his head to disagree. You crossed over to him and placed your hand on his head, 'Trust me. He has a large heart.' The fourth son said, 'Then why don't we feel it? He does not spend time with us. He remains in his room drinking or out walking. He is so quiet as if he does not exist.' You assured them. 'He does love me and all of you.' At this the Second Born got up, pushed his chair violently. It fell. He walked past brushing you and angrily started circling the holes in the courtyard that had already been circled.

When the Fourth Born was fifteen, he fell in love with a boatman's daughter who was thirteen. She was Rewa, who sculpted millions of marble Shivalingas in all sizes but the same shape. She knew about him and wanted only to see the fish. She would sit mesmerised watching him swim naked. Other fish would come and attach themselves to his belly, to his thighs, to his chest. She felt strange waters emanate from her whenever she saw him thus. One day, she got the courage to get in the water with him hoping that her waters will attract his fish. They did not. She got out and he looked at her deep brown skin with such love. His fish still refused to respond. She realised she would not be able make his fish swim in her waters. She jumped into the Narmada with a stone tied to her waist. She drowned and was never found. The middle one was miserable for many years after.

'She must have been taken by Narmada to the sea,' people said. He felt sad. Many days passed in sadness. One day, while swimming on his back he was being taken downstream swiftly, the sun was in his eyes, and he squeezed them shut. In his shut eyes he saw the ghats, the jungles, the ravines, the rocks and the hills and he saw swarms of people and temples and dead bodies burning and the flowers and the earthen lamps floating, the statutes of Ganesha and Kali being drowned, and he saw baptisms taking place and saw the gurudwaras and the mosques lining the water. He saw the kirtan singers and the sadhus chanting shlokas and the prostitutes singing thumris. He saw the traders and the sailors and the divers and small children. He saw the naked Jain munis[1] and the Christian nuns. He saw *shraadh*[2] being performed and *mundan*[3] being performed and he saw the wrestlers and washermen and the drug addicts and the suicide jumpers and the dead bodies of animals and people floating. He saw the green fields and the mango orchards and the fish farms. When he opened his eyes, he said to the river, 'You are gorgeous.' The river beckoned him, if you must watch my glory, walk with me it said. He agreed.

When he announced that he is leaving in search of himself along the Narmada, you broke down. He was only seventeen then. You implored and cried and scolded and cajoled and hugged. The First Born tried to dissuade him. The Second Son was indifferent. The Third Son said, 'I will come with you.' The Fifth Son said this is reckless. The Sixth Son asked, 'How does one find oneself? Aren't you here and can't we see you?' The Seventh Son asked, 'What will you bring back for me?' I said, 'Join me in my political work and when you see other people's woes, you will forget yours. You must serve the people.'

He was adamant.

Alfie said, 'Son, go but be careful. This is your home, and it will always be here for you. Come back whenever you are

---

[1] Ascetics.

[2] A Hindu ritual performed to pay homage to one's ancestors, especially to dead parents.

[3] A Hindu ritual where a baby's head is tonsured for the first time after birth.

done.' For Alfie, who hardly spoke these days, it was like a full speech he had delivered. His voice was warm, decisive, and encouraging. Frieda, you were surprised, but you did not contradict him. All you said was, 'I walked along the Narmada with Alfie when he was in my womb, that's why he wants to go.'

When he left, Alfie asked his place to be set at the table. It would be empty. No one was allowed to sit in his chair or change its position. The son remained present at the table in his absence. 'He will come back,' Alfie assured us all from time to time in his absence.

He walked days on end. When he got tired of walking, he descended into the lap of the fast-flowing river, and let it take him where it wanted. He encountered crocodiles and snakes, and none would touch him. They seemed to have a disdain for him for being a hybrid fish-man. He met tigers and leopards and monkeys, and they would not touch him. They ignored him as an untouchable. The more he dared them the more they ignored him. He had not yet encountered human beings and yet he knew that he was moving with the Narmada to the sea. Only when he slept, did he see people. He ate what he found which was little. His hair had grown, and his beard was thick and dark. Semi-naked and hungry, he proceeded with an empty mind. He would cope with whatever nature presented to him.

He reached the city of temples. He was a bag of bones and skin by then. He sat on the opposite bank watching the aarti happening. In the few moments when they laid the lamps down and there was absolute silence, he saw her. Rewa. Golden in the reflected light, shining in the middle of the river. Her bosom was wet, and his fish got startled. He felt life creeping in him with the warmth of the sun rising from his groins. He dived stealthily and swam to her. It is you, he whispered. The voice that he had not used for so many months seemed someone else's. Hoarse and expectant and coming from deep inside his gut. He extended his hand and touched her wet skin. She was real. She seemed oblivious. He swam even closer. He touched her hair. She was still like the air around. And then he bent his head and kissed her on the lips. She kissed back, and he closed his eyes. When he opened his eyes, there was nothing. When morning came, he started walking again.

Now he saw her often and the more he ignored her, the more he saw her. She never came close and remained at a distance. Exhausted, he now wondered about what he was seeking by doing this. He was a recluse with unkempt hair. His skin was bruised and dry and exemplified a strange shade of bronze. He remembered his brothers and that he had left them all for no reason except to seek out Rewa. As he had walked, he felt Rewa's love, and he remembered instances where he should have reciprocated. Was it his youth and his pride that he did what he did and why he was roaming the riverbank semi-naked and forlorn? He sat and wondered about what his purpose was, and he meditated on that for many days in that spot.

Then he saw her beckoning him to go downstream. He stopped. 'What are you doing there?' he asked. 'Go where the river meets the sea and I will meet you there,' she said. But you are not real. You are my imagination. Be it as it may, I shall meet you at the sea. You cannot stop now. 'I am going mad,' he thought and sat down and whimpered. What is happening to me? It was all clarity for a few days and then suddenly these hallucinations again.

Now as he walked the last hundred miles to the mouth of the sea, there were no hallucinations, no Rewa. A sort of calm had descended over him. He walked without expectations. It was just something he wanted to complete. He would decide there what can be done next. Maybe go back home to his mother and her lover. And his father who may not be his father.

He had reached the end of the river.

He sat down and watched the setting sun. He was at peace. There was nothing he wanted from life or had anything to offer to life. In the golden blue light, he saw her swimming towards him. He sat still ignoring his hallucination. It would be dark soon and then this vision would disappear. She came close and extended her arms to embrace him. Her touch felt like redemption. It was cool against his warm body. She raised her neck and kissed him. He reciprocated, and his arms lifted to cup her face. In that kiss he found immeasurable love. He let the feeling absorb him into his bones. His goldfish was alive again after many months of hibernation.

He was sucked into the sea. He clung to her body for this seemed like the end. He was drowning in the ocean that was made of Rewa and of love. When his legs touched her, he felt the scales. He held his breath, and took his hands down to touch her between the legs. It was all scales and the knowledge dawned. She was a mermaid. He went under and put his hands between her legs and ripped it down to her fins at the tail end. She shrieked in agony, and he held her tight skin to skin, and they swam towards the surface. There was a trail of blood. The sea turned red. She was limp and unconscious when he laid her on the sands at the shore. He had broken the membrane that held her legs together. Now she would be human again. Now she would be able to live in the world with him. Now his fish desired her waters, and she let her waters embrace and swim his golden fish.

She is your mermaid daughter-in-law. She still has scales on her legs and occasionally when you see an abandoned scale shining in the house, you smile.

Much had transpired when the fourth son was away for two and a half years. The First Born had brought Urja home. Badi Bai was hiding Jamuna for the second son. The third son was involved with Maya and writing copiously. Alfie had his first heart attack. The fifth son and his stories had become wilder. The sixth son took care of Alfie all the time. The seventh son was a teenager now. I was an elected member of the municipal council and my political work emerged as promising. I was on the verge of getting a ticket from the Congress Party for the legislative assembly elections.

Rewa and the Fourth Born were married a year later in a simple ceremony because that year India was at war with Pakistan over Kashmir. Lal Bahadur Shastri was the Prime Minister.

THE FIFTH SON

When you carried him, you smelled ashes on roses and then there was a silver rose, like an albino in our garden that year. It was not white. It was red drained of its pigments. It reflected light.

This was our Fifth Son, born the year India gained Independence from the British. He talked in his sleep and narrated stories…fiction and facts mixed. His brain sloshed in his skull and spit out fables. He had a mirror which he had received and that captured images and memories. He who could exist in two places at the same time…in my head, in my head…he would say. He met the girl incarcerated in a mirror who was happy in the world of her illusions and images…

When he was growing up, the boys missed a lot about Alfie, who now looked more at the ground than things at the eye level. He was so quiet like he had ceased to exist. Often his door was ajar a crack with the light falling like a sabre on the floor the end of the corridor. For them, maybe everything would be all right if he emerged from that room and sat with them. There was always an anticipation in their eyes for Alfie. Once when the fifth son who was ten years old, he said, 'We should have been born in a better family where the father would be a real father.' We were at the dining table. You were taken aback, 'What do you mean? Daddy is a real father. He is fine as he is.'

'No, Daddy is not fine. He keeps himself confined to his room or to his mynas. He does not go to the church with us. He does not come to our school. Nothing!' The sixth son added.

'Some daddies are like that. He does brush your hair on Sundays.' I said this to support you.

'That's not enough! And why do you do all that you do, Uncle?' He asked with angst.

'What do I do?' I asked.

'You earn the money for the house, you go to the market, you take us to church, you come to meet our teachers at school, you take Mummy to the cinema. You do so many things that Daddy should be doing.' The fifth son added.

'See, your daddy is my friend and friends do that for each other.' I spoke.

'That's wrong. What does Daddy do for you?' At this, the First Born got upset and raised his voice, 'Enough. Daddy is fine and not replaceable. We are thankful to Uncle but he is not Daddy.' That scalded my soul.

The First Born and Second Born left the table. Frieda, it shattered your heart and you had tears in your eyes.

'Daddy is fine. And we will only talk good things about Daddy,' you said with a finality. From then on, conversations about Alfie were different on the dining table. They were about his hunting anecdotes, his job as the sanitary inspector, his handsomeness in his youth, his gallantry at the wedding and about everything except his veracity as daddy. That is how we built the myths of parenthood in our family.

One of his stories that became a folklore was...

In that world, women were infected with a bacterium that made them speak angrily all the time. Before that they spoke with deep affection. After the infection struck their throats, even though they spoke with affection, it came out angrily. Their anger made men tamer. The tamer the men got, the angrier the women became. And in that world, it was a cacophony of noises: shrill, loud, rough all day long.

Their land belonged to a King who discovered that if you lock the people in a room, they evaporated. Since the doors and the windows of that world were open all the time, the din of women made the King mad, and he shouted orders for them to be locked up a batch at a time. When the first batch of twelve women evaporated, the anger in the population increased manifold. When the other batch of twelve women evaporated, the noise levels rose such that it could now be heard from twenty-five miles away.

Among the women who evaporated, there was the wife of the court magician. After his wife had evaporated, the court magician was afraid for his daughter. It was in these circumstances that one day he designed the plan wafting between dreams. He went and picked his beautiful little daughter whom he called Darpana and whom he loved the most. He tied the voices in her throat and incarcerated her in the mirrors. He did not want his daughter to be evaporated by the King. She now roamed in the mists of reflection and was happy in the illusion. With her voice choked, she only smiled in the mirrors and the images of that imagery-ridden silver-plated world smiled back. She would spend hours appearing and disappearing from the mirrors, conjuring faces and personas that she forgot about instantly.

While she travelled in the imaginary world, the women were getting angrier, and they accosted the King accusing him of being a misogynist and their loud angry voices led him to lose his temper and raise his gun at them. They descended on him like locusts, and they shut him in his bedroom and shot him through the door. Later, they found him splattered in the room, stuck to the walls by the bullets, still alive. The courtiers put him together in an unsavoury mass. He still rules. Because they never found his tongue, he could not shout orders, and no woman disappeared after that despite their cacophony.

In the meantime, Darpana continued to make reflections and rarefactions, refractions and resolutions and shone through the mirrors.

In my dreams, in my dreams…he said.

He was mesmerised by the mirror gagged luminescence… like a child by the flame of a lamp, like a thief by the shine of gold, like deer by a mirage. His eyes fixated on the mirror's surface and if only he could pass through glass, he would touch her and smell her. She was oblivious of the eyes and lived immured in that scintillating cage of light and shadows, of glass and silver, of ether and shine. Her cage had expanded as the mirrors started to break with the noise in that place and she inhabited many mirrors at the same time and in many images in one mirror.

In my head, in my head…he said.

He always kept the mirror with him. And looked at it when he yearned for her, and she appeared. She had conquered the world of the mirrors. Every time he shook the mirror, she changed shape and colours. Her world of mirrors was a kaleidoscope and only he had access to it.

He would show people the mirror and tell them of her beauty. Now she has put her leg on the chair and is applying oil and her calves are shining. Now she is putting the musk in the valley of her milk-coloured breasts. Now I can see the nape of her neck with the valley at the top of her spine and she has fine delicate hair that is reflecting the sunlight. Her ear lobes appear alluring, and her tongue is pink, shining with moisture as she sticks it out as she is trying to put on her earrings.

He would slap his head and say in my head, in my head…

As the sun splashed orange on his windows, his eyes would sparkle with her moving in and out of the mirrors, appearing and disappearing and then appearing again. He would sit and watch her move in his iris. She would dissolve in the cones and rods and be formed there again in a new avatar. If someone looked into his eyes, they would see the kaleidoscope of images floating through it like a movie screen.

He would distractedly slap his head and the image would change. But it was always her. He would desperately try and reach her, but his lips would always touch the cold glass leaving smudges and then he would wipe it clean so that she became visible again. He was animated with the mirrors and would chat and interact.

Until one day, when he was twenty-one, he decided that if he could not get into the mirrors to reach her, he would push the mirrors in himself so that he absorbs her with the mirrors. And Frieda, you remember, when we found him, he was suspended on a frame made with the large shards of mirrors that had passed through his viscera and muscles. And he had the most endearing smile on his face.

That day, you asked all to leave the room he was found in. You removed every shard from his body with affection and you kept saying soothing words to him, words that appeared incoherent and yet they meant something. And the words rose in a crescendo.

The Sixth Son, who was there, said, 'There is a beautiful woman in a pink saree dancing to Mother's words.' She was wrestling with them, catching them, and throwing them around for them to crash against the walls. Hence the words shattered and reverberated and folded on themselves confusing the listeners. The battle between you and her went on for a long time till the black plumes with burnt pink ash spiralled out of that room. In that black plume, the Sixth Son saw the beautiful woman leave hurriedly, smiling but with embers in her eyes.

Then you came out with the Fifth Son as if nothing had happened. The Fifth Son started living not in his head but in the real world.

You had used your last prayer that was given to you ages ago under the banyan tree.

After a year of this, Alfie would die one evening.

THE SIXTH SON

This one was a happy child. And you smelled everything pink all the time. This child could predict death. He was born three years after the Fifth Son.

I remember there was a wedding in the family. There were folk singers called to perform on the evening before the wedding day. There were drinks and cocktails, and your youngest sister's husband, Rajan, was in a great mood. There was perfume burning on every skin. The light of the oil lamps gave colour to the eyes. The night had converted the skins and eyes into things of beauty. As the evening set in, Rajan began to dance. He was not inebriated and yet there was rhythm in his limbs. We all knew he did not drink. He lifted the evening and other folks joined him in the dancing. There was laughter and food and chatter and banter.

This child, who was seven then, sat next to me. He was clapping and enjoying and hooting at the dance moves. When I looked at his face, he locked my gaze and smiled, 'Uncle, do you see that beautiful woman in pink saree dancing with him?' I did not see anyone in a pink saree. I looked at him puzzled. 'Rajan Uncle will die soon.' He predicted. The Sixth Born, still a boy, was nonchalant and kept enjoying the evening. It made me uncomfortable. I looked at Rajan and his youth brimmed full of life, in a film of sweat, dancing to the beat of music happily, cheered on by the others. I asked him to repeat what he said. And the sixth one said that again. It was bizarre and chilling. I felt nauseated and went out of the courtyard for some fresh air.

Two days later, Rajan died. He had driven his speeding car into a truck.

When the news reached us in the evening, our son was playing with his friends in the playground. They were running around, and they were calling each other names. He was being called SOB. I took him aside and told him. 'I knew,' he said. SOB… SOB… SOB…resonated behind us from the boys in the evening air.

He looked at me. His pupils were dark. He told me he saw it. That Rajan Uncle was sad. But to me Rajan was the happiest man that evening, I reminded him. Our son told me what he had seen. There was this young woman. Beautiful. Shining. Translucent. In a pink saree, doing a slow tango with him taking his hands in turn, one after the other. He had remembered. Our son said, 'Rajan Uncle's dance the other evening was the invention of his sadness. He loved the edge, the wound, and drew his limbs in space in tandem with the lady in the pink saree. Their forms fused in a yearning beyond visible expression. She had kissed him with a breath of death.'

He was speaking like a connoisseur of sadness.

It was the same woman in pink saree that he had seen the other night when he was smaller. He had come charging to your door drenched in sweat and terror and was banging the door in the deep of the night. Your door was bolted. I had come out and gathered him in my arms. He was just five then. He shivered like a reed in the wind in my arms. The leaves were swirling in the courtyard silently. The clouds had gathered dark and without rain. The lightning crackled and lit his face. He was terrified. He whispered; "I saw pink sadness in colour of ash pass by my window in the street. She was looking inside our home." We both sat down by your door, and I touched his forehead. He was burning with fever. That was the first episode. I did not know how many times he had seen her since then. Then he forecasted the first death and connected it to her taking away Rajan.

He had a lesion of sadness in his heart. But he was always happy because he thought that his smiles would heal the wound that could never heal. That was his dilemma and his oddness.

That evening, as we walked back from the playground, I said, 'So, your friends call you SOB.' He looked at me and said, 'Yes. Short for Son of a Bitch. It's for fun.' I felt hurt, bewildered, and speechless at his naïveté, his disparagement, and his happiness.

He grew to be a good young man. Cheerful. Helpful. A bit pensive at times. His nightmares continued. I always observed him closely whenever there was a death in the family or the neighbourhood. He never let on any signs that he knew. He knew them all. I suspected. For he had his bouts of sadness when he was tormented. When he was happy, he felt high and then without any premonition, he felt low, and he rode the roller-coaster with calm and stoicism. He had adopted an ingenuity of strength to remain happy to solve for that unsolvable knowledge of sadness that he carried inside him.

At sixteen, the year the Fourth Son married Rewa, he became friends with Aslam, a tall lanky teenager with sad eyes. Aslam was one year senior at school. He had said through the smoke filtered face, I do not have a father. The Sixth Son understood, and they developed a bond. They pinned their loyalty on the walls and their empathy on the windows. They were together most of the time. They did not talk much but had the comfort of sharing their silences that the other understood perfectly. One would look at the intensity of sadness behind the smoke screen, and the other would understand the sadness that was not being spoken about. Aslam would seek out girls and women to share his sadness; Neena, Amina, Sonal, Kanika, Ruth, Lakshmi, Manjulika, Nazneen and others. He got bored with air and sunlight they brought and found himself covered with fine grey ash of sadness in fleeting time. The only person his sadness resonated with was with our son. This continued for seven years. When people asked, 'You love Aslam?', he said, 'Yes. I do.' He was not embarrassed. And they asked whether he was his lover, he said as much as Sudama was of Krishna or Shams was of Rumi. And the gossip continued unabated.

He met her when they had gone to meet Aslam's sister at the Girls' College hostel. The girl with crows in her eyes. As Aslam chatted with his sister, our son was drawn to the singing voice in one of the dorm rooms. He stood there listening behind the door that was slightly ajar. The singing brought forth a surge inside him. A surge of sadness that travelled from the soles of his feet to the tips of his hair on his head. A force more mysterious than thought started welling up in him, like the sad spirit of the earth had entered him. He pushed the door open to the dark room and said, 'You have the sadness that I am looking for.' She turned enveloped in the greyness of the room. A shuddering descended on him like an earthquake, deep, dark, dank, disconcerting. She had the yellow eyes of crows. Next instant she switched on the light, and they were light shades of brown. Did he see what he saw? Then he heard the crowing of a flock of crows that had descended in the trees outside for the night. Maybe he was thinking of crows. He was fascinated by the pearlescent skin, brown eyes, black hair, and liquid waist.

'It's my blood,' she said. He looked at her confused. 'The singing. It comes from my blood,' she said. 'My mother conceived me while singing. The men raped her, and she distracted herself with the singing. Over the course of her pregnancy, she distracted herself with singing. When the nurse pushed her hands in her vagina as she pulled me out, she sang. Her breast milk was mixed with the songs that I sing. She sang all her life to forget me.'

In her songs he heard sounds burning in the blood like powered glass. In her songs he heard the shattering trigonometry of a sad universe. In her songs he heard the bitumen black eating away the primary colours.

'I see crows in your eyes,' he said.

'You are mistaken,' she said. Then she asked him, 'What is the reason for your sadness?' He said, 'Death is a beautiful woman in a pink saree. I see her lick away breath with her slithering split tongue. I can do nothing other than be an audience. I collect the sadness she leaves behind.'

Alfie passed around this time and the mynas were gone.

When she finished college, her money was cut off by her aunt who was supporting her till then. She was supporting her on the promise that no man enters her life. He brought her home. He told you she needs a home to live in and he gave up his room. You welcomed her. In that fully occupied house, he moved into Alfie's vacant room. She took up a job where she had to sing blues and jazz in Jackson Hotel every Saturday night. The Sixth Son would sit at the corner table with Aslam and listen to her through the night.

She sang trembling like a professional mourner, looking like a fiery spirit in the skin of glass, singing with a desiccated throat, without colour, without music but with a sadness that came from the pits of her gut. Her singing radicalised old men, brought pristine and unsettling sensations on the skin, created fresh roses in the air and generated an almost religious fervour in the audience. Her sadness swept the earth, on the wings of crows made of dark feathers like rusty knives.

There would be a silent flock of crows with yellow eyes all over the Jackson Hotel. These crows, in those times of political emergency imposed by Indira Gandhi, stayed till they squeezed out those yellow lemons of dawn, in a country of poverty and restriction, a country open to death and resistance, a country where men were neutered, and sane voices choked. As the country and people were suspended in emergency, she sang like a scar.

Each Saturday night at Jackson Hotel, her singing brought forth an unknown edge, an unseen blemish and drew him close to her with a yearning that was beyond visible expression. Each Saturday night, her songs worked on his skin like wind on the sands. It changed him into a lunar lunatic for the rest of the week, sometimes behaving like a beggar at the wine shop asking for alms, other times like a sad blushing adolescent, sometimes like a gypsy with his ektara, enraptured, other times like a confused afflicted mad man. He would pass her closed doors in the week and hear the songs in a sad humming. The thing was that the sadness that had been part of their existence was ever changing and never repeated itself like the waves of an ocean in a storm are never repeated. He discovered dark sounds, behind which in tender intimacy existed volcanoes, ants, zephyrs, and the vast night pressing its waist against the Milky Way and Black Holes.

Frieda, now that you have moved into the casket, she comes and sits by your side every day, singing softly. I hope you hear her voice.

Their magical power of sadness became imperative, impervious, irredeemable, and he eventually asked her to marry him.

THE SEVENTH SON

When you started smelling burnt wood, you knew. Smells had never betrayed you.

You wanted this constant burning furnace of your uterus to stop baking more little people. You desired that this one come out early. You were tired. Alfie had given up drinking miraculously one day. Your financial condition was not good. I could not do much.

You started eating raw papaya. Everyday. You knew that it creates heat in the body and helps abort. Then you started jumping walls. You would sit on the highest wall with your sons and jump. For others it seemed that you were playing. You would climb walls and jump over fences to steal papayas from the neighbourhood. You started eating spices and your face would be flushed. Ginger and turmeric and garlic in copious quantities, all of which went into food. Hot spices with nutmeg and cloves and nigella and poppy seeds were consumed daily. Asafoetida was used in curries and lentils. Everyone stopped eating the food you cooked. Badi Bai had to make fresh food every time for the children.

You did not say a word to anyone about the new smells. But when you started eating excessive spices, you developed a sustained high temperature. Badi Bai found out that you were tucking a raw peeled onion in your armpits to bring up your temperature. Then she understood. She called the Gypsy. This was two years after the previous son was born.

He came and sat outside the door and sang on his ektara for two days. He was flushed, and he did not eat or drink anything. Then he asked me to have a word with you. Does Alfie know? I asked. He did. I came to you and asked you to bear this one. You were angry and upset. The baby was still firmly rooted in the earth of your body even after four months. You asked why? 'So that you give this one my name,' I had said. You looked at me with anger and tears welled up in your eyes. You stripped and said, 'See! My abdomen is flat. There is no baby.' I looked at your beautiful, smooth, dough-like abdomen, with no stretch marks after six children, and said, 'Frieda, this will be the last one!'

Eventually your abdomen started showing the bump and the baby started kicking. You continued in your stubborn ways. You now despised your red roses so much that you had set them on fire one night. It was Alfie who never slept much now, pulled water from the well and saved them.

I remember I had filed my nomination as a Congress contestant for municipal elections when a perfectly healthy boy was born. When the blue-red-pink-black vagina expanded like a universe between your legs, Badi Bai had to use her hands to pull out the baby. Peeped first the mop of flame coloured hair, then came the little head, then the flopping brown-white arms and then slipping and swimming fast in an instant came the block of heat in the eager arms of Badi Bai. When she wiped him with a clean, soft cloth, he shivered and shook involuntarily in a spasm of surprise after surprise. When she used the wet towel to clean the vernix, the towel sizzled and sent tendrils of steam shooting in the room. She stopped and looked into the eyes of the little boy. They were golden brown reflecting licks of flames. When he urinated, it scalded her chest. The tiny penis, directed there, emitted a hot burning liquid like acid.

The day when our last son was born, all your hair turned white and you knew that your womb would not bear fruits anymore. 'Babies don't inhabit the wombs of women with white hair,' you said, relieved.

That day I had claimed your last son when your youth perished.

It was an autumn day and daylight curled into itself shortening steadily and turned the day crisp on the edges. That day your long waves of hair changed to silver all at once like darkness turning to light. Your skin furrowed with thin lines like someone had dragged the tip of a pin on the clay surface. The muscles under your jawlines sagged like someone pinched and pulled them down. Your face developed a shadow under your chin like the time that clings to bodies.

It was autumn with vermillion and ochre colours hanging from the trees.

On one side of that day, you were warm, youthful with a child in your belly and on the other, you were empty, withered and old. After I asked you to give that child my name, all the colours and water drained out of you. You became a replica of your mother, shrivelled and afraid. You knew that your womb would wrinkle up now like a dried apricot. That the juices of life will evaporate from it.

The kindling of my demand burned your fingertips. The agony shrivelled you like parchment in the sun. You did not mourn your extinguished beauty. There was still some water left coursing your organs. Tears rushed to fill the hollow of your eyes, now red-like autumn. You no longer recognised yourself in the mirror. 'I am spared the slowness of time, long agony of little deaths of tissues, that gradual fading away.' Is all you said!

I had waited patiently. I had given up my six sons to Alfie. I lived heirless with all my sons playing around me. Each smile of theirs seemed to clutter my heart with joy and constraint. I lived with corroding loneliness among my own as a second-hand father. Each day I assured myself that if I breathe, it will be enough. The desire to name one child after my own, the last bloom of your belly, to claim him as mine had overwhelmed me. My need to name him after me was a cry for the love that my other children will never give me freely because their names and the blood would be conflicted. Only the name binds the blood.

Alfie and I had both waited outside your door as Badi Bai delivered our seventh son. Hannah was no more. She had passed due to consumption a few months back. No one came from your family now. All the sisters were settled and away. Your father was too old. The Mother had lived up to her promise to Alfie of never visiting your home. When Badi Bai left, the night squatted around. Alfie met you and the baby first and thereafter he went to water the roses. I pressed my lips against your skin and asked you to name him after me. I wanted one flower in my chest that would not lose its bloom even after I was gone. You inhaled the air and closed your eyes. You did not say anything. I picked up the baby and held him to my chest.

'You do not have to hold him so very tightly, this light, that is yours.' You spoke. And I cried. I had finally found home in my skin under this roof.

It was autumn and there was a young moon hanging in the sky outside the window.

This was the one who needed constant cooling. Your favourite son. You would wash your laundry and put it on him one apparel after the other. It would all be crisply dried up. Monsoon was the best season for him. In summers we had to get slabs of ice to keep him cool. I remember you were upset with the Second Born once when he and a group of boys had asked the Last Born to remove his shirt and lie down on grass on his stomach when he was three years old. They had broken an egg on his back and had sat waiting for it to cook. It sizzled as you passed by and got upset. The little one was unaffected. He enjoyed being the centre of attention. But the Second Son got a scolding worth remembering.

In his teens, the first time he held a girl by her wrist, it left his mark on her and it was found. She was forbidden to meet him. 'He will scald your uterus,' her mother said. And then it all started. That he will scald and singe and burn the insides of a woman if ever he made love to one. And so, he remained loveless for a long time. Till she came, light as a feather, levitating above the ground.

She had learned ballet as a young girl from the age of two, from a Russian émigré, who had fallen in love with an Indian painter and come to India. Her parents were gardeners in the painter's house. The Russian wife of the painter taught her how to pirouette and rise like a butterfly above the ground. She taught her how to burn light in her body. She taught her to power the sinews and tendons to stretch the limbs and muscles to lift herself. She told her that under your shoulder blades, there are stubs of the wings that never grew out otherwise you would have been a butterfly. And the little girl believed her. She would bend one leg and touch the thigh of the other. She would point the other foot and touch just its tip to the ground. Then she would spin. Arms raised. She would spin like a top and become a blur.

By the time her Russian teacher died, she was already an orphan. She started performing in the travelling theatre. The Last Born was often called there to dry the clothes. He would stand naked, and they would drape him with clothes one after the other. He was paid for that. That day he was standing steaming when she passed by in a blur. She was looking for her tutus that were missing. She circumnavigated him a few times and he found his temperature dropping. It was pleasant sensation that ran in his veins from the foot to thighs to groin to abdomen to chest to his head. He felt giddy and cool despite his rising pulse. It was a kind of euphoria that he could get used to. Just that the clothes were not drying anymore.

Then he went to see her performance, he was smitten by the blur of the butterfly. He stole her tutus. All of them. He could since there were no clothes that he did not have access to. She got new ones and they went missing and this went on.

You found a heap of tutus in his room and wondered at your son's strange behaviour. The waist of the tutus was slender, and the colours were majestic. When you asked him, he told you these belonged to the girl that he loved. You were not perplexed but pleased.

Frieda, you have moved into the casket now. Do you know, the Last Born spends his nights sleeping on the floor by your casket?

FOR LOVE OF THE SONS

Umbilical cords are the lines that connect this world and the other and pulls the souls from there to here. Only mothers are blessed to build these ropes in the deep earth, buried in their bodies. And Frieda, you were blessed seven times.

Our sons were the gifts of our souls and bodies. Look at them, all seven of them tall and handsome. I have seen the pride in your eyes. And the hurt when the world called them names. But it did not matter what the world said. These are just the tags bursting out of cruelty. The sons are very dear to you and to me. They were to Alfie when he was alive. Whatever the world thinks, they are ours and invaluable. Dreams soft as flowers and brittle as glass floated in the liquid of your eyes when you saw them. They were the reason that Alfie lived, and they were the reason that I lived with you.

The boys grew healthy with a world of their own. Hugs were acts of piety between them. Children shared their clothes. Because they were only the custodians till they grew out of them and the real owner was the next one in line to get those hand me downs. We hardly had money to buy with cash and you would buy on credit from the cloth merchant in Sadar Bazaar once a year for a shirt and pair of trousers for each son. You bought after Diwali so that the clothes were stitched ready by Christmas. You would pay a monthly sum to clear your debt till it started afresh again the next year.

Breakfast was always savoury porridge and a boiled egg. Only the younger ones got a cup of milk while the others got tea with jaggery. The eggs were from the chicken that you had reared in the backyard. But it was the lunch every Sunday that we all looked forward to. There was always different dishes;

mutton biryani, mutton curry and pulao, mutton keema and tandoori roti...it was always mutton something. Badi Bai and you would spend Saturday marinating and preparing the spices and you would start early Sunday morning to prepare the lunch. Being a Hindu Brahmin, I did not eat meat, fish, or poultry and Badi Bai made vegetarian food for me.

You remember, I had moved into the annexe after the first son was born, we had so much joy that it could not contain itself. It started creating ripples outside your home. Alfie had gone quiet, but he would demand his bottle of rum every evening.

I had become interested in political work. India had been dragged into World War II without any discussions with the Indian leaders. I started taking part in all the satyagraha that were called during that time. It was a period of great conflict for me. I worked for the British Army Supplier Contractor and however small my contribution to the establishment, it was becoming morally unacceptable to me.

When Gandhiji called the Quit India Movement, I gave up supplying to the British Army. This was in September 1942. Things went downhill from then. You never complained because you understood. This was after our third son was born.

Alfie had started walking all over the town after that.

I remember after the first son was born, I had brought a Murphy's radio. It was large with fancy dials and enamel panels. It had a long antenna. You placed it in near the dining table. We all listened to the news on All India Radio diligently. Alfie seemed happy only with the children. He would sit by the crib in the mornings as the children were massaged and given a bath. Badi Bai had started serving me breakfast as we listened to the news. She sent the lunch to my room. I got the grassroots news as I volunteered at the local Congress branch in the mornings and afternoons. You worried about my not working, but you never pushed it. In the meantime, you listened to the national news while looking after the babies.

In the evenings, I would come down again and then you and I would listen to the news. Alfie would be gone to the club by then. That was the time I could spend with the First Born freely. Badi Bai, you and I discussed the political developments so fervently every evening as I held the First Born and you looked after the Second Born. I would play with the First Born, now two years old. His smiles fired my spirit with unfathomable affection. It became my responsibility to rock him to sleep. I would pick him up and carry him in my arms and rock him to sleep. Then Badi Bai would serve us dinner. I had started eating at your dinner table.

Remember, Frieda, that day when there was commotion in the house with the eldest crying as Badi Bai was shouting at a man who stubbornly came in and sat in the drawing room and refused to go away? He was tall, fair, muscular with a big moustache, large clear eyes and *paan*[1] stains on his lips. He smelled of some local perfume—*itr* and seemed to have filled up the drawing room with his presence. He had come to get his money for the credit that Alfie had run at his liquor shop in Sadar. You were heavily pregnant with the third son, and you came to see what was happening. While he was rude with Badi Bai, he changed his tactics with you, and he fell at your feet.

'Like you, I have children,' he cried. A petite pregnant woman and a massive muscle mass of a man at her feet. Badi Bai told me how incongruous it all seemed.

You asked, 'How much does my husband owe you?'

He said, 'Five hundred rupees. He has not paid a penny for two years.' That was a lot of money back then. You took off your gold bangles and gave them to him. Gold was Rs 100 for 10 grams then.

Badi Bai was aghast. She said, 'What are you doing, Frieda?'

---

[1] Betel leaf.

He had taken the bangles quickly and put it in his pocket and said shrewdly, 'This will not be enough.'

'These are 60 grams. You don't need to come back here again.' You were smarter.

'And don't give him any liquor henceforth.' You said as he turned to leave. 'If you give him liquor, charge him there else don't come back here for money.'

He left. You sat down on the sofa. You were short of breath and had broken into sweat.

In the evening as you served food at the dining table, I remarked, 'Your wrists are bare.' Badi Bai was in the kitchen making chapatis and the second son was sleeping in the crib beside me. The First Son was in my lap.

You said, 'I like to wear glass bangles.'

I had seen all married women in my family with gold on their wrists. I had never seen you without those gold bangles. As I finished food, you said, 'Mahesh Babu, could you give some money to Badi Bai? I will send her to get me the orange, red, maroon, and green bangles from the market tomorrow.'

That night, I came to your room. Alfie was still at the club. The First Son was sleeping, and the room smelled of Johnsons' baby powder. You put a finger to your lips and said, 'Shhh...' And indicated that you would come out.

In the dim light of the veranda, I waited. When you came, I told you that I gave the money to Badi Bai. And I also told you that I know now as Badi Bai had told me about the alcohol creditor and that you had given your bangles to him.

You pulled the wooden stool that usually lay in the veranda and sat down. You were tired and upset. I could see that. I sat on the steps.

'I find it humiliating when the creditors come asking for money. He was rude, and he had contempt as if we are trash.'

You looked sad and beautiful in that dim light with flies circling it. I offered to find a solution. I did not want you humiliated. That night you and I agreed that I will provide for his liquor.

I used my contacts from early on when I used to work for army canteen supplies. I knew people and I reached out to them to arrange for his needs. We would get the supply of cartons of wine every fortnight. I kept it all under my bed and would keep a count of the number of bottles consumed.

Those days I went to meet my mother once a month. My brothers had stopped speaking with me. One day as I sat with my mother, my eldest brother came and sat quietly with us. Then he said to me, 'Mahesh, do not come here. We have daughters-in-law here and it becomes difficult to explain your situation.'

'I come to meet mother. I can meet her somewhere else if you agree.' I spoke. I understood his position.

'Our mother is a respectable person. The town still gives her love and respect despite the reputation you are building. We must think of the future of the children here. They are all girls. Please do not tarnish your family,' he said.

My mother held my hand tightly, and she could not say anything. That is when I stopped going to my mother's home. You always asked after her. You always respected her.

We had Badi Bai. And, of course, the Gypsy. Remember, how every morning he would present himself with some fresh vegetables and seasonal fruits from people's farms on the road to Narmada? How jubilant he seemed as he presented those? He still spent his evenings-nights-mornings at the ghats of Narmada looking for his lady love. He would come only mid-morning till mid-afternoon. Occasionally, he would get the colostrum from the people whose cows had given birth. Badi Bai would make mithai out of it for the children. She would boil the colostrum till it split and then she added the sugar we got from the government ration shops. When there was no sugar, she would add jaggery. She would reduce the liquid till it became brown and thick. The children loved the sticky sweet mithai.

Badi Bai did not lose her charm in those days. She still wore her sarees neatly and would starch them once a month with rice water. She still oiled and flattened her hair neatly. Badi Bai still went to the pawn shop to sell something or the other. There was nothing much left in the house. But whatever she could, she sold. Your sarees, one at a time. The gold and silver were long gone. The clocks and watches. 'Good, now we will not have to see the face of time,' you said when she sold the last watch in the house. And then she would go out intermittently to get the rations from the government shop. She would cook whatever she could for all of us. And she delighted in giving the children small pleasures. Gulgule, panjiri, cutlets, maleeda, purees made from boiled sweet potatoes, sweetened saffron rice she called zarda etc.

The radio was a blessing and it kept a semblance of normalcy in our home. You listened to the Hindi film songs of Noor Jehan, Shamshad Begum, Manna Dey, Pankaj Mullick and others. The gramophone was rarely played now. Alfie did not like its sound anymore. I still have that radio in my room as a relic of that time. I must bring it into your room and play it again.

Your relationship with Alfie was the same. You cared for him and looked after him. You ensured that his needs were met. You were affectionate towards him and never once blamed him for the condition that his family was in. I marvelled at you.

There is something that I will never forget about you in those days. It made me believe that we would come out of this condition somehow. I did not know how, but I knew somehow. I still remember your acts of kindness. And then there was a blind Muslim fakir who came to our door every Tuesday those days. You always gave him a small bowl of *atta*[2]. However bad our situation may be, you never turned him away.

You did not complain. I had nothing to complain about. Alfie was too drunk to complain about anything.

[2] Wheat flour.

THE BEGINNING...

IT WAS A SIGN

Frieda, you were sixteen then. In the church, you had not noticed DC in the congregation. He stood next to you in the parallel line proceeding to the altar for the communion. You were on the right, and he was on the left. You had your head bowed, and hands folded in reverence. He was standing straight with a tranquil face and hands at the back holding one in the other. DC wore a brown linen suit and brown loafers. You got a gentle whiff of his Old Spice, and you noticed his brown shoes. The ushers helped the congregation to the altar and when your turn came, you both kneeled next to each other at the centre of the altar, with you and your three sisters on the right, him on the left. The communion of the body of Christ as a circular, coin-sized rice wafer was put in the mouth of the congregation by the deacon. The blood of Christ as red wine was offered by the pastor. You had raised your right hand cupped by the left under it to receive the rice wafer as the body of Christ. Your eyes were closed in piety and anticipation. The deacon placed the wafer in your palms and between that and your mouth as you lifted the cupped hands, the body of Christ slipped from your hands. The deacon was wide-eyed and open-mouthed at the mishap. Falling at the feet of people was an utter disrespect to the body of Christ. DC, with a swift motion, caught it on his palm before it could touch the earth. Reflexively he offered Christ's body to you. You opened your eyes and then your mouth spontaneously. He placed the rice wafer in your mouth, and you received it with devotion. It was all so instantaneous. You then closed your mouth, and the sensation of the dissolving wafer was still lingering in your mouth when you received the wine offered by the pastor as the second part of the communion. You closed your eyes again. The red wine was sour and watery. You kept kneeling longer than others more out of the commotion of nerves than the focus on the Lord. He, who had offered you the host had entered your heart. You thought that it was a sign. You, who had stubbornly refused the advances of all the young men till now, it seems, were ready to fall in love.

Through the rest of the service, you sat with an uneasy restlessness. You could still see the pores in the skin of the hand that held the host. You felt strange warmth at the back of your neck from the direction where he sat a few rows behind. This warmth reached your bosom and rose to your face and flushed it red. Because your skin was translucent, there was not much you could do to hide the refraction it created of what was passing through your mind and heart. You turned your head slightly intermittently to get him in your peripheral vision to affirm his presence. You did not dare to turn and fill your retina with his image. Your propriety and dignity prevailed. You restrained yourself so as not to attract attention and to avoid an explosive gossip in the community.

When the service ended, after the benediction, you were the first one to walk out after the pastor. You waited for DC outside, hoping to say thank you. The first thing you noticed was his brown pair of shoes as he walked out of the church. Then you saw his chiselled face basking in the sun, and you had difficulty taking your eyes off it. You lowered your gaze in modesty. You could hear a hammering in the distance. That was but just your own heart drumming in the ribcage. He walked past you without acknowledging. He did not consider it decent to speak with girls unescorted by their parents. And he did not want to create facetious rumours in the congregation. You had stood there with your dress fluttering in the winter breeze. You thought his ignoring you was cruel and his indifference, inappropriate. It immediately blew away any illusion you were building about him. You saw him walk past the front garden of the church to his red and black Austin car parked outside. Your face became withdrawn and sad. A film of water formed in your eyes giving it dark luminosity.

That Sunday, DC was with his friend Alfie, who noticed it all. Alfie had seen you, Frieda, at Russell Square a few days earlier and recognised you. He did not know your name yet. DC and Alfie had planned to have lunch at the club after church service and then head to YMCA for snooker.

When you reached home, your mother raged at you. 'What's going on? What were you thinking when you walked out like that? You should have eyes only for God in the church and no one else.'

You did not answer. You avoided verbal and emotional skirmishes with the Mother.

'Don't be stubborn…answer me!' the Mother demanded. 'I have six other daughters to marry off. If you spoil our family name, your sisters will either remain spinsters or become prostitutes.'

'I have not done anything wrong,' you wanted to shout back. But you knew that it would aggravate the Mother further. 'He had just looked past me and walked away. There is nothing there,' you thought. Mother's yelling grated your soul, but you maintained a stifling stubborn silence.

'What's between your legs is only for your husband to open and discover,' the Mother continued berating.

The Mother reminded you sisters often of the thing between their legs and every time she said that you wondered what's between your legs. Of late it had become a powerful source of mysterious energy that churned your mind. You had seen what was between the legs of other women and it was the same thing. You wondered how the men opened it and what they discovered there. Wasn't it strange and profound that it was your body but someone else needed to discover it? So far, you had decided that you would never allow any man to do that. But today when the Mother said that, the image that conjured in your mind was that of a strong hand with a rice wafer discovering what's between your legs. You smiled.

'What are you smiling at? Here I die with anxiety about what the future holds for the seven of you and you are smiling? You uncouth girl! There are all kinds of predators out there. You have heard of the Orchard Man, haven't you? And how he picks up girls at his whim. No one can save them then. God forbid he sees any one of you!'

'Does the church and the sermon give her no peace?' you thought.

IT FLEW AWAY IN THE WIND?

Alfie had seen you earlier when he was at work. He was the Sanitary Inspector in the Cantonment.

Alfie had to give the summons notice by hand to the businessman who had sweet shops all over town and whose shops had hygiene issues that had been notified. Alfie had agreed to meet him that Saturday at his office in a placed called the Russell Square. It was a rectangle where two roads crossed, obliquely at thirty degrees. It was cobbled with smooth stones and had a line of silver oak trees in the centre with benches under it. The sparse traffic of bicycles, tongas, and very few cars skirted around this area. Beyond the wide footpaths were red tiled verandas with slanted roofs, leading into the shops and offices. In the by-lanes were the bungalows of the British gentry. The Square was a cheerful place on Saturdays, as it was a market day, and all the local artisans and farmers put their colourful stalls with local produce on the footpath.

Alfie had left his horse tied in the shade in one of the alleys between the shops. He waited in the veranda, smoking. He was early. Men and women in their colourful best were all about. Some examining the wares at the stalls, others chatting with one another. There were parasols, now made of nylon rather than cotton, more austere than fancy, without all the lace trimmings as had been the fashion a decade earlier. Children played with colourful balloons. Two men pushed a small, hand driven Ferris wheel, sweat dripping on their faces and squeals and peals of laughter from children on the wheel. The people's attire was a strange mix of western and local. Women were either in saris or frocks or ankle-length skirts and the men were in either cotton suits or open-collared shirts and baggy pant or dhoti kurta. It was early 1930s and fashion was changing. It was festive with the young and old, rich and poor, British and Indian all in the pursuit of enjoying the market. Diagonally across at a distance Alfie saw the seven sisters come out of the French photographer's studio and a horse drawn Victoria emerged and stopped near them. Happiness was the colour they wore. He could not but smile as he waited.

Alfie was about to cross the square when the air dropped suddenly, and it was still. He could see everything but could not hear anything. He then saw the white galloping horses turn at the far end of the square, pulling a shiny black open Victoria, carrying the seven sisters in his direction. He saw the trail of wind and dust following the carriage, and as they approached him the squall hit them from behind and out flew the dupatta of one of the sisters. It was like a red wild spirit that floated and danced in the air. It seemed in a frenzy. He had moved a bit inside the veranda to avoid the dust storm and bent to follow the dupatta that hung about in air like Aladdin's carpet. In the stream of the squall, it floated along the carriage with the seven sisters, and he saw you lunge up to grab it, only to have it evade your hands. He could not see your face as it was turned the other way upwards, but he noticed your beautiful hand.

And just as soon as the squall had come, it left with equal haste. In its aftermath, it had left minor chaos behind. All the young men in the square were whistling, catcalling, and fighting for the dupatta and a few moments later, each had a piece of it in their hands. Just then the carriage passed by Alfie. The air carried the giggling words, 'How can you marry one of these men? They can't even save my dupatta.' That is when he saw you, Frieda, for a moment. Laughing and happy. The tonga passed by and with it the colourful seven sisters. He also noticed the youngest, not more than six or seven years old, had the bunch of balloons tied to the string in her hands.

That day Alfie decided that he would perhaps marry you one day. He did not know your name then.

He was strangely euphoric that day and walked with a sublime bliss that he had not felt before. Nothing exceptional had happened; the squall passed, Alfie served the summon notice and came to the YMCA. DC was already there waiting. They said their hellos and sat on the sofas around a large tree trunk centre table strewn with magazines and a chess board.

DC was Peter Barnes, the District Collector. They were friends and knew each other while working on inspections. DC was tall, broad shouldered and often turned lobster red in the bright sunlight of the hot town in central India where they lived. He had an impeccable grooming and forbearance. He had come from England five years ago at a young age of twenty-one as a young Collector in this remote part of India. He was not very social but was quite visible in that rather small town, riding the streets on his horse for inspections. DC came across as enigmatic as he spoke little and had that distinct arrogance of a civil servant about him. The DC had an official car, but he was fond of riding on the horse.

On the other hand, Alfie was a free spirit, warm and amicable and prone to conversations with strangers. While Alfie's parents were both English, they had died when he was a baby. He had never been to England and was brought up in foster care by Badi Bai, his ayah. Alfie, in his late twenties, was a handsome man with blue eyes and a complexion that comes with baking slow and long in the Indian summers. His job as the Sanitary Inspector required him to be on the horse while inspecting the abattoir, the vegetable mandi, the public sewage canals etc. He wore brown Jodhpur breeches with tan boots and a crisp white cotton shirt with a short navy-blue tie and a bowler hat on his inspections.

It was hot and humid. The monsoons were just around the corner. As it was early evening, Alfie wanted a snack of sandwich and coffee and to play some snooker before he went home. There was jazz playing on the gramophone. YMCA had the latest collection of jazz and other music from Hollywood and was the only place in town to listen to the current music from the West. The YMCA was still quite empty as young men came in only around six or seven for an evening of fun, games, and camaraderie. DC played crossword and Alfie flipped through *Time* magazine lying on his table till his order came in. He was enjoying the music when Wilson, the Anglo-Indian boy, served Alfie. And he served black coffee to DC.

After, when they started playing snooker, DC kept winning. They continued playing, DC kept winning. Alfie did not show any emotion, but DC knew that he would not stop till he had won the game from him. They had interludes for a quick dinner and two short breaks between the games. DC still had a better score than Alfie. As the evening tuned into night, the lamps were lit, and they got their drinks and kept playing. DC liked scotch with two ice cubes precisely. Alfie liked rum. Old Monk, with water. They had been playing for many hours and had barely spoken a few words. They could play on but now Wilson was standing in the corner, an indication that it was late and that they would close soon. Yet, they played on. Alfie had gained a few games but overall, DC was still leading by a thin score. DC was playing because he enjoyed the game and Alfie was playing because he wanted to win.

'Do you want to go hunting?' DC asked Alfie.

'Hmm...yes,' Alfie said, concentrating on the red ball.

'Where do you want to go?' DC continued to distract him.

'There are quite a few options...Sita Pahar, Pariyat and Kandhari close by...' Alfie took a shot and missed the putt. 'Mandla and Sagour as well.'

'This weekend? Sita Pahar?' DC asked, as he putted.

'Yes...why not?' Alfie said as he lost. The DC had won. 'You were not your best today, Alfie. Anything the matter?' Alfie only smiled as he pulled out and lighted a cigarette.

Today, Alfie did not mind. He was still carrying his exhilaration at seeing you earlier whose name he did not know yet.

They were good friends. Winning and losing in snooker was fine.

This is how Destiny was to play out its game by bringing you in their lives.

It had been raining furiously. The monsoon had been quite belligerent that year. While coming from school, you three eldest sisters were huddled together under a large umbrella as the wind rose and the rain lashed. The eldest, Hannah, had started wearing a saree. Frieda, you were wearing a white salwar kurta with a blue dupatta and Sarah was still in her frocks. Hannah's saree was wet all the way to her waist, and she had wrapped the pallu around her to keep the weather at bay to no effect. She was drenched. And so were you and Sarah. Hannah and you two were in the front and Sarah was walking close behind them. You walked against the wind clustered together. The trees were swaying like they were inebriated, and the wind was running amok as if it had developed feet, pushing the three of them back with its raving force. The umbrella was barely able to contain the three of you against the wind. The road was empty with no soul in sight. Initially you all had waited at school for the nature's fury to subside but then you had to reach home lest your mother becomes hopping mad with the three of you.

The Mother was always worried about her seven daughters. What if one of them was deceived into falling in love with a plebeian young man? What if one of them besmirched the reputation of the family? She wanted her girls to preserve their virginity at all costs. And so, she had become your ruthless keeper with strict diktats and stricter punishments. Stymied, her daughters became like icebergs floating around at sea with just the tips visible. The Mother was afraid of what lay beneath in the depths of your hearts. She had no access to your minds and souls.

The school bags were dripping wet with all notebooks soaked. Sarah was crying and wanted you to take shelter somewhere. You refused because you knew that the Mother would be provoked and would find a way to make it your fault and then her fury would have no end. There was no shelter in any case on that lonely patch, except long eucalyptus trees and some mango trees on either side of the road. The sides of the elevated road were already filled with deep waters and Hannah feared the creatures under the murky surface. Snakes, crabs, scorpions, frogs, etc. This made those trees inaccessible. You walked on stubbornly. You did not like the situation, the Mother's anticipated belligerence, Sarah's crying, and the fact that you worried about Hannah's health. You disliked the wet clothes sticking to your bodies, making the contours of the chest, legs, and waist visible. It would be a never-ending scandal if someone saw anyone of you in that state. It will become a saga of shameless exhibitionist sisters.

Hannah's protection could not do anything. Your anger did not keep the rain, wind, and storm at bay. Sarah's crying did not alleviate anything. A rush of wind came riding on thick and heavy drops of water and took away the umbrella suddenly with an unforeseen gush. Now exposed with no protection, Hannah collected the two of you in her arms. Sarah hid her face in her hands to protect the rain from lashing at her face. You raised your head and looked in the direction the wind was carrying the umbrella. You kept staring till the umbrella became a speck in a distance and was lost behind the thick curtain of rain. You asked the sisters to keep walking fast. You were distraught but you did not cry.

When you turned the corner, you saw the Mother in the veranda pacing up and down. She stopped when she saw you three girls. From the way she was standing, arms akimbo and posture ramrod straight, you knew she was fuming. You knew she was angry because all the three of you were young and beautiful, and she could not control that. You all had managed to reach home safe. She knew that there will be no rumours because no one saw you, but the Mother was still scared of what the people might say.

When you three entered the veranda, with a halo of steam emanating from your warm bodies, she looked at you smouldering and riding the beast rising in her. She looked into Hannah's eyes and said, 'Go in and change.' Hannah looked at the others with timid empathy and left without saying anything.

She then had turned to Sarah, who was trembling and whimpering like a wet puppy. 'Where is the umbrella?' She thundered. 'It flew away,' she said sotto voce. 'What did you say?' She asked. And Sarah was shivering and did not say anything. You said, 'It flew away in the wind.' The Mother slapped you and pushed Sarah to go inside.

Now you waited for the Mother to unleash her wrath on you as you nursed your cheek. The Mother stared with dilated eyes that had embers flashing in them. Then in severely low hissing voice, sharpening words with her teeth, the Mother commanded, 'Go back, search and bring the umbrella from where you lost it.'

'What if the Orchard Man sees me?' You asked, scared. The Mother did not reply and stood stubbornly spewing fire from her eyes.

You looked at her helplessly, your bones and muscles felt cold and wet and you wanted nothing more than a change into dry clothes and a warm cup of tea to feel cherished again. But that was not to be, the Mother pushed you out in the rain without saying another word, still scalding you with embers in her eyes. Frieda, you stood in the rain, hoping for mercy. None came. You then turned and started walking back to the school. You shed a tear but then they came uncontrollably. 'Why am I such an unloved one?' you wondered. The Mother could have allowed you to change and take another umbrella or a raincoat. But no! Only the rain carried away your tears with it.

You walked in a daze. It was a long distance back. The day was threatening to turn deeper grey and purple like a bruise. You trembled in the cold wind with hair plastered on your head and clothes on your body. The rainwater ran all over your skin leaving tiny tingling whirlpools of shivers. Never would you do such a thing to anyone as the Mother did to you. You thought.

You reached the spot where the umbrella had flown away. You stood in the sheets of rain and thick droplets that felt like pellets of steel. You tried to remember the direction where the umbrella had flown and all you could visualise was the swirling of winds and the fervent chasing rain. Then you spotted the black canopy of the umbrella wedged sideways in the branches of a bushy tree some distance away beyond the water trench that Hannah had been so scared of earlier.

You were so relieved at the sight of the umbrella that you had dived into the water and waded across and reached the tree. You did not think about all the water insects and organisms that could attack you. You reached the tree but could not climb it as the mud under your feet was squishy and the tree under your hands, slippery. You could not get a proper grip either on the earth or on the tree to hoist herself. You slipped and fell in the water trying to get a hold to climb. Your clothes, skin and hair were smirched brown with the muddy slush. You were not discouraged and you tried again. You slipped and fell again. This time when you came up from the water ditch, a hand grabbed your hand and pulled you up. It was a man's hand, you knew, with its broadness and firmness. Before you could clear the water from your eyes and look at him, he had pulled you on the back of the horse to sit in the front of his saddle, without slipping. You struggled to clean your face and eyes and look at the Good Samaritan.

'You are safe now,' he said. The voice that seeped into your ears was deep, baritone, clipped and firm. Your back was pressed against his body, and you could feel the rising and falling of his chest with his breathing. It triggered a strange desire and a fear that made you tremble.

You turned and looked at him. The same handsome face with brown eyes, and streaks of water gliding across the smooth-shaven skin. You were tongue-tied. All the words were lost now in so much rain, water, slush and wind.

Both of you sat like that for a few minutes and as he pulled the reins to turn the horse, you pointed desperately to the umbrella, and he looked up. He gave you a broad grin as he understood what this solitary girl was doing in that raging storm. He stood up on the horse, which wobbled but remained steady and he extended his hands to retrieve the umbrella. You promptly folded it and clasped it to your bosom under the folded arms.

He started laughing. 'It's raining. You can open that.' You shook your head in a firm no. He looked at you amused for a moment and then sat down and guided the horse around onto the muddy road.

The dusk was turning a deeper shade of cerulean grey and dark blue. On the road, he removed his hat and put it on your head. He got down so that you could sit comfortably in the saddle and removed his thick raincoat and covered you with that. You had already sneezed a few times.

You looked at him with gratitude and he just nodded. 'I know where you live. I will drop you.' You wanted to talk to him, but it seemed that words dissolved in your throat.

And that day, when DC dropped you at the corner that turned to your house, he said, 'My name is Peter Barnes. We go to the same church. I saved the host for you the other Sunday.'

'Thank you,' you said. 'My name is Frieda. I am grateful to you.'

He laughed at that. 'Frieda, the peaceful. That's nice.' You read warmth in his eyes.

You turned the corner clutching the umbrella to your chest. There were lights flickering in the homes around and in your heart as you realised that you were completely besotted with this man. You felt so calm and so wonderful having finally met him. You wanted to stay and speak more but that would have been inappropriate.

The Mother's anger abated at the sight of the umbrella, yet she did not speak with you the rest of the week. That week you thought about him many times impulsively and inadvertently and waited to see him again in church on Sunday.

When he met Alfie in the evening at the YMCA, DC had a cold and was sneezing. When Alfie asked him, he told him about this determined girl called Frieda who had braved the weather just to retrieve an umbrella. He told him it was the same girl from the church whose host he had saved. That's when Alfie came to know your name!

THE PROPOSAL, THE TANTRUM, AND THE LETTERS

When you turned seventeen, a red and black Austin came and stopped on the dusty road outside the house of seven daughters.

The DC stepped out. He was wearing an open-collared light blue linen shirt, striped cotton jacket, a high-waisted, stiffly creased and ironed baggy trouser and black shining leather shoes. Sarah noticed him coming to the gate and the entire house was in a nervous flurry when she announced that. They had never had a visitor in a car. The shining car seemed out of place in their dusty lane. DC knocked at the gate and waited for some movement in the quiet house.

After some time, Hannah and the Father came to receive him. Hannah was composed. The Father's surprise and anxiety were betrayed by his accelerated speech and uncoordinated actions. They took him past the courtyard painted in white lime, and a flowering orange tree. They took him to a spartan room with three chairs in which they received an occasional visitor. It was dark and Hannah opened the only window in the room. She got the whiff of frankincense, sandalwood and musk from his perfume. She noticed the neat straight parting in the dark brown-black hair and a skin golden pink in the diffused evening light as it poured in from the window.

The Father suspected that he had come for you, Frieda. He knew Hannah was not interested in marrying and the others were still young. Hannah had decided to become a nurse and was undergoing her training at the local hospital. It was her day off that day.

The Father and DC sat in that room with one window and three chairs and made an intermittent conversation.

'How can I help you?' the Father asked.

'I was passing by and thought about introducing myself,' DC said.

'You are the District Collector. Everyone knows you. It is an honour that you came,' the Father said in humility that comes from being a father of seven daughters and from knowing one's place in society. The Father sat at the edge of the chair with his hands on his lap.

'The honour is mine that you have welcomed me,' DC said with warmth. He realised the discomfort his unannounced visit was causing. He had not been able to stop thinking about you since the day he had helped you retrieve the umbrella.

Hannah served tea. It took a while as she had to send Tamara to fetch biscuits from the corner shop. The Mother joined them in the third chair, wincing and complaining about the pain in her joints and sat stiffly to convey the impression of an advancing age. She was only forty.

'A woman has to give birth and the more children she has, the more her body is destroyed,' the Mother said. 'Life obliges a woman to multiply and give birth again and again.' She continued to ensure that her importance is registered in that small gathering. DC nodded understandably.

The Father sat with a lump in his throat for the first visitor in a car, overwhelmed by his own poverty and the aroma of camphor on his clothes. He was surprised by his own indomitable ineloquence. The late afternoon heat of mid-April in India was covering the DC with a fine layer of perspiration making him seem shinier and his chair creaked like lizards in heat as he shifted his position. The parents both sat still and expectantly with arms folded, making an effort at continuing the ensuing silence.

The DC, not used to situations such as these, gathered his courage.

'I want to marry your daughter,' he said.

'Which one?' they both asked at the same time.

'Frieda.'

'Why her?' the Mother asked acidly. 'There are others, prettier than her.' She had lost colour with her silent rage. She knew it would be wrong to create a scene in front of the highest district officer!

'I have seen her in church,' he said. 'I like her.'

The Mother was now more upset.

And he waited patiently in the quagmire of grunts and eviscerated sentences of the Mother, bile and disgust apparent. At first, he tried to listen with respect to that confusing semi audible monotone but then his imagination went after you, following you in the rooms and the courtyard. And he sat there listening quietly to her litany. He was afraid of the humiliation of refusal. The Mother was carrying on as if in trance and he saw that her eyes were twisted like a fish and that the words did not correspond to the movement of the lips.

When Hannah started lighting the lamps in the house, he saw a lizard on the wall that crawled lazily and then stopped. He controlled his herpetophobia and decided it was time to leave. He stood up with a strange feeling that he had risen from a body that belonged to him but was still left behind seated in there, warming the chair waiting for an answer. The Mother continued speaking with her eyes fixed to the floor.

The Father followed him past the hot fragrance of orange blossoms in the summer evening. DC paused and turned to see if he could get a glimpse of you. But the house was dark, and the sky had just suspended the moon. The Father accompanied him to the car. 'Forgive her temperament, her thorns,' he said of the Mother. The DC turned and shook his hands.

The DC sat in the car and turned the ignition. He heard the Father say something. He was not sure with the engine coming alive right at the same time. He turned off the engine and looked at the Father whose face was in the dark shadow with the moon behind. 'I agree to your proposal,' the Father said. The DC nodded with delight. 'Thank you!' He said and while he was perfectly sober, he felt dizzy with delight, and he imagined himself hallucinating. Was the last hour real?

He drove away.

He saw the slightly bent figure of the Father still standing there in the rear-view mirror. He stopped the car, got down and went to him.

'Do I have the permission to visit her?' he asked excitedly.

'Not at home. Not with the Mother around.' The Father said in a calm humble voice that betrayed the understanding and empathy he felt for this young man. The DC withered with a sigh.

'Where would you like to meet Frieda? She can only meet you either in my or Hannah's presence,' he said.

'Can I meet you at the officer's club for lunch tomorrow?' he said, almost imploring.

'Let me see what I can do.' The Father replied.

That evening the engine drone was music to his ears and the fumes smelled of warm orange blossom scent.

Next morning, you woke up with light in your soul. Hannah had told you the previous night what the Father had told him. But all hell broke loose in the house when they found a black rag doll, three pieces of mirror and three incense sticks, stuck in a half-cut coconut outside the door.

The Mother went hysterical. 'This is a bad omen. This is witchcraft. Call the priest. Nobody will leave the threshold of the main door till the holy water purifies this house,' and she started throwing all the meagre things of the household in the courtyard for purification and started looking in the nooks and crannies of the house for any other signs of witchcraft.

You knew. This would be the first of the many theatrics and hurdles you would encounter.

The Father went to call the priest and, on the way, stopped at the Collectorate to let the DC know that the afternoon lunch was impossible that day and that he would help organise it later, perhaps when the shock of the proposal settled down.

The Gypsy came that evening. He sat outside the door and played his ektara. He smiled only when he saw you.

DC was encouraged with the Father's approval and started sending letters to you through his driver. The driver would deliver the letter to you near the school gate routinely at least once a week and sometimes twice. The letters had a steadfastness of his feelings, honesty of his thoughts and sometimes had emotional poetry. The letters were sincere and contemplative.

Hannah knew about the letters and the happiness they gave you. She protected your happiness from the Mother, who was oblivious. Hannah would do your portion of the housework, so that you could read and re-read the letters. Hannah would stay close to the Mother and would keep her engaged so that her attention would not go to you. Hannah thought it important that you find happiness.

You believed every word in his letters; that restrained sentimentality, those written meditations of the heart, the gentle insistence of the future together, the male honesty of an impending permanence of their relationship. Your belief had simplified your love and made it easy to accept DC.

You got restless when a letter got delayed. You had never felt like this before. Each letter brought you closer to DC and you were surprised at your vulnerability, and the beauty you felt for yourself through those letters. You looked forward to seeing him at the church on Sundays and an eye contact, a smile and an exchange of a few words after provided you enough patience to sustain herself till next Sunday. It was all very discreet for you knew the unreasonableness of the wrath of your mother.

You were determined to marry DC, since now no person had the power over your heart like him. He was your only beacon of happiness.

THE SPECTACLE OF THE WHITE SAREE

The white silk saree with a thin gold zari border was an heirloom that no woman in your family had worn. It was a saree not meant for weddings. It was a saree of mourning that your great-grandmother had been given by the royal family of Orchha, long time after the death of the prince, when they were clearing away the clothes chest. It was one of the sarees the princess had worn during her mourning period. Your great-grandmother was a Hindu Rajput woman. The saree had remained languishing as the family heirloom for nearly eighty years. You were given the saree by the Mother when your marriage date was fixed. You had noticed the bizarre condescension in the Mother's eyes. You knew the family folklore around it, but you chose not to be superstitious because you were marrying the man that you loved. You had closed yourself in your room and shrieked and jumped with joy. When the Mother heard you in the kitchen, she said to Hannah, 'This is what I am afraid of. The hormones of my daughters!'

When you opened the saree, you realised the sad state it was in. You saw patches of discolouration in the silk and some fine tears in the folds. The zari had come off in places in spirals of fine golden thread. You did not bemoan the hand me down but sat thinking of how you would make it worth the occasion, the most important day of your life. You had a magnificent vision of your marriage saree. However impossible, you decided to work on it to make it grand for the occasion.

Every night when the house slept curled in the dreams, you spread it and removed the creases with the cushions of your palms. You moistened it and then stretched it gently to remove the supple corrugated waves of ripples that the silk had acquired. You soaked it in herbs and let it dry in the soothing moonlight. You collected the sun's rays in the warmth of marble stones and ironed it gently. You let it fly in the early mornings on the twine clothesline so that it could be saturated with the dew that fell. All that the saree did was change randomly. In some places it was white as the moonlight, in some places it held the warmth of the sun, other places the softness of dew and yet others it stubbornly refused to change. Exasperation enveloped you, Frieda, but you were adamant to make it what you wanted it to be. You held all your disappointment at bay because every time you received his letter, your heart thrummed like a galloping horse. The only message you ever sent back was thank you. That summed up your feelings and choked eloquence.

The Mother refused to help. You went to the elderly rangrez[1] in the old quarters of town who could mend and recolour it. When he saw the saree, he refused to take it and said that it is too delicate and too deteriorated to mend. When you insisted and negotiated, appealing to his expertise and exquisite art, he said visibly distressed, 'This saree does not feel auspicious. It reminds me of death. You should burn this thing.' The rangrez left to attend to the vats boiling with colours and dyes.

An old woman was sitting inside the shadows of his dilapidated house who saw and heard the conversation. You noticed her only when she emerged from the depths of the room. As you gathered the saree untidily, the old woman looked at you with glassy, rheumy, deep-set eyes piercingly and said, 'Meet me when the moon is half eaten and visible over your head.' She had a strange metallic flat voice neither a woman's nor a man's. The old woman was untidy, and her kohl was dark and wide around her eyes. You looked at her and a shudder ran through you. As you stepped out, the old woman said, 'Not here,' and as you turned and looked at her and she said, 'At the mazaar under the banyan tree at the far end of the fields.' You did not say anything but walked away feeling

[1] Person who dyes fabrics.

strange, as if sucked of all the energy. You felt like you were being strangled by those piercing eyes. Your hands trembled and you felt palpitations in your heart. The presence of that eerie old woman was surreal, and it scared you. You decided that you will not meet her. However, as the days passed and when you could not fathom how to mend the saree, your resolve weakened, and each passing day drew you closer to the thought of meeting the old woman.

In the meantime, the whole town was intrigued by the spectacle and visions of the white saree in your house. Sometimes draped to the rosebush in the front. Sometimes flying on the clothesline in the backyard. Sometimes draped around you, and other times fluttering between the posts in your front yard. Your obsession was becoming a lore that turned into banter for all to enjoy. Some even perpetuated by the Mother herself. But you were oblivious and impervious to it all. You only wanted your imagination to transcend into reality.

The night when the moon was half in shadows, you rose in the stillness of the night. You gathered the white saree and stepped out. The night waited for you with bated breath. You felt an uneasy restlessness. It seemed completely incongruous, that the night be so still when your heart was beating so wildly, and your mind was working so furiously. Not a leaf shivered in its branches, not a speck of light rose to greet you, the wind had frozen in its path. You walked in the darkness and shadows of the streets devoid of all life and totally deserted, no dog barked, no cat crossed the path, no cow lay in the middle of the road. When the fields started, you thought about turning back but something propelled you to carry on. You had beads of sweat on your forehead. You were scared and yet determined. You walked through the wheat field as the bristles of the seed pods scratched your ankles and shins. The stones and dust entered your flat sandals like little universes and poked your soles, but you walked on. Your clothes got caught in the crop and it seemed as if someone was pulling you back, but you walked on. In defiance. In tenacity. In a daring daze.

The darkness changed its tone when you saw the silhouette of the big banyan tree with shadows caught between its trunk, branches, and descending roots. It was a large sinister tree with many roots that reached the grounds and found the earth to anchor in and some still hanging in the air at myriad lengths above the ground threatening to bury their ends in time. But all; leaves, branches, roots, all were still as the breath of the dead. As you got closer to the big banyan tree, you perceived movement in the dark shadows. When your eyes adjusted, you saw the outlines of a rectangular-shaped mazaar[2]. There was a small earthen pot at one end that held the embers and emitted thick woody and sweet-smelling smoke. It was the incense burning. The old woman waited for you and when you reached her, she extended her hands and took the old white saree. Then she tied your eyes with a large strip of cloth. She was chanting something, and you were not sure if it was just her or if there was someone else there.

She held you by the shoulders. You felt the hard, calloused, and gnarled fingers that pushed you forward, neither gently nor briskly. By now you had lost the directional orientation and was enveloped in another thicker layer of smoky airless darkness. You smelled an alluring fragrance of heady tuberoses and subtle cinnamon and cloves. The old woman continued to chant in an ineligible tongue.

When the old woman stopped and started to remove your clothes, you were startled and lost balance and your hand found the support of the tomb's edge. You felt scared and tried resisting, but with firmness and without changing the tone of her incantations the old woman peeled them away. When you stood naked there, the old woman started moving around you in circles, chanting in an elevated tone. Some

[2] A Muslim shrine or enshrined tomb.

time passed, and you sensed that the stillness was changing into something dynamic. It was not the wind. But sounds, of the leaves and the soft movement of branches and the roots. Her pitch had changed, and her voice had acquired a duality. Initially it was indecipherable but then as the loudness and the hoarseness increased, you heard a softer incantation alongside. You spread your hands and turned around and touched the old woman's face and throat. You pulled her face close to your ears. Both the voices were not coming from her mouth. You were startled. The old woman's face was smooth like that of a child. You touched her hands, and they were smooth as well. The incantations continued in a hoarse and a soft voice.

The sounds became louder and urgent, and the earth started shaking. You felt panic and just when you thought you heard a third sound like a wail, you felt burning on your skin at the back between the shoulder blades. And then it was all frenzy. The wailing sound seemed to be leaping around you high and low and it made your hair stand on your arms and legs. The confusion of sounds, the shaking earth, the rising wind, the flowing hair, the strange incantations in two voices interspersed with a third one, which made you feel giddy and nauseous. Every time the third voice was high and felt close to you, there was deep burning on her skin. After what seemed like eternity, you fell to the earth exhausted and singed. You were drenched in sweat. It all stopped suddenly.

There was the stillness of the night and nothing else. You could sense the old woman around you. A few moments later, the old woman pulled you from under the armpits and stood you up. Still blindfolded, she poured cold water on your head, and it traversed the neck, shoulders, breast, torso, stomach, and limbs to your feet and then the earth. You started shivering wildly as your body cooled down suddenly. You felt the fabric of the old silk saree wrapping you up. After the old woman was done wrapping you, she put an arm around your waist and said softly, 'You are blessed.' She continued to hold you upright and did not remove the blindfold. You both stood like that for a long time and when she opened your blindfold, the sun was blue, grey and orange in the east. Eagerly you looked at the saree. It was in the same condition as earlier. When you looked at her confused, complaining and helplessly, the old woman gave you an assured smile and said, 'It will mend but come back again for the next two nights.' You started crying in panic and pain. It had all been futile, you thought. Nothing had changed, except the dark fear and burning you felt under your skin.

She handed you the clothes and when you were dressed, the two of you walked together to the edge of the town and then the streets and then to your doorstep. The old woman left you there at the threshold. Later, when you examined the burning sensation on your back in the mirror, your peach-coloured skin was all bruised with symbols and alphabets of a language you did not know.

You had been restless and scared but nonetheless you went for two more nights as the old woman had suggested. The same ceremony happened each day. She said the same thing at the end of each ordeal. You are blessed. And you found that hollow and strange as it was your body that was burnt and disfigured while the saree remained in the same condition as before. The first night it was your back, the second night it was your chest, and the third night was your inner thighs that were marked as if in dark blue ink. Your body had been burnt and disfigured and it was painful. You started crying at your own recklessness in frustration. You felt taken advantage of by the old woman. On the third night, the old woman gave you a small locked wooden box and its key.

'Keep this with you. But you must not open this box for the next forty days. When you open it, it will tell you what to do.'

'What about these marks?' you said indicating the tattoos that infested your body.

'You are blessed,' is all she said. You looked at her incomprehensibly.

'The prayer on your arms will help you with the flowers. The prayer encircling your body is one with immense power and you will be able to use it three times. When you have used it, you will lose it. The prayers on your thighs will give you sons as many as you want.'

'What flowers? And what prayers? I do not understand. I do not understand anything of the last three nights.'

'About the flowers, it will be a gift to help others. You will know in time. About the prayers, when your heart beats for a solution, the resonance will make the prayers surface from your body to your tongue, and you will know what to pray. You don't have to do anything about the prayers on your thighs.'

When you started to leave, she said, 'Do not open the box for forty days, otherwise you will lose all your blessings.'

When she left you at the threshold as she had done the previous two mornings she said, 'Blessings come with challenges. Your life will not be an easy one.' And she kissed you on the forehead with her chapped lips and left. When you turned a few moments later, there was no one there, just a dusty swirl in the early morning cold breeze. You stood there and thought about the flowers, the prayers, the burnt marks, and the box, the things you had acquired in return for the three nights. All strange things. The saree was still in the same state. You started crying as you walked back home.

The Gypsy had followed you at a distance all those nights without you knowing it. He was not the one to interfere. He only wanted your safety.

THE WHOLE TOWN IS GATHERED OUTSIDE

You gave the box to Hannah and told her not to give it to you, come what may, for the next forty days.

'What's in the box?' she asked.

'I don't know,' you replied.

'I cannot take care of it if I do not understand what I am doing,' she said and then you led her to your room. You bolted the door and removed your clothes. Hannah raised her hands to her mouth and let out a gasp. Your body was all marked blue-black and thickly welted with an exotic language. Large tears brimmed in her eyes. You told her of the events of the past three nights. You told her about your desperation to go each night and about feeling deceived when it ended.

'You love him so much?' Hannah asked as she grasped the box tightly. Hannah had never felt that way for anyone. She needed to hear your answer.

'Yes,' you had said with a calm pride.

'Then this is safe with me,' Hannah said. She unbolted the door and took the box away.

Giving the box away was like giving away a part of your body. Every day you would go and ask Hannah morning, afternoon, and evening if the box was safe, and she would say yes without meeting your eyes. After one week you asked her, 'You don't look me in the eyes when you say yes. Is the box safe?' And she simply said, 'Yes' again.

'Look me in the eyes and say that.'

'No…you will read it in my eyes where it is.'

Then for the next week, every day you would turn Hannah's room upside down looking for the box to make sure it was safe.

Hannah would put the room back again. The Mother sensed that something was amiss because while you had gone quiet, there was a wildfire in your eyes and your hair was unkempt, and Hannah was forever tidying her room. You did whatever the Mother asked you to without arguing and the Mother missed your defiance.

The third week, you started crying and begging Hannah for the box. When no one was in sight you would hold her hands or waist or feet sometimes and beseech and cry for the box. Hannah would refuse. You had stopped eating and bathing and finding the box had become your sole objective. Many times, you thought of beating Hannah and forcing her to reveal the whereabouts of the box. At the end of the third week when all your begging and crying did not help, you picked up the hockey stick the Mother kept behind the front door for any unwelcome intruder. Frieda, you swung it and landed it heavily on Hannah's shoulder. Hannah doubled over in pain and looked at you with surprised anger as you were not a violent person and wanted to give in but when she saw your madness and rage, she decided not to and told you that she had buried it in the backyard garden.

The fourth week, the garden was full of craters and mounds. The soil was moved and moved again. Your solitary figure constantly dug the ground at regular lengths to find the box in the bosom of the earth. All the marigold bushes and the chrysanthemums had been demolished and the Mother was hopping mad with anger after two days and she tied your leg to the bed post. But after a struggle with the captivity, you escaped in the night after a few days and started digging again. You dug the neighbours' gardens and your house had become a glorious battlefield of the neighbours complaining and fighting with the Mother and asking her to give them compensation to mend their gardens again. And the Mother feigned complete ignorance and fought back hard. There were noises and stone pelting and abuses, cacophony, bickering, accusations. Only the nights calmed the passions, but the craters kept emerging.

The Father went to the Collectorate to call on DC and to explore if he could knock sense into you. He was told that DC was away on an administrative tour for two months and that he could meet him only when he was back. He returned disappointed.

In the fifth week, the Mother slapped you and beat you. You had stopped eating and cried for the box all the time. You were locked in your room, tied to the bedpost. You constantly howled for Hannah and the box. The Mother, exhausted with trying to control you, turned on Hannah and told her to give back the box. And that entire week Hannah claimed that she had forgotten where the box was and kept searching in a new place every day under the Mother's supervision. Rest of the sisters too joined in the search, but no box was found. In the last few days, you calmed down and seemed to have given up.

When the sixth week started, you got ready every morning and waited for Hannah to bring the box. In the last five days to complete the forty days, you sat like a statue and waited. Not eating, not drinking, not doing anything. Just waited with a shallow breath. Hannah had stopped going near you after the third week when she had been hit. But you knew of her presence in the house by the sound of her feet. The Mother would come and sit by you, glaring, trying to fathom your madness and then she would start speaking with you calmly first, then agitated, then angrily and finally violently rant, none of which had any effect on you. Then the Mother would place her hand on your head as if commiserating, as if accepting her defeat, as if holding herself responsible for your state. But her touch only gave you the courage to go on with stubbornness single-mindedly.

When the fortieth day arrived, you had no strength. Early in the morning, Hannah came into your room, and you could not get up. It was still dark. She called the Mother and the two of them picked you up like a feather. Hannah sat you down on a low chair in the courtyard and the Mother fetched water from the well. They removed your clothes and poured the water over your head. Your jaw clattered and your body shivered violently in the cold water. As Hannah soaped you gently, she noticed that there were no marks on your body. The Mother poured the water again. After the bath was done, Hannah wiped you and rubbed your thin body with almond oil. The Mother stood and watched with sad eyes. Hannah wrapped you in a towel and took you to your room. She oiled and combed your hair in one tight long plait. Then took out a fresh set of clothes to put on you. When she removed the wrap, your peach-coloured skin shone smooth and translucent in the orange morning glow. You shivered, and your skin got the goose bumps, as Hannah put the clothes on you. She put a thin line of kohl in your eyes which shone bright and alive, beckoning Hannah to return the box. Hannah smiled and patted you on the shoulders. Then she left the room.

When she came back, she had the dirty wooden box with her. She placed it on the low table beside your bed and stood away.

'Go on…open it,' Hannah said.

As you extended your arms to open the box, your hands trembled. When you touched the box, all your energy gave up. You sat with your right hand on the box, feeling the roughness of the surface. You felt something moving inside.

The rest of the house and the town was still sleeping. The Mother had come up with a cup of tea. She stood looking for a place to lay it down.

'Unlock it please,' you gave the key to Hannah. The Mother stood rooted in curiosity with the cup of tea emanating tendrils of steam. Hannah unlocked the box and waited. You opened the box. A shriek of hysterical laughter went up from the Mother and a wail went up from Hannah.

The box was full of crawling, wriggling and hairy moist worms!

Frieda, you were not perturbed. You closed the box and sat down by the window sipping tea that the Mother had brought. That morning you went back to the rangrez where you had met the old woman. He told you that the old woman was not there. When you told him what was in the box, he did not say anything but asked you to wait. He went to his backyard and came back with bunch of twigs which were loaded with fresh green leaves.

'Feed these to the worms,' he said.

'What leaves are these?' you asked.

'Shuhtoot[1] leaves,' he said. And he told you to come every second or third day to get more.

In the room, you laid out the leaves in a wooden crate and poured out the worms into it. There was a small cotton pouch at the bottom. It was soggy and dirty. When you felt the pouch, it seemed to contain some seeds. The entire day you sat watching the ugly creatures wriggling there, holding the cotton pouch in your hands. Nothing happened. They only wriggled and burrowed in the leaves. But that night you slept peacefully. And so did Hannah. The Mother was very amused with your suspension of sanity in the last few weeks and with the outcome of it. She walked around smiling the entire day.

In two days all the leaves were gone. In the morning, when the dawn was just a smudge in the sky, you walked to the rangrez and knocked on his door. It reverberated loudly in the silence of the morning. When he opened the door, he was naked except for the dhoti, with mark of the folds of his quilt and bed sheet embossed on his dark brown skin. With sleep laden eyes and without saying anything, he gestured you to wait. Standing outside, you could not make out anything inside

---

[1] Mulberry.

the room as it was dark inside. The rangrez came back with a much larger bunch of leaves, neatly tied with the jute cord, and gave it to you. Before you could say the words of gratitude, he turned and started closing the door and the words that were beginning to emerge from your throat just hung in your mouth. Silently you too turned back and headed home.

This became your routine every second or third day. You would leave silently in the morning and come back with the bundle of leaves to feed the worms. As weeks passed the worms became furry and grew. There were different kinds of worms. You were fascinated by their growth. From thin scrawny worms they had grown into fat furry caterpillars that walked all over the crate devouring the leaves. As more days passed, they attached themselves to the twigs, and released wet fibrous saliva and enveloped themselves in it. You did not know what to do and asked the rangrez and he told you to put them in hot water after a few days and then pick one or two strands and roll them on a spindle. You became curious.

When you put one of the rough balls in the hot water, you struggled to find a strand and then you saw a beautiful, winged creature emerge from one of the other cocoons which was a different one. You caught a few strands and started spinning that on a spindle while keeping your eyes on the winged creature. It dried its wings and then spread them and waved them. You were mesmerised by the colours therein. Suddenly, it moved in the sunlight and the wings reflected a kaleidoscope of colours across the bare lime painted white walls and tiled ceiling of your room. It was like thousand mirrors reflecting a thousand colours and you sat chasing the colours with your eyes while moving your hands on the spindle. You did not know when the day passed. When twilight fell, there were more winged creatures in your room than you could behold. And in your hand was a spindle full of rough thread.

That night you slept with the spindle lying by your pillow. There was a soft flapping of wings in the room that soothed you. Next morning, you slept late and were woken up by a furious banging on your door by the Mother.

'What is happening in your room?' the Mother asked.

'Nothing,' you said without opening the door.

'Then how come there is a coloured hue around in your room? The whole town is gathered outside. Open the door.'

When you opened the door, the Mother stood rooted at the spectacle. There were large, beautiful moths filling your room. As they flapped their wings, the moving geometry of colours created a hypnotic effect. There was a fine mist of sparkling multi-coloured dust suspended in the air covering everything.

Then came Hannah and the other sisters. They saw the vision of a girl in white night dress in a rainbow mist surrounded by the magical winged creatures. The word spread like wildfire and people from the neighbouring towns and villages started coming to see the spectacle.

Rumours started that you, Frieda, were a goddess, and people started to bring offerings and started praying and doing aartis outside your house. The priest of your church came and said that this was a miracle. People lit candles and diyas outside your window. The priests from the local Hindu temple came and said that this must be Krishna's blessing and set up a site for their rituals. People brought offerings and the Mother was happy collecting and hoarding all that.

Gypsy playing his ektara outside your window accentuated your magic and the crowds swelled.

On the third day, DC came. He had come back from his tour the previous day and the news had reached him. When he found that you were at the centre of it all, he knew he had to take you away from this frenzied commotion. He was not surprised at the Mother's cunning and enterprising encouragement of the chaos. When he asked you, 'Will you come away with me to calm this frenzy?' You simply said, 'Yes.'

He whisked you away from the back door. All the winged creatures followed you, and the coloured hues stopped from your room. When the Mother found that you were not there, she was enraged. All the gathered people started going away, and by evening the house had a deserted look like death had visited the place. The Father and sisters were much relieved.

DC took you home. But not without Noa, the littlest sister, now eight. The Father would not allow you to go alone and insisted that you take a sibling along. DC got his house help to make the guest room comfortable for you and Noa.

'You both can stay here as long as you want,' he said.

You both just nodded, relieved to be away from all the brouhaha and yet anxious to be staying under the same roof as him. You saw his affection in his thoughtful actions, and the warmth in his eyes.

You had carried only three things with you: the spindle of raw silk, the white tattered saree, and the wooden box which had the pouch of seeds in it. Later that day, Hannah bought you a small bag of clothes and toiletries.

You did not know what to do with the coarse spindle, and so you asked the rangrez. You also asked for the old woman insistently explaining how she looked and how she dressed, and he said, she was my *bua*[2]. She is dead now. She is buried under the banyan tree in the wheat fields. You were perplexed because the old woman had held the saree and had draped it around you as she had chanted for the three nights. The box from which the moths and silk had emerged had been given by her. 'You must be mistaken,' he said. 'She died when I was a young man. Anyway, what can I do for you?'

And you showed him the spindle. 'I don't know what to do with this,' you said, helplessly.

---

[2] Father's sister.

'Ah...this is silk. You must wash it with soap and remove the coarse fibres.' He said after looking at it carefully. You stood looking at it not knowing how to wash the spindle of silk. He understood. 'I will do it for you, but you must help.'

You washed the silk fibres in a vat with him and stretched it tight between two horizontal sticks of bamboo. After he repeatedly washed it, the silk fibres started shining clean and smooth. He laid them out in the sun to dry. 'You can leave it here. Take it back after three days.'

When you returned and saw the silk drying in his courtyard, it shone as light ran in its veins. It looked pure and pristine. The rangrez took a thread's end and rotated it around the spindle till it was full and bulging. 'Now you can stitch and darn your saree, and if you need help come back,' he said.

You tried. And got frustrated. You did not know how to stitch. When you sat in tears, the DC asked you what happened, and you told him the whole saga of the saree and troubles you had gone to get it mended.

'After all that is the only saree I can wear,' you said.

The next day, mid-morning you saw the rangrez at the front gates. You ran to him as he came in. 'I came to see how you were getting along with your saree,' he said. You were ecstatic like a saviour had come. He spent the entire day helping you with stitching and darning. You learned fast and started putting the weaves of fine wefts and wraps through with the needle to mend the tattered parts. You were delighted with the work and the effect it produced on the saree. The rangrez did not tell you that the DC had requested him to come and help.

After that day, you stitched day and night and many days passed. You mended the large tears by putting a fine silk net, that you made of crochet behind the tear to give support and then stitching the seams. You went methodically from one end of the saree to the other till all of it was mended. Noa played around you, oblivious to your obsession. When you laid it out to see how it all looked, you were pleased. But there were still some colour patches that distracted the beauty of the saree. You called upon the rangrez again.

'Take the skin of the whitest of white onions and boil them in water, till the veins of the skin are shed. Then drain it and soak your saree in it, while still hot. Leave it overnight and then wash with water from the Narmada and let it dry in the moonlight for thirteen nights.'

'Why thirteen nights?' you asked with curiosity.

'Because this saree has souls trapped in it, and because after thirteen days the souls leave for the nether world.'

You remembered that this was a saree for mourning. You did as he told you. When the silver moon hung in the night sky, you asked DC to take you to the Narmada River. You took the onion skins in a large bag. You had asked the housekeeper to put the logs for fire, and the pans for boiling water in the car. That evening when you drove with the DC, people of the town saw how happy you looked. They felt strangely betrayed by their absconding goddess and it did not seem right that you looked so radiantly happy. They followed.

At the riverbank, you lit the fire and put the onion skins in water to boil. When the water was reduced, and all the pulp separated from the skins, you filtered it with a sieve and dipped the saree into it. A dense steam rose hissing from the pan and spread like a cloud around you, hiding you from the world. It was some time before you emerged with the limp saree splayed in your hands like a dead child. You looked flushed. Nothing seemed to have changed in the saree. You sat down and stared at the saree and started mumbling strange words. You went into a trance and kept saying words that did not make any sense. A strange, sweet smell of tuberoses and cinnamon and cloves wafted as you mumbled. Your voice was soft and hoarse, coming from the pit of the stomach. You washed it in the flowing waters of the Narmada and as you opened the saree like a skin on the surface of the river, you saw a white wake of amorphous cloud escape from the saree and flow away in the river.

You had used the first prayer given to you by the old woman that night.

You felt tired and sick as you washed the saree. Later, you tied its two ends between the car door handle and a tree trunk and let it flutter in the moonlit wind. You sat down taking the support of the car tyre and dozed off. It was only when the liquid golden light fell on your face that you woke up and collected the saree. It was still damp and cold, but you folded it and put it in the wicker picnic basket and closed the lid. DC had slept in the car. Noa in the backseat. DC looked unkempt and rugged, and yet quite handsome in the morning glow. You wanted to touch his face but resisted the urge. As he drove you back, you wondered if he thought you were mad.

'I like your madness. I am the cause of it.' He said with affection reading your mind. Then he touched your lips lightly with his index finger and smiled as he drove. He was kind and indulgent and showed you how deeply he felt for you.

'I could buy you a new white saree,' he offered.

'Mother would not like it. It's best this way,' you said.

While driving, you thought you saw the Gypsy walking ahead. The car passed by quickly for you to be sure about that.

Each night you spread the saree in the moonlight and protected it from the sunlight. On the full moon night, you had completed thirteen nights of drying. When you spread the saree on the bed the next day, you were mesmerised by it. It was glowing white like the colour of swan's feathers, and it had patches of light woven into it where you had mended and darned it. Silver light radiated from those patches.

One evening, the Mother came. 'Enough of this nonsense!' she said and took you and Noa home. Noa excitedly told the Mother how the saree had transformed. The Mother listened to her with a stoic face and thereafter asked, 'Has the DC seen the saree?'

'Yes. He saw it fluttering in the moonlight and said it is the most beautiful thing he has seen,' Noa replied.

'It's a bad omen for the groom to see the wedding saree before the wedding!' the Mother said and smirked with satisfaction. She could never appreciate anything you did because of her dislike for you. She thought you were strong-willed, disruptive and destructive.

You had a lot of silk yarn remaining in your spindle. You decided to crochet a net in a hexagonal weave. You started at the centre and crocheted round.

The date of the wedding had not been fixed. The reason was that the Mother did not want to spend money on hosting a dinner for the family and well-wishers. 'I have seven daughters...I can't go around throwing lavish dinners each time one gets married. I will be reduced to grovelling and poverty,' she declared. The Father, one day, bought a male baby goat and said, 'We will wait for it grow up so that the dinner can be organised.' It needed to be fattened up to be enough for the community. And till the baby goat grew into a Billy goat, you crocheted the net. You decided that you would wear it as your wedding veil.

When the baby goat was no longer small but young with a shiny coat and firm rippling muscles, the Father said, 'We can decide the date now,' and he went to the priest to confer. The priest said that the best time would be in March. The winters would have abated and that the wedding could take place before Lent. March was still three months away. So, you continued to crochet the veil with fine silver of silk.

One day when DC came to meet you, you had the veil in your hands, and you were crocheting. DC looked at you and said, 'You will be the most beautiful bride in that veil.' You felt happy and cherished. The other sisters joined you, and they chatted and laughed with the DC. When he left, the Mother was angry and accused you of being a wrong influence and spoiling the rest of your sisters 'See how they have learned to talk with strange men!' she accused.

'Mama, DC is not a stranger. He will soon be your son-in-law,' they said and laughed at her unreasonable worry.

'He is a stranger till the day they get married! And the way Frieda has been accumulating bad omens, I am not sure!' she said, bitterly.

But these days nothing perforated your happiness. Every time your sisters saw you smiling, they said, 'She is so happy.'

Few days later, DC came to your house and gave you a box and a letter. When you read the letter, you smiled more. And then the Mother came and snatched the box from you in anger. It slipped, fell, and opened and out flew a river of sparkling pearls across the floor like tiny moons littered about. You did not react to the Mother but smiled in the comfort of his love and bent to pick them up one at a time. They reflected in your eyes lighting them up. It was a pre-wedding gift from DC. You knew that the Mother's obsession will pass once you married him.

From the next day, you started weaving the pearls in the veil that you were making.

I WILL MARRY HER

Finally, the day of your marriage arrived.

All this while you had not thought of the blouse that you would wear with the saree. When you asked the Mother a few nights before, she gave you an old coarse cotton white blouse that was smudged and discoloured with age and use. You accepted it not knowing what to do with it. That night as you were about to sleep, the epiphany happened. You knew what to do with the blouse.

On the morning of your wedding, you went to the backyard where the Father planted flowers. Gardening was the only thing that gave him peace in the house of seven daughters and their anxious mother. You got a bag full of white and yellow frangipani and white jasmine flowers. The whole morning, you pinned them on the blouse. You stitched the frangipani at the neckline and the edges so that it formed the borders of the blouse. Then you filled the rest of the space with white jasmine and tucked them so close together that not a shred of cotton fabric underneath was visible. You liked it when it was completed. You sprinkled some water on the flowers so that they would remain fresh for the evening.

The marriage ceremony was to be solemnised in the afternoon around four. The Mother did not help you get ready for the ceremony. The sisters were busy getting ready themselves as they were the bridesmaids. You were unfazed.

You took a warm bath, wrapped yourself in the cotton towel and came to your room and shut the door. You stood in the middle of the room and removed the towel and looked at your beautiful peach and cream naked body and said, 'It will never be the same again after today.' You touched the moist core underneath the dense fuzz and wondered why it had such a warm feeling, and if yearning was the emotion, it lay in there waiting to be unlocked. You touched the soft breasts gently wondering what his touch would feel like there. And then you looked at the eyes in the mirror. How peaceful and yet how animated they looked. You could not read the other emotions that flew past your black-brown iris and bluish-white sclera. You plaited and tied the hair in one long braid.

You slipped into the petticoat first and tied it low on the abdomen just on the pelvis bone. Then you stretched your hands above your head and slipped on the blouse hands first and then the head. It fit you snuggly like another layer of her skin. It was still moist with the water you had sprinkled earlier. It gave off the aroma of fresh jasmine and frangipani flowers. You did not wear any underwear. Then you took time to wrap the saree around such that it highlighted the contours of your young body. The smooth, pale midriff was exposed, and a fine line of down was visible from the navel downwards that disappeared into the edge of the petticoat. There was no jewellery to wear.

That afternoon as you searched for pins to tuck the saree, you found the box that the old woman had given. When you opened it and out flew innumerable butterflies with myriad-coloured wings and created a canopy around you through which the soft hues of light filtered and fell upon your beautiful face. You stood mesmerised by the translucent wings and the butterfly dust that hovered suspended in the air and reflected the light as it turned on its axes. You tried touching one of the blood red butterflies and as you touched it, it shed red dust like dried haemoglobin, and it turned yellow and fluttered away. You followed it with your eyes and then when you touched it again, it shed the yellow dust the colour of sunflower petals and turned blue. The Mother knocked on the door, 'We need to leave for church,' she announced. 'Give me five minutes,' you replied smiling, thinking that you had got distracted with butterflies.

You took the red butterfly wing dust and applied it on your lips and took the small round box of kajal and applied it with the end of a matchstick to the upper lids, stretching it out a little upwards on the edges. And then you opened the pearl encrusted round veil and put it a sideways shifted from the centre on your head. When you put on the veil, the butterflies descended and created a colourful wreath on your head.

Frieda, you had a serene look and you glowed with happiness. Then you looked at yourself again in the mirror. You smiled. You were an exquisite bride.

When you stepped out into the veranda, Hannah looked at you with admiration and gave you a bunch of blooming white tuberoses that she had cut from the Father's garden. You took those and balanced them inclined on your white wrists, as you stepped out into the courtyard to walk to the church.

The Gypsy was standing quietly in the corner with his ektara, and people jostled to look in at the bride. A collective gasp went up from the women waiting outside. They had never seen such beauty and such splendour.

The sparkling of the pearls, the elegant shine of the silk net, the tiara of butterflies and beneath that your dark luminous eyes and the red lips. You were the most beautiful bride and it seemed that suddenly the world was drained of its beauty and all of it had concentrated in your being. The long saree that you had mended covered you with delicate passion and its thin tender folds moved with the movement of your muscles. The darning and stitching that you had done had blended with the texture of the fabric and the white and gold made gave you a pristine beauty. You walked the street with the Father who was proud of you. The Mother and the sisters followed behind. The Gypsy was also there followed by a beautiful woman in a pink pastel saree. You were the princess, and they the ordinary folks following you.

The word had spread in town about the vision that you had become, and the street crowded with people on both sides.

Their goddess of a few months ago was now a bride. They were jostling to have a glimpse of her. Hands flew to mouths in adoration and surprise, eyes widened with wonder and hands inadvertently extended to touch the grace that you presented. Except the Father, in white dhoti, a navy-blue achkan and a light blue *saafa*[1], who had his hands around your elbow, nobody had dared to touch you, lest such radiance scald them. Each step that you took robbed the world of a bit of beauty and faces directed to you started turning ugly with spite. Your beauty made them feel deprived and jealous.

And then, the first spit flew with its tentacles spread out. It landed on the side. A voice rose. 'She is a prostitute. She has already lived with him for a month. Now look at her!' After a brief lull as if the crowd was imbibing the full significance of what was said, there rose of storm of malice, leering and nastiness. You had walked steadily and gracefully because you knew that you had done no wrong. You walked with the confidence of all this culminating in betrothal to him whom you had dreamt of for so long and who had been tender and kind to you unlike these imbeciles. You knew all will be fine once the marriage was solemnised. And so, you walked with the head held high and the dignity intact.

The ugliness increased as the sun bent low on the horizon and cast a golden March light on you. The slight breeze made your veil shiver just like you were shivering inside the white flowers of the blouse. Your luminescence increased in proportion to the jealousy and the rancour that spread like a disease. In the cacophony of the crowd, you noticed the beautiful woman in neat pink pastel saree smiling at you. She seemed the only one smiling at you. As you passed her, you smelled a familiar smell of tuberoses and spices. You turned back to look at her. She had stood there smiling. You had

---

[1] A headscarf or long cloth used to form a turban in parts of India.

reached the small church, and as you entered the porch, you felt a stone of impending doom drop in your chest. It was a strong sinking feeling. You said a small prayer which did not seem to rise from the lips but stayed stuck in the throat, choking you. The priest and the best man were standing outside with expression of anxiety and worry.

'DC left for England in the afternoon for some urgent family matter. It was an emergency. He could not come as the train for Bombay was leaving in 30 minutes when he received the telegram. He said he will be back and that you must wait,' Alfie said, as he was the best man. He handed you the letter that DC had left for you. 'This will explain everything,' he said. At that, all the butterflies flew away, leaving your head stripped of the tiara.

You stood behind the veil, insulted with the spit and jealousy of the town. The philistine town had won against your beauty. The Mother and sisters had caught up with you and were milling around to fathom the implications. You lifted the scintillating veil and looked in the eyes of the priest and Alfie questioningly. Just then landed a tight slap on your cheek. It was the Mother.

'After all the reputation that you have acquired, who will marry the rest of my girls?' Her fury was hoarse and vicious.

Your spirit broke and all the flowers on the blouse wilted in a moment. Tears welled up in your eyes. The iron metallic taste emerged in your mouth. The slap had cut your inner cheek. Before you could implore the Mother to be kind, she had landed another one and the blood dripped from your lips onto the blouse and one by one the flowers turned red with shame and embarrassment. The slap had chipped a small triangle of your front tooth and cut the lip.

The Father stood shocked, drained of all the blood from his face. He removed his *saafa* and held it in his hands. Hannah took your arm. The other sisters were crying. The Mother was livid with anger at the insult, the embarrassment, and the gossip it would create for her and the rest of the daughters.

'You will get married today,' she declared, and then she turned to the crowds. Before she could ask the crowd, Alfie said, 'I will marry her.' He was the best man of your fiancé. You looked at him with blazing eyes. 'This cannot be. I will wait for DC,' you spoke. The Mother raised her hand again. But before she could land another slap, Alfie had stopped her and gently but firmly pushed her away. The Mother was humiliated and would not speak with him for the rest of her life.

Alfie, in a fine blue suit and a carnation on his lapel, held your hand and walked you up the aisle. The priest solemnised the wedding with a small, hushed audience. The crowd outside was pleased. You were in a state of disbelief and your mind blanked. You had to be nudged to say yes to the vows. Alfie looked serious but had affection in his eyes when he looked at your face as he said his vows. He held your hand firmly. He could feel the cold sweat and a racing pulse on your palms. He noticed you were holding DC's letter in the other hand folded in a tight fist. As you walked from the altar after the marriage was solemnised, the atmosphere in the church was like a bereavement service had taken place and that the coffin was being moved. The sisters closed their palms so tight that the confetti in their hands was squashed and destroyed. Hannah cried silently. The Mother was wildly upset. The Father was helpless and looked broken and stood with his *saafa* in his hands with a defeated look as they passed by. The retribution was done. The feast of the goat happened as was planned. A town legend was created that day of the bride that wilted in a moment.

That was just the beginning.

You have only one wedding picture. It is a bit yellowed and stained now but Alfie has always treasured it. In that black and white wedding picture, he looks content, and you look away from the camera frame like there is someone else you are seeking. There is the backdrop of the church, small, simple, made of rough stones trying miserably to emulate the magnificence of a cathedral in a small, condensed format. There was a large patch on your saree as your womb decided to weep too. You had stood at the altar with a sweet fragrance of tuberoses and the metallic smell of the blood in your saree and spirit. You borrowed the muslin dupatta from Sarah to cover the red colour because that was abominable. He could sense the tension in your muscles as he put his arm around yours. Yet, Alfie was genuinely happy.

The Mother, when she saw the red stain, said, 'That is another bad omen! Misfortune just follows her!'

You went back home to change. As the Father and Alfie waited beside each other, the Father said, 'Marriage changes everything. You will now not be the same person that you were before your marriage. Your relationships will change; what you had till now will be different in the future. All you will be left with from before will be shadows that will not be easy to recapture. You will together ally against the rest of the world and hopefully not against one another. Prolonged proximity will make it bearable and even interesting at times. Just don't give up; that's the secret of surviving a marriage.'

When you reached home, you shut yourself, tore the letter without reading it and let out a wail. Hannah and Sarah had accompanied you. They got worried and knocked on the door, but you would not open it. They kept knocking and shouting entreaties to you. Quite some time passed. Hannah shouted, 'If you delay, Mother will come.'

You opened the door and went and stood stark naked in the middle of the room in the dark diffused light that stole in from the open window at the back. Only your silhouette was visible. Hannah rushed to light a candle. The warm yellow glow displayed the ripped off blouse and the petticoat. You had torn the flowers off it. The white turned red flowers lay strewn in the room. The delicate silk saree that you had spent so much passion making, looked ugly and old. 'This is my shroud that I spent decorating in my madness. The lengths

I went to, to make it perfect!' You said in abject disdain. You tore it in the middle. Then took the scissors to it. 'This will not destroy another girl's life with its curse,' you said as you cut is. Soon it was in shreds and lay strewn among the white turned red flowers.

You stood with sweat and tears on your face. You had blood between your legs. Blood was a symbol of sacrifice and you had been sacrificed at the altar of your mother's wrath, at the altar of DC's betrayal, and at the altar of blind acceptance by Alfie. You were the sacrificial goat, and this was your blood. You loathed yourself and your own blood. Your hair was in a disarray and your veil was in a devastated state. There was a red puddle where you stood breathing heavily, disorientated. Suddenly your life had changed from one of infinite bliss to one of infinite uncertainty and confusion. Only the bouquet of tuberoses that lay in the corner of the bed still looked fresh among the red and white mess in the room. Outside the window a smoky ink blue darkness was descending with easy stealth.

'What will become of me now?' you said looking terrified, helpless, and racked by a suppressed sob that rose from deep within your chest.

Hannah gathered you in her arms and said, 'Hush... hush...all will be fine!' You stood straight with arms hanging indolently by your side. After a while, you bent your neck and placed your head on Hannah's shoulder.

'You will learn to love him. He seems like a kind man.' Hannah said after some time.

'Let me clean you,' she said and went to get wet towels to wipe you. By the time, Hannah wiped your face and body clean, the blood had started to run down your legs again. 'This is bad,' Hannah said and went and brought a large wad of gauze cloth that she placed gently between your legs and held it with a string tied around your waist. 'Now let's get you dressed,' and she went to look at the gifts which were given to you by the DC.

You looked at it in disdain and refused to wear it. Hannah brought you her best cotton saree and draped it on you. You were without any makeup and dressed in a resolve of mourning. What you did not realise was that your anger made your face glow red and made you more beautiful in a daring sort of a way. When you were ready, Hannah and Sarah opened the door to take you back for the reception dinner. The reception was in the large colourful canopy just outside the house that had been cleared of the shrubs and bushes. The smell of spicy goat curry and the vapours of the pulao rice attacked you as they opened the door. You felt nauseated. Anger welled inside and you wanted to break everything around in the tempest that raged inside you. But the only thing that you did was pick the bouquet of tuberoses and fling them out of the window with as much force as your anger could muster and then you walked out.

The Gypsy walked behind you quietly at a distance. His ektara silent.

The bouquet had landed on me who had stood motionless outside on the path watching you. I was there because the window was open, and I had seen you tearing—the flowers, the wedding saree, and the veil. I was there because I was worried when I saw you smearing your veil with blood in such vehemence. Blood was sacred and a symbol of life to me, and when I saw the blood, I was petrified. It was a lot of blood from such a fragile body. I stood there because your vulnerability had rooted me there. I stayed to ensure that you do not do anything that would harm you physically. I moved in the shadows when you opened the door and Hannah and Sarah entered the room. I stood there in the darkness watching you getting wiped and cleaned and I stood there then to see you change. I knew DC and through him I knew you. I also knew Alfie. We were all friends—DC, Alfie, and I. And I felt deep empathy and the sadness for you, Frieda. I knew that DC had left that afternoon, and that it was unfair for you to be married off like that. I picked up the flowers that had hit me and that lay splayed in dust.

I had witnessed the marriage solemnised with a sombre and quietude that precedes a disaster. I had been in the church because I had received the invitation from DC. When I had seen you enter the church yard in splendour, I was unable to take my eyes off. I had been surprised at Alfie's impetuosity, unaware of the episode at Russell Square where Alfie had seen you more than a year ago in a black Victoria with your sisters and was besotted by you.

The reception was a calm affair. A local band called 'Catholic Boys' was playing songs. The band was invited by Alfie at the behest of DC for the wedding. Alfie knew the band and had enjoyed them play at the YMCA. The band played the cover songs of Jimmie Rodgers, Frank Luther, Carter Family etc. and while the band played, the feast of the goat progressed. The guests greeted you and Alfie solemnly and gave you gifts or envelopes with money. They shook hands with Alfie and kissed you, Frieda. It was hard for you to smile with the churn in your heart and temper in your head. You and Alfie avoided eye contact with each other, and sometimes Alfie tried to touch your fingers to comfort and assure you that it will be all right, and every time you moved your hands away telling him that this is a disaster. Alfie acted cheerful but he had the premonition of a deep impending trouble lurking among the guests. Alfie was to attend the wedding with someone he was very fond of and had left behind.

There was a lull in the guests approaching you. The music played on. Alfie was looking at the band listening to 'Sweet as the Flowers in May Time', you saw the woman in a chiffon saree tied so low at the waist that the curve of her hips was beginning to emerge. She was walking towards you both. You saw that her ivory saree had sequins with a wide deep orange sequinned border. The sequins reflected the lights and dazzled your eyes. She walked like a young girl holding the pleats of the saree in the front with just the slight fluid roll that seemed charming. Like reeds in the water swaying in the wind. You were distracted by Hannah who asked if you needed anything to eat. The bride and the groom had not eaten yet.

The next moment, like a hurricane she was at Alfie's lips kissing him lusciously and lavishly, holding his face in her hands and saying, 'What have you done?' repeatedly. You noticed her silver jewellery—large danglers in her ears, multiple silver bracelets, choker, rings in the fingers, her red lips, and beautifully made-up eyes. Her neck and chest had a glistening sheen of health. She was distressed and crying and hugging him and kissing him desperately. 'What have you done?' Hannah saw it. Everybody saw it. The band stopped. A collective gasp of yet another surprise escaped the gathered guests. I emerged from the guests and gently took away the distraught, shimmering woman. Alfie was shaken and wiped his lips to remove the stains of her lipstick. You seemed indifferent and looked at her shining midriff and waist as she was walked away with her hourglass figure.

Things calmed down after a while and the feast of the goat continued.

Alfie took you to his home that night in a black Victoria. His bungalow was in darkness except a small light in the veranda. There was only Badi Bai who waited with a burning earthen lamp on a brass plate with turmeric and rice to welcome the bride.

That night Alfie said, 'I am sorry for what happened.'

You did not say anything as you did not understand what he was talking about. So much had happened that evening.

'About her kissing me like that.'

'Oh that!' you said and continued to sit at the corner of an unfamiliar bed looking at some vague spot on the floor.

'I had promised to pick her up before the wedding, as we were attending it together. I got caught up in DC's departure. She must have been waiting for me. We are just friends and there is nothing more to it.' He clarified. You thought the mouthful of kisses was more a demonstration of deep physical intimacy.

'I have made no promises to anyone but you.' Alfie continued to assure you but more to break the silence of the room.

'What have you done?' you said remembering what the other woman had said but thinking more about yourself. You turned then and looked at him with a hurt that he can still see in your eyes whenever you are alone. You never asked him about that incident again. You did not know that you would have to reckon with the nemesis that the sequinned woman would create later in your life.

YOU DID NOT LOVE ALFIE

You felt profound indifference and he felt the formidable passion in the early days of your marriage.

You had married a stranger. Alfie had not. He had seen you in the town square when a dupatta had blown away and he had fallen in love. He had retreated after DC had told him about his affection for you. He knew he could love you and make the marriage work.

He knew why DC had left and his distress. His mother who was in an institution had had an accident when the building had caught fire. She was in a serious condition battling for life. DC had to go. He was the only kin.

Your indifference made him aware of the betrayal he had committed by marrying you. He had given DC's letter to you and hoped that you would have read it by now. How was he to prove his love when the barrier of indifference was so high? Life seemed regular. You dressed like a new bride. You both had breakfast, lunch, and dinner together. You slept in the same bed. But the shine in your eyes was missing and it seemed that the words that came out of your mouth though appropriate had no soul in them. His name was not precious in your mouth. He suspected that it must taste bitter.

How much Alfie had wanted to know more about you. How much he needed to learn about you.

That first night, when you slept on the same bed, you did not remove your clothes. 'It is the time of the month,' you told him. He understood. Alfie changed into his pyjamas and lay beside you. He could see your contours and smell your hair and body. But he dared not touch you. You seemed so fragile, and your fragility devoured his desire that night. He had not slept. He realised that he will never sleep alone now; that you would always be by his side. You lay quietly by his side. He knew that you too had not slept. Sometimes you wiped the tears. You wondered if this was the first one of many nights till death did you apart. That is what you both had promised to each other in the church; he faithfully and you disdainfully. You would be by his side now and his desire and yearning had found a home. The first person that he would see every morning would be you. That was an exhilarating thought for him, and he spent the whole night contemplating that. He thought that from this day onward he would be with you for better or for worse, for richer and for poorer, in sickness and in health, to love, cherish and to obey till death does you apart. He had taken these vows.

He probably would not want to know about your faults. But he would be obliged to know as the days and years passed. He just hoped that the faults that you exposed to each other were contained between the two and not visible to people who knew you both. He was keen to know your virtues and talents. He found it strange...the use of 'us' to denote two people. He didn't know how much of 'us' would be possible all the time for you both would be individuals too in your own right, in your liking and disliking, in your choices however limited they may be, in your preferences for things mundane.

He now wondered why he got married the way he did. Was it the logical thing to do given his infatuation? Or was it because it was inevitable, some larger force that decided it for them? Or was it because it was something that everyone does? Or was it to experience something that he had never experienced before? Was it his destiny or was it for the incredulous excitement of the moment? Was it an impetuous act that had led him to a binding and abstract future of marriage? What if he had not stood up to your mother...what if...what if! And suddenly, he could no longer tell if it terrified him and if he no longer seemed to want what he had seemed to want just a day ago.

He wondered what you had been thinking. If you would like the sound of the razor scraping against his skin in the morning. Or the sound of him brushing his teeth. Would it be all right if he did not shave for a few days since he liked the stubble on his face as a reminder of his youth? He generally did not take a bath daily and would that disgust you? You had agreed to share your life together, but he did not like anyone to use his towels or his slippers.

When two people share a pillow, they become a pair against the rest of the world. They share their dreams. They share their worries, and they share their future not the past. But you were not like that.

When the dawn walked in the street outside your window, and the furniture started emerging from the obscurity of darkness, he waited to see your face. You had walked away to the bathroom without showing your face or looking at him.

It must have been nine in the night, on the third day after your marriage. Alfie was sitting on the bed in his pyjamas, reading. Jazz played on the gramophone at a low volume. Frieda, you sat in front of the mirror; your dark wavy hair ran loose over the shoulders to the floor. You were in a nightgown. You had collected your hair in the left hand and brought the brush down with a smooth fluid stroke with the right, starting at the nape of your neck to the edges at the end. Alfie looked at you and found you outrageously desirable. He noticed traces of despair and melancholy but also the resolve to still look beautiful to the night. He was learning about you.

You opened the grip and the hair had fallen like a curtain across your back. You continued to brush. When you gathered it again at the nape of your neck, your back was slightly arched, the fabric of the nightgown followed the curve of your breasts, and it took Alfie's breath away with the simple force of that gesture. It signified in you a finality or an invitation or a promise. You continued brushing, the silver brush like lightning gliding on dark waves.

You released the hair, put the brush down and then brought your hands to the forehead and gathered the hair carefully, more carefully than necessary he thought. You tilted your head back, running your hands over it, looking straight up. You had your chin slightly raised and you drew a brief sigh. He looked at your profile, a sharp nose, curved lashes, and full lips. You pulled up the hair and slowly arranged it at the nape of the neck, in what seemed to Alfie like an implausibly expanded moment. It aroused desire but ensured no memory remained of it. It was like having seen you naked.

Then he noticed the mouth, half-closed. Alfie realised that it was your mouth that had attracted him. He wondered if it would burn his fingers if he touched your mouth. He began to understand what came before the genesis of his impetuosity in marrying you. That raw animal rhythm that has to do with the salvation of bodies. It was a primitive feeling.

Your fingers were gently locking the stands into a braid. You were solemn and magnificent, elegant, and calm as you finished. It broke his reverie as you stood up and tidied the dressing table. You turned on the table lamp at his side and shut the lights in the room. Then you lay down on your side of the bed, said goodnight and entered the night. The braid lay coiling on your pillow like a snake.

Even though it must be a few centimetres apart, there was this distance the size of continents and oceans that lay between you two. He knew he must be patient. He wanted to tell you he understands but the formal civility between you prohibited any intimate conversation. Sometimes he tried covering the distance by lightly touching your back, but he would immediately sense the cold tensed-up bunch of muscles and that you were holding your breath waiting for his fingers to lift. His arms were not long enough to cover that continent. And you continued to drift away to the other side of his horizon.

This repeated night after night when you would turn away and pretend to sleep. And his desire would die a silent death each night. He wanted you to want him. He did not want to claim you as a matter of right. His chivalry of marrying you had recoiled you in a shell of silence. He did not want to break you again. He would wait. He decided.

More nights passed like this.

While you stubbornly refused to get into the rhythm of married life, you had once told me that you were so shocked with the way you lost DC and the way your mother forced your marriage with Alfie, that you lived in a vacuum for a long time. No thoughts crossed your mind, no activities interested you, every day descended like a stone born of the darkness. You did not reach out to your friends or to Hannah, though she visited you sometimes. You felt betrayed by all. You were embarrassed about the madness you went through to marry DC and with what end? You isolated yourself from the world.

In the early days of your marriage, the house was full of silence. The only voice that was heard was that of Badi Bai. She had brought him up. He never told you how he came to be in her care, but Badi Bai did.

The bungalow was at the edge of the town with a dense forest beyond. He was found suckling at his dead mother's bloodied bosom in a room washed by the morning light. It was his parents' bedroom decorated with furniture and linen brought from England as part of his mother's wedding presents. The white lace curtains on the open windows had stirred in gentle breeze. In the sitting room lay his father. He was a trader in British goods and had come to India in search of adventure some years before World War I broke in Europe.

When the police came, their bodies had already turned stiff. The thugs had raided the house and spilled blood around as a sign of their brutality. He was spared. Badi Bai had been his ayah and nurse since Alfie was born. Alfie had no relations in India. So, she took care of him till his grandfather came from England. The grandfather had no children apart from Alfie's father. When he came, he was old, suffering from consumption. He was a widower. His grandfather decided for him to be looked after by Badi Bai. The grandfather spoke to the pastor and made him Alfie's guardian who was then deposited as his ward. Badi Bai and baby Alfie moved to a small room in the parsonage near the church. He set up an allowance for Badi Bai to take care of baby Alfie. The grandfather went back. He died a few months later.

She was his sole companion and caretaker since he was eighteen months old. When he was growing up, he looked up at her as his mother. She never allowed him to call her anything but Badi Bai, even though she was the only parental figure he had. Alfie had a fond relationship with her. He was close to her and could not fathom life without her. Even after he received the inheritance from England when he turned eighteen, he did not let Badi Bai leave.

Frieda, you liked Badi Bai. She had welcomed you like she was waiting for all these years for you to come and take the reins of the household. Badi Bai had this karmic detachment about relationships and things that was so endearing. She did not possess anything, yet was possessed by all. She had welcomed you into the house in a traditional Hindu way. She did aarti and then made you throw rice over your head. She did your tilak with rice and turmeric. Then she made you stand on the brass plate filled with vermillion water and made you step into the house. She saw your footprints and said, 'You are very auspicious. You are the Grihalakshmi now,' and handed you the keys of the house. Badi Bai was not a Christian. She was a Muslim woman, but she knew more about the Bible and Christianity than most people. She gave you a Bible saying, 'This belonged to his father.' Though you found it difficult to love Alfie initially, you kept it with you all your life. These were small proofs of the connection; these mundane attachments that were created easily. It still lies on your bedside table as it did all your married life.

She would dote on you. She would oil and comb your hair and he liked it when you two sat in the veranda leading to the courtyard on a sunny summer day and Badi Bai would plait and decorate your hair. He wished you would see then what he saw. You looked beautiful and the veil of pain that you put on with him was not there with Badi Bai. Badi Bai would help you put on the saree and fuss over your appearance. She would take you to the market to buy new clothes and stuff that the house needed for its lady. You both chatted and giggled like schoolgirls. You two would potter around in the kitchen and prepare meals together. In fact, you learned a lot about cooking from her. The roast meat, the shepherd's pie, the stew, the apple pie, custard flan, cakes and north Indian kadhi, kheer, biryani, fried fish, and baigan do pyaza. She diligently and innocuously moulded you to Alfie's food habits and tastes. You seemed cherished by her maternal affection and basked in it without remembering your own unloving mother. Soon, you began to love her like one would a mother.

Like the rot eats away the wood without it ever showing till the wood crumbles, Alfie was being eaten away by your indifference. After the initial silence, you had started talking with him and yet it was plain civility and sociability. Like you would speak with any person on the street or on a social setting. You did not love him, and you had not yet made love. It was nearly two months after the wedding. It was starting to get suffocating and then one day Alfie decided that the only way he can hold himself from crumbling was shikar[1] and friends and YMCA and parties and work. He started staying out late and would come home drunk so that he would fall asleep. But the irony was that whatever he did, you loomed in his mind like an illness. During shikar, he would miss you suddenly and a sense of incompleteness would emerge from his gut. When he was with his friends, it was all alcohol-fuelled flamboyance to distract and yet that could not be. When he was at a party every beautiful woman reminded him of you and what he could not have, every song, every game, every fashion, every dish reminded him of you. You had become his neurosis…

---

[1] Hunting.

When Alfie would go for shikar, you would tend the earth in the backyard. You cleared it of the undergrowth and pebbles and raking neat rows. You would bend over and spend hours in the sun preparing the earth and then you planted part of the seeds from the box the old woman had given to you as a blessing. The seeds sprouted into green shoots. Every new leaf gave you a joy that distracted you from your marriage. In a few weeks the backyard was full of young plants and soon there were buds that were ready to burst open.

Badi Bai had understood that you had not yet consummated the marriage. She encouraged you to accept that it is an important part of marital life. She knew about Alfie's raging desires and conquests. She also knew about his affairs before marriage and was surprised how he had such patience now and valour to wait for you. She feared that your marriage would fall apart soon enough if it went on like that. She cajoled you gently. She told you that men have needs and if they are unfulfilled, they find ways to fulfil them. You had flinched at the thought. 'Good!' you thought. 'I don't care.'

Badi Bai did not know that the vows Alfie had taken in the church were the only truth in his life now. He loved you irrationally. That he had resolved to stand by his vows come what may. After all you had an entire lifetime to consummate the marriage and to fulfil those vows.

One night, couple of months into your marriage, Alfie woke from his fitful sleep, he saw you had turned towards him. He lay still, lest it stir an emotion that would make you turn away. You are shorter than him. And your head was at his jaw level. He was able to see your face from an angle above. You both remained like that for a long time. When the light broke, he saw disgust on your face at the natural reaction of his flagrant manhood of the morning. The enormity of his impetuosity, his mistake dawned on him. He realised you could not be man and wife, if your body and soul were not into it. A ceremony, a signed paper, many witnesses, a common pillow, and a shared bed are all futile, if the heart does not bind the two together.

Therefore, he was surprised that day when you made love to him. The roses in the bushes had burst suddenly that evening and the air was saturated with its fragrance.

It was June. The days were hot, but the moon still cooled down the nights. Separate beds were laid out in the courtyard at the back. Badi Bai slept in the front of the house with another house help. Alfie was tired and had slept fitfully. He was now always anxious about your indifference. He was perturbed about your lack of affection. He was beginning to feel guilty for having broken your spirit. He may have been dreaming because when amid wakefulness and sleep, he saw you holding his head in your lap. You had bent over him looking at his face and your hair was loose and fell in a dark curtain blocking the light of the moon on his face. He felt you unbutton his muslin kurta and pull it over his head gently. You loosened the cord of his pyjama and removed that too. Alfie felt a shiver run up his body from toe to the scalp. Then he saw you remove your clothes and lie next to him. He felt your smooth and moist trembling touch on his chest and then you buried your face in his neck. As you lay there, the sinews and blood vessels charged up, a flare-up, and that night, you made a gentle but urgent love. Afterwards he fell into the deep abyss of sleep cradling your head in his arms. When he woke in the morning, he saw you lying asleep under a crumpled saree next to him. You both were naked. He lay there without disturbing you…he could not see your face. He felt happy and lay there basking in togetherness. You stirred and woke up suddenly, got up with your back to him. He could not see your face. He reached out and put his arm around your waist as you sat there. He kissed your lower back between the dimples of Venus. You covered yourself. Your hair was still splayed. You got up resisting his soft grip. He let go thinking that you must feel shy about your lovemaking. When you got up there was blood on the sheet as the flower of consummation. You pulled away and he remembers how you had looked at him. Just for a quick passing second. With total contempt!

It had seared him to the core. It was a consummation out of obligation than love.

LETTERS BELONG TO THOSE WHO WRITE THEM!

It must have been a year of your marriage. It was a bright winter morning and you were sitting arranging freshly cut roses. You were making a large bouquet for the church altar and a flower decoration for the temple door. Each time before picking your scissors and accoutrements of flower art, you bowed your head, touched the flowers, and said a small prayer to the souls of the flowers, seeking their blessing to help you make something exquisite and to magnify their glory.

You were about to begin this reverent art when Badi Bai entered with a plate of pink fresh guavas and put them on the table in the lawn near you. "Oh ho, I forgot the salt!' She called out to the maid, 'Lalli! Get some rock salt.' And you shouted, 'And black pepper too!' and you both looked at each other and giggled. Alfie was away at work completing the sanitary inspection of the civilian areas in the cantonment. Badi Bai would tell him all this later, much later.

The main gate opened, and a car drove in. It was an Austin, red and black in colour, broad with shining silver fenders. The driver came around and opened the door and out stepped a dapper gentleman and when you saw him, the blood drained from your face. Badi Bai knew DC as Alfie's friend and your ex-fiancé. She went to receive him and chatted with him brightly as she brought him to the lawn. Frieda, you stood there like a white statue, like a taxidermy art. The colours drained from his face too when he saw you. Badi Bai noticed both.

You were civil and shook his hand and asked him to sit down. He looked handsome and your heart raced. You made some small conversation about the winter days and the guavas. 'You must have some tea with us,' you said and looked at Badi Bai, who knew what that meant. She left to organise tea.

There was a palpable tension when Badi Bai left. You were surprised to see DC there. You kept your poise.

'You look more beautiful,' DC said.

'I am a married woman now,' you replied.

'That knowledge does not reduce my loss. I remember you every day, Frieda!' He implored.

'You could have stayed one more day,' you said, coldly.

'There was no train for the next three days, but I wish I could. I lost my mother and you the same day when I boarded the train.'

'I am sorry to hear that,' you said and placed your hand on his hand that held the armchair.

'I left you a letter. I gave it to Alfie.'

'There was no time. I was at the church doorstep when we found that you had left, and my mother would hear none of the reasons. Alfie gave me the letter there. I tore it after without reading. There was no point to it then.'

'I am so sorry, Frieda. I wish I had done things differently.'

You both remained silent.

When Badi Bai came back with tea, your eyes were red, and DC was visibly distressed. You served him tea and asked Badi Bai to join. She asked him about England. She resumed the conversation about the acquaintances, about the town and other small talk.

Badi Bai knew from your demeanour that you both needed more time. She picked the tea service after you were done and went back to the kitchen.

'Why did you come?' you asked with tears in your eyes.

'I don't know,' DC said. 'I knew Alfie married you, but I had to see you.'

'May I have those letters back?' DC asked after some time.

'Why?' you asked with a calm that belied your sense of loss.

'They will be my solace and a reminder now. That there was someone who deserved these and I faulted her.'

'They are mine. Did you not write them to me?' you spoke.

'The letters belong to the one who writes them. You never wrote.'

'I could never write my feelings on paper. I was madly preparing to give my life to you. In any case, I have destroyed your letters. There was no point holding on to them. Once they gave joy. But when they became a cause of my distress, I burnt them.'

DC sat with you for a while and then left.

You retired to your room and when you did not come for lunch, Badi Bai came to get you. Things lay scattered on the bed. You simply embraced Badi Bai and cried with deep sobs and tears. The only thing you said was, 'I was meant to marry that man.' When you composed yourself, you picked all the things that were lying on bed and put them in a box. Badi Bai understood that these were the things given to you by DC. It had a pouch full of pearls, some books, gifts for the wedding dinner, a black umbrella etc. You asked Badi Bai to burn them. 'This is the carcass of my past. Cremate it for me. Please.' And you gave it to Badi Bai. 'I cannot do it myself,' and a sob escaped from you.

Badi Bai took the box. She did not burn it but kept it. She left it behind when she died many years later. Urja had found it and all hell had broken loose.

A few days later, Alfie mentioned that he knew that DC had come home. 'Today he left for England.' He told you. 'He had come to resign and move back to England forever.'

After you had taken the initiative to consummate the relationship, Alfie took charge. A need, a desire had opened in him. While still apprehensive of your disgust, he took the first opportunity he found to kiss you on some part of your body, with gentleness, with a naturalness that belied the lack of love in your marriage.

Then night after night, he would patiently break down your defences and cultivate confidence in you to partake in the adventure of the bodies.

He knew that you did not love him.

During the day, you killed time with mundane activities. Chatting with the fisherwoman (Alfie liked fish) who came twice a week, speaking with the vegetable sellers who told you stories about their families and farms, haggling with the fruit sellers. There came children from the Convent School selling raffle tickets, beggars with their litany of misfortune (them, you always gave something—money, flour, rice, old clothes etc.), knife grinders, kalaiwalas[1], the man who bought old newspapers and bottles, the woman who took old clothes to barter for utensils, the palm readers, the hawkers of sweet caramelised sugar figurines, the ice-creamwala, the dhobi to take linen for washing and ironing, the itrwala and so many more. Once a month there would be a tribe of hijras who would descend and sing and dance. Both you and Badi Bai would enjoy such mornings, amused with their exaggerated gesticulations and resonant clapping and paan-stained laughter and their ways of embarrassing the affected. Occasionally there would be someone selling a chit fund or Kashmiri shawls or Bombay Georgette sarees or dry fruits from Afghanistan.

Badi Bai would be constantly opening and closing the main door to either chat or chase them away. She would be muttering in annoyance or announcing in anticipation.

The days passed and your emptiness increased. Your only respite was the occasional flower bouquet that you made with the roses.

---

[1] Those who polish brass and copper utensils.

Alfie was busy with his work as a sanitary inspector. The public disposed garbage in the drains choking them. Dirty water overflowed. Rats the size of rabbits ran in the sewers with conviction of their hegemony. Half-naked or naked children played in dirty puddles all over. People defecated in the open. There were no proper toilets either in homes or communities of the poor. Amoebiasis and dysentery were rampant, and the side of the streets smelled of liquid shit. He had to pass orders to get it removed weekly.

There was a mound of garbage where people dumped their waste both wet and dry. It was an open space and in time it had become a mountain where eagles and crows and rodents and bacteria and all sorts of infection flourished. His team tried to burn that but then there was a revolt of the scavengers as this garbage mountain provided them a meagre inhuman income by collecting what was worth redeeming and selling it to the kabadi[2] shops. Despite that when there was an outbreak of cholera, he had it all burned down. It simmered in a blanket of low flames and a heavy cloud of smoke enveloped the town. People's skins and clothes smelled of fetid garbage smoke for weeks after.

Your heart softened for Alfie the day he cried after culling the dogs. Alfie would tell you about it over a few days. He was so upset it that he could not eat a morsel for a few days.

The bolt pistol was placed on the head of the first dog and the trigger was pulled. The dog went limp with unconsciousness. He was taken out of the pen and his neck cut with a sharp machete.

'The first dog has gone down,' the superintendent announced. His voice was hoarse. Alfie stood behind the glass window with the tea flask in his hand. The inspection cabin was on the first floor with large glass window overlooking the culling area. In the white-tiled culling area, the dogs who had

---

[2] Scrap sellers.

been captured from the streets were packed in a large metal pen. There was a cacophony of cries. Dogs are intelligent, and they knew what was happening. Terror was visible in their anxious eyes and in their nervous howls and in the way they desperately tried to escape the pen.

Another dog had fallen on the ground with its blood spurting out. The staff with plastic gloves and long boots to the thighs and plastic aprons lifted the dog and dropped it into the loader.

The next dog was lassoed and put in the smaller pen with its head in position. It was trembling and stared feverishly at the culling staff. The bolt stunner was placed on its head and shot. The dog whimpered as blood poured from its head. This one had gumption and its feet continued to run after it was slaughtered.

The moaning and desperation increased to a shrill pitch in the large pen that held the dogs. This was the first batch of about thirty or thirty-five street dogs captured in the past week. There was an outbreak of rabies and the health department had passed the order to cull all the strays.

The dogs collapsed one by one, slaughtered, and thrown into the loader. The smell of the blood sharpened. Blood marks had splashed all around on the white tiles. The blood flowed into the drains and mixed with water running from the tap to flush it.

As spittle collected at the edges of his mouth, Alfie retched.

The superintendent said, 'Sir, wait in the office. I will oversee this.' Before he could ask anything, he saw another pen being brought in. This had pups and younger dogs.

Alfie flew out from there to his office and sat there trying to control his rage and helplessness at the killings. He ran and vomited in the toilet bowl. Saliva ran down his mouth and tears from his eyes. 'So horrific!' He thought. 'So awful'.

The only thought that kept running in his head in a loop was 'Thou shalt not kill'. He walked out and stood in the morning air inhaling deeply. He then lit a cigarette and smoked hungrily to clear the stench of death that had congealed in his throat. He gulped clouds of smoke and blinked to take away the image of the pups. The tears that welled up could make those images disappear.

Thou shalt not kill. Thou shalt not kill. Thou shalt not kill.

Alfie, unable to calm down, started sweating. He continued smoking.

'It's done.' The superintendent informed.

'Let's go and see.' Alfie said with a heavy heart.

The staff had cups of tea in their hands. And they were sipping it contentedly after the killing.

'How many?' as Alfie shouted from the inspection window, a few white pigeons flew up from the rafters shedding white feathers. Peace always comes in white, he thought.

'Total seventy-nine, Sahib,' one of them replied. Alfie saw more white pigeons in the ledge above the tall glass windows of the culling shed as he registered the information. A few of the staff had started removing the disposable plastic overalls.

'I am going home.' He told the superintendent.

The sadness with which Alfie related this made you think, 'Perhaps he is a good man after all!'

It had been three years of your marriage. In those days, your sadness was more than you could handle. You had grown reluctantly affectionate towards Alfie. Your affection ignited desire in Alfie that he had supressed. Now, you never denied his desire. Subtly, you encouraged him to help you find love in you somehow. You dressed impeccably not letting anyone know how discordant the situation was. Alfie would send away Badi Bai for different errands and spend the day naked like a child in the house, smoking and making love to you. Insatiably. You never denied him. There was no conversation. Alfie was gentle, never rough; insatiable, yes!

After making love, you would find him with his eyes closed, breathing lightly, with cigarette smoke wafting, caught loosely in his fingers while the gramophone played Frank Sinatra. That made it difficult for you to make conversation. You would remember that he made love with the cigarette in his hand. Cold ash on the bedsheet afterwards was evidence. He was always careful that you were not touched by the burning cigarette. He could never make love without his cigarette. Every time you looked at his smooth skin, his face, and the sinews that ran across the topography of his body lying there naked, you wondered what it would be to fall completely in love with him. There was no companionship. You yearned for companionship.

The gramophone played jazz or western music when Alfie was home. You liked KL Saigal but there were no records of his in the house.

What you started liking was smoking. Sometimes you would take the cigarette from his fingers as he slept after sex and would take deep drags to calm yourself. Sometimes you would hide in the bathroom and smoke.

One morning, about four years into your marriage, when it was just turning pearl grey from inky blue, Alfie happened to pass your room. By then, you had started sleeping in separate bedrooms because Alfie came late from the club and it disturbed you, you had said. And it did not matter because you never refused his lovemaking now. Your window was open as it was still September, and the days were warm and muggy. The darkness brought a gentle breeze. He had not been able to sleep as he realised what Sheila Aunty had said so innocuously.

Sheila Aunty was the only friend you had. She visited you often. She spilled the beans during one of her visits. She made papier-mâché masks and sold them in shops. She sat speaking about her masks and then mentioned that she had made masks for you and me.

'I am sure you will love those. Mahesh will look like such a contrast in the African mask compared to your Venetian mask,' she mentioned to you.

'You know Mahesh Babu. Don't you?' she asked Alfie.

'He is a friend of many years. We play snooker often,' he said and smiled.

She had hinted at the affair innocently and without malice, and Alfie had taken it lightly then. He had not broken your faith despite his colourful bachelor life. And he firmly believed that you would not betray the vows you had taken together in the church.

'What bouquet are you making for Sarah's wedding?' Sheila Aunty changed the topic. Sarah was getting married in a few weeks in October and she had asked you to make her the wedding bouquet.

'I haven't thought about it. But the red roses are blooming profusely now. I will make it with those,' you said.

You would create such an enchanting bouquet with red roses, green fern, and morning glory that it will make Thakur Rudra Pratap, the Orchard Man, become besotted with you. More of that later.

One night, Alfie saw you curled up without clothes on what seemed like a wine-coloured thin quilt. He saw your flesh and it awoke a desire in him. It reminded him of the nights when you lay together. After your contempt had dissolved, Alfie was still careful. His touches were tentative, but the humidity of your skin was always perfect. He would invariably curl and fit into the curve of your body. You always slept with your face away from his. He smelled your hair and it always smelled of roses and sunshine. His nose was always on the curve of your neck. When you complained of his stubble once or twice, he started shaving in the night before going to bed.

You were away every afternoon to Sheila Aunty's. He was glad that you were stepping out of the house and socialising. Alfie did not know that you were meeting me there.

Over the past year, Alfie had become an archaeologist of every place in your topography. He explored and discovered your secret folds and deep crevices, the curves and valleys and wanted to get into your gut, heart, blood, marrow. He began to embalm you under his skin. You would let him make love to you. Alfie did not know that I had started lingering beneath your long lashes and closed lids in those moments of lovemaking.

You did not seem sad anymore, if not completely happy. You were embedded in his home like a diamond in a ring. Your flower art enchanted him and just watching your fingers play with the flowers and create something beautiful brought peace to his soul. That assurance that you were there for him changed his anxious, impetuous physical desire into an elegant, restrained desire.

His desire was implicit and always there. His eyes were the tools to visualise and analyse the physical diagram of your cellular and ocular topography. He was so besotted that he would have disintegrated himself to penetrate each cell of your body, to reach your heart and be pumped out and be the runner with your blood cells, be the calcium in your bones and the electrical impulse in the synapses of your brain. He may have held you intimately in his heart, but he knew you were never there. Not in your soul, not in your muscles and skin and not in your cells and spaces in between when you made love to him.

You were so perfect that all he had was admiration. And denial.

ART OF FLOWERS

It was after a few years of your marriage. You did not have children yet. One day after the church service, the children pestered their elders for coins to buy ice cream, lemonade, chips, sweet orange candies, pinwheels, paper snakes at the cart shop opposite the church. Pestering turned to begging if the elders were busy socialising and greeting each other and then it turned to outright tantrum. You would meet people and watch the children as they laughed, cried, jostled, and played. There was always an emptiness, a yearning. Alfie continued to be affectionate, but the house was quiet and incomplete.

A woman in a peach georgette saree, with bright marigold tucked in her hair, came by and stood next to you.

'You are Frieda, right? The bouquet maker? You made the bouquet for Sarah's wedding a few months back. I remember.' The woman challenged before you could deny. She smelled of Yardley Lavender perfume.

'I do it sometimes. Sarah is my sister,' you said.

'My daughter may need your services then.' For a moment you were stunned at the haughtiness. You were about to say something when she said, 'You don't speak much. Do you? Anyway, I know where you live. I will come in the afternoon on Tuesday when it's quiet.' Then she hopped into her chauffeur driven car, 'My name is Marjorie.' She declared and went away leaving a wake of dust, fumes, and perfume.

Sarah's bouquet would also lead Thakur Rudra Pratap to unleash his lust. More of that later.

You were anxious all morning on Tuesday. Marjorie came in the afternoon when the sun was hot and air still in anticipation.

Her daughter, not more than sixteen, followed. You saw her round belly as she removed her stole, and you knew you had to help this girl.

'I want your discretion,' Marjorie said.

'You will have that.' You spoke. 'What can I do for you?' You were not sure what was expected of you. The girl was distressed and fidgeting with her fingers under the belly.

'Her wedding is coming up in a week. You heard the banns in the church on Sunday. I want you to make a bouquet that will hide the sin she is carrying behind the flowers.' The daughter stood squirming with shame.

'We barely spoke or touched and now I have this whirling inside,' the daughter said whimpering. 'If only I had known that soft words said with kindness could lead to this...'

'Liar!' Her mother slapped her shoulder. 'If only words could make women pregnant, all the women would be getting pregnant after the priest's sermon in church. You careless lassie! You should have behaved. It's fortunate that Nathan still wants to marry you. But this swelling must be hidden till you are married.'

You extended your hands and felt the movement beneath her tight skin. She was well into her seventh month. There was a shifting movement, and you could feel a small foot. That was a healthy baby inside.

'I try to distract myself and forget about it, but this thing moves all the time,' the girl sobbed.

'I will make the bouquet for you. But you must hold it all the time on your wedding day,' you said to the girl. Then you turned to Marjorie, her mother, 'I need some money to buy material.'

'I am aware you are not exactly rolling in money,' she said condescendingly, taking out a 100-rupee-note from her purse.

'Send me a strand of your fiancé's hair and a button from his coat in five days,' you said to the girl.

'Why?' she asked, behind the veil of tears.

'Because I will make the most beautiful bouquet for you. People will forget what's behind it.'

You started spending time in the garden. You took the seeds from the wooden box you still had, the one which you had given Hannah to hide. You planted a few seeds. In five days, you had lovely bright red roses. You got pale tuberoses and cream-coloured carnations from your father's garden. You created a starburst of a bouquet with tendrils of climbers and asparagus fern that extended both sides, from the midriff to the bosoms and from the midriff to the thighs. It had a hollow behind that fitted neatly on the curvature of the swollen belly. You had tied it in silk lace supported by a transparent netting behind and embellished it with artificial pearls. On the front you had sewed the groom's button with his hair.

The girl looked dazzling with her bouquet. The pearls reflected the light and made stars on the bride's face and a twinkle in her eyes. The sin was invisible and forgotten that evening.

People who had seen the bouquet were in raptures and brides all over the city dreamed of your bouquets for their wedding and started coming to you. The mesmerising bouquets you made became the reason for the girls to get married and the church was continually busy with all the marriages taking place.

But it was not enough. You made the bouquets because you loved the flowers and the joy they brought to the young women's lives. The joy that you did not have at your own wedding. You did not charge much then. Later, when fame was not enough and your family had grown and times had turned bad, your art of the flowers brought some income and helped sustain us.

It had been more than three years of your marriage. Around that time, I had entered the house like the floating kite that landed in your backyard. A squall of children was left outside the gate. I came in hesitatingly and undecided like the kite. I entered the veranda. The main door was open. In twilight, the darkness had crept in the rooms. In the far end from the main door on the other side, there was a framed rectangular door which still held the promise of fading light. I dared not enter inside the bungalow. It had a sloping, red-tiled roof veranda on four sides supported by round pillars. I walked to the end of the right side of the veranda. I could see your dark silhouette, standing there taking the support of the door frame at the far end. I could hear the echo of silence that emanated in that bungalow. I crossed the veranda's length on the right. I was afraid to speak and break your reverie. I came closer and stood behind you, thinking about how to break that serene sheet of silence.

I could hear a muffled tinkling of cowbells with rising clouds of dust in a distance. The kite was trembling in the rosebush near the boundary hedge at the back some yards away. The sky was turning orange and red. Frenetically thinking about how to retrieve the kite, I cracked a knuckle inadvertently and your head turned. Tears that brimmed in your eyes caught the sun's rays. In an instant, you wiped your eyes as if caught guilty and you regained your poise.

'The kite...' was all I could mumble pointing in the direction of the rosebush. You looked at the kite and made the gesture with your hand that I could take it.

'Just be careful. Those roses are precious,' you said, as I started in that direction.

I walked across the back garden. The roses were spectacular and radiant as if emitting light, as if whispering in the breeze. I stood looking at them enchanted. Then I retrieved the kite. Just then squeals and peals of laughter exploded at the front garden. You turned and saw a swarm of children all no more than twelve years standing there with jubilation at the retrieval.

They had entered the main gate and were milling in the front part of veranda.

'My mouth is dry with the dust and heat. Could you please give me some water?' I had asked. I knew you, Frieda. I had seen you at your wedding and at the club with Alfie, but we had not been introduced yet.

You were standing straight now, without the support but close to the door frame.

'These children can be tiring. They have unending energy and I have been playing with them for quite some time. I don't mind it. When I see their smiles and their laughter and how happy they are with the kites soaring and their anxiety and worry with the kite dipping, I don't have the heart to stop the play. Only the invading darkness breaks our spell.' I said jovially explaining myself.

You nodded slightly and went to the kitchen. When you came out you had tidied your hair and the pleats of that peach paisley saree. You handed me a large brass tumbler of water.

I drank greedily and as I did so, I looked into your eyes and stayed there. I saw the flush of pink rising in your cheeks, but you did not lower your gaze.

I handed you the tumbler.

'Do you know what pencha is?' I boasted.

'Yes...I know!' You said with a tinge of exasperation.

'Then you know how to fly kites. Do you know the technique?'

You chose not to respond but looked at me with slight amusement. I was being condescending, I agree.

'You first entangle the opponents' kite string and then let them be. Loosen and release as much line as you can. If you are using a good maanja[1], give it a sudden jerk and...*wo kata*!'

---

[1] Glass powder coated kite flying and fighting string.

I said with excitement echoed by the 'Wo kata' chorus by the children. They were all jumping and dancing.

'Is this your kite?' you pointed to the kite I had retrieved from the rosebush.

'Umm...yes,' I said embarrassed. I understood. It was my kite that had been cut and I had come chasing it to your house to retrieve it. You looked at my face with a stoicism that resembled a smirk, silently saying what kind of an expert at pencha are you if your kite gets cut. You turned and went in.

'Let's go.' I told the kids. The swarming children were jumping and shouting with glee all around me for having retrieved the kite. Other kites were fluttering around in their hands, and some carried the spindles of lines that was tied to the kites.

As I walked out, you said, 'Stop! I know you. You are Mahesh Babu.'

I turned and was delighted that you knew of my existence, 'Yes! I am.'

'Alfie speaks about you sometimes. I had seen you at our wedding...and the club sometimes.'

That was the first time we spoke.

I flew the kite late into the night that evening in the grounds behind your bungalow. It glowed in the sky in the dark with the rosebush dust.

That is how our story began.

You had slept well and had bathed before coming into the kitchen. You were fresh, and your skin looked healthy. As you cooked breakfast with Badi Bai one morning, you asked her, 'How was Alfie as a baby?' Then you added, 'It would be nice to have children in this house too.' Badi Bai remained quiet. You continued, 'With the amount of effort Alfie is making, I should be pregnant by now.' The quiet house and the days progressing at the rate of mundane were becoming unbearable.

You had never denied yourself to Alfie. You wanted a baby for your heart to have a reason to be. You wanted a baby who would fill in the spaces and silences that seemed to be clotting in your heart.

You stepped out and went for a walk. As you walked near the ground where the children flew kites in the evening, you looked at the kites that get cut and are blown away. You felt like a kite broken from its string ever since you married Alfie. DC could have been the string to hold you steady and let you fly. And you stood there looking at the sky remembering DC and your fate.

I was passing by. I recognised your silhouette. I decided to come your way. When you heard my motorcycle, you turned. I could see the shining streaks wiped quickly and incompletely on your cheeks. I saw you that you held your breath. I asked you what happened. You did not reply. You looked at me so helplessly that I got off the motorcycle, put it on the stand and came to you. 'Is everything all right?' I asked tenderly. You burst into tears. I stepped forward and stood trying to figure out what to do.

'Come, I will drop you home,' I said. You shook your head and started walking. I walked beside you, dragging the motorcycle along. I remember you were wearing a white georgette saree with pink, blue and green flowers. I remember an end of your pallu swaying in the breeze as you walked, I remember the white Bata leather sandal you wore on your feet. I noticed the delicate filigree silver jhumkas[2] in your ears. How young and beautiful you looked. How disoriented and sad you seemed.

I walked with you to the gate of your bungalow.

Every morning thereafter, I waited at that spot on the road hoping to see you. It always left me with a strange mix of undefined feelings. I was glad that I did not see you for you

---

[2] Earrings.

must be in the safety of your home. Yet, I was disappointed that I had not seen you. This went on for a few days.

That year there was bountiful guava on the trees. Yellowish brown on the outside and deep red inside. I got a basket of those sweetly aromatic guavas and came to your bungalow. I was hoping to meet Badi Bai and give those to her. When you opened the door, I felt elated. 'I got this basket of guavas for your home.' You looked at me and then at the cane basket.

'Mahesh Babu, that is too much. There is only Badi Bai and I who will eat this. Alfie does not like fruits.' You spoke.

'That's all right. Make guava jam out of it. I can get you more if you want.'

'No, thank you. This is enough,' you said. I think I saw a shine in your eyes and a feeble smile on your face. You stood there waiting for me to leave.

When I turned back at the gate, there was no one at the door. You had taken the basket in.

I started coming every week with a basket of fruits or vegetables or sweets. Mostly, I was received by Badi Bai but the days when you received me, I was happy through the day. I felt elated and time passed quickly. In that time, I found that you liked mangoes, and guavas, and ber[3] and tamarind and bael[4] and lychee and amla[5] and jamun[6]. I had started receiving gifts from your kitchen; jars of homemade jams, preserves of fruits, chutneys, murabba[7] and pickles. Always accompanied with a rose from your garden. I took them home and my mother and I had them as delightful accompaniments to our meals.

---

[3] Berries.

[4] Stone apple.

[5] Gooseberry.

[6] Java plum.

[7] Marmalade.

One day I heard the gramophone playing Frank Sinatra and it gave me the idea. I brought you a KL Saigal record of *Devdas*. It was a rage then. You were delighted.

'Mahesh Babu, let us listen to it together,' you said. You called Badi Bai too. When the music played, you closed your eyes and it seemed you were transported elsewhere; a happy place for you. That day we listened to it three times.

The other gifts that I gave you were the 78 rpm records of Rasoolan Bai, Bade Ghulam Ali Khan, Janki Bai and others of Indian classical genres. I started visiting your home to listen to music. Often you kept a basket of flowers and your tools and materials and made the flower bouquets while we listened to music. I would watch you mesmerised as you worked.

Marriage and its demands had reduced your friends to a few. Sheila Aunty had remained the best one. Your sisters visited you sometimes. Your mother never visited you. Your father came often. Your favourite sisters Sarah and Mara were stationed in other towns. One day, when I came with a basket of jamun, you asked me if I could drop you to Sheila Aunty's on my motorcycle. Alfie has taken the car, you told me. Badi Bai came to the gate, and I could feel her gaze on my neck watching us till we turned the corner. You sat carefully without touching me, and I sat on the edge, nearly on the petrol tank, lest you feel offended by my touch. We rode with a partition of air cushion between us. After dropping you, I went and waited under the shade of the tree at the entrance of the street hoping to take you back later. But I saw Alfie in his car driving towards Sheila Aunty's place, late in the afternoon and I left.

SHE WAS A WITCH

Everyone believed that Sheila Aunty was a witch.

You went to her place every afternoon. She would give you sweet lemonade. You would add a pinch of salt and stir. She would smile with melancholy. Dissolve your sadness and drink it, she would say. And she would continue to make her masks of papier-mâché.

She lived alone. She was happy.

She would sit holding your hand in hers. Letting the moisture come alive between the skin of your palms. She would kiss you sometimes. On the forehead like a mother does. Sometimes on your cheeks. Like affection does. Sometimes on your lips. Like a lover does. Sometimes she would say, you have always been my favourite since you were a little girl. Even more than my sisters? You would ask. More than anyone. And she would kiss you again. She was only a bit older than you.

She was beautiful. People stopped in the streets to look at her. Admire her. When they did that, caterpillars crawled on her skin. Therefore, she had several masks made and she put one on every time she went out. She kept the town guessing who she really was and where she was coming from.

She lived alone. She was happy. She wore masks. She was a witch.

Wrap your soul in cat's fur. She would say. It remains soft and warm. If you leave it to men, it will turn cold and hard. She would say. You would smile. Your smile those days seemed like an accident of fate.

When I gave you the cat's fur as a gift you saw that as a sign. But that was later.

She stopped staying with you in the afternoons when we started meeting there. She would raise the end of her saree and fly away like a single winged butterfly. Showing the white-blue skin stretched over the cage of her ribs from under her thin, slim blouse.

When the old leaves ran with the new wind and new cold came riding on the back of old warmth, you and I had started meeting. You asked me to come there. At Sheila Aunty's house in the afternoons. No one will see us there, you said. Each afternoon as you waited for me, love electrified the synapses of your brain and its charge traversed down your face sparkling your eyes, to your chest between your breasts accelerating your heartbeats until it reached the pit of your stomach and knotted itself so tight that it hurt. It squatted there solid, static, stuck, unwilling to resolve!

We would sit together under the tree dappled in the afternoon sun. On the wooden bench in the garden with the tall green unkempt hedge. Our faces so near that you could see the pores on my skin where the bristles on the face, right that moment too, were trying to push through. You could see the dust caught in my long lashes. You could see the liquid in my brown eyes. The faint lines on the side of the eyes, the soft skin of the eyelids, the dark hair of the brows. And then you would lower your eyes and look at the stitches at the seams of your saree pallu. The knot tightening in the pit of your stomach. I wanted to touch you and hold you, but I did not dare. Those moments I would open my mouth to speak only to find that I had lost my tongue. Only the apprehensive afternoon breeze sang of our longing. We had scoured each other with our gaze and left marks all over our exposed body parts, mapping territories like cartographers. We wanted to fit in each other's body; in every curve and indentation. We were inundated with desire but held back. You were married.

One winter afternoon I gave you a coat made of cat's fur. I had purchased it from the British shop in Sadar Bazaar. Frieda, wear this as you wait for me.

One day when the kissing distance was hard to withstand, I touched the same end of your silk saree's pallu in a leap of faith. You withdrew your hand. But then you felt my long fingers and hard skin on the sides of your head and my thumbs under you jaw as I brought your face near and drew a kiss that was urgent and desperate with desire. Slowly I unrolled the silk saree from your body, layer after layer, pleat after pleat until it lay in a heap on the grass. You were trembling. I undid the string of your satin petticoat. You removed the blouse and the brassiere. You stood fresh as a flower in the sunshine in front of me. Your skin shone like burnished marble. We made love. 'You smell of earth after the rains,' you said as we lay there, you on me. 'And you smell of roses and nutmeg.' I said as you buried your passionate damp face in my neck.

That was the beginning.

Every afternoon we made love. In the garden, where no one came. Our hearts like Sheila Aunty's garden, bloomed. It became a riot of colours in a profusion of bloom.

Then came the plague of the butterflies. Cloud of butterflies descended in multi-coloured plumes. They could be seen from miles and miles. They covered your naked body as you lay waiting for me. I saw the butterflies embrace you. I blew away one after the other. Gently. Playfully. Do you know a butterfly lives but a few days? I said. Later, with you covered in the butterfly dust, we made love. It was deep. It was strange. It was desirable.

She had stayed that afternoon. Sheila Aunty. Sitting making her mask. Mixing mashed paper and water. She sat on the bench watching us gathering each other rhythmically and frenetically. She made two large holes in the place for eyes. She carved the smiling lips. When it was done, she put the wet deformed mask on her face and began her dance of glee. She danced for a long time. Rhythm. Pace. Feverish frenzy. You and I stayed in the garden. That evening. That night. We were two butterflies drinking nectar from the flowers of each other's bodies. We were like famished animals, gobbling up time without chewing. She danced like a mad woman. Only we could see her. There was going to be no tomorrow. When she left, she took the night along and left two masks: one for you and one for me. 'Wear these when you go out together,' she had said.

When we kissed in the morning, my lips tasted of sin and your eyes were lit with guilt. That was the moment that our happiness began. You had conceived that day but how were we to know.

She was a witch!

The French photographer was back in town. You wanted a picture of us together. For keepsake. You spoke. You knew that while we met discreetly at Sheila Aunty's, there could be no display of our affection beyond her garden. Beyond, you were Alfie's wife, and I was Alfie's friend. You remembered the day a few years back when you had come with your sisters and had a group photo taken. You shuddered at the catcalls and the jeers that followed but then you wanted to feel the exhilaration of holding your breath and staring straight at the lens waiting for the smoke of the flash to go off. You liked the smell of the flash powder and the suspense that the photographic plate captured.

We went discretely in the afternoon to get our pictures taken. In one photo we wore the masks that Sheila Aunty had given and in another we stood close together without the masks. That was a mistake that Sheila Aunty had cautioned us about because she knew the fallout of exposing our faces to the world. It would have consequences.

She was a witch!

MAY I HAVE A FLOWER?

His father was a landlord who owned large tracts of land and many orchards of mango. His mother died in childbirth but not before naming him Thakur Rudra Pratap. His father had other children from his other marriages after that. But he remained the special one. From the young age he suffered from an ailment where the connection between his will and desire was broken. As a result, he yearned for what he did not desire and pursued what he was not passionate about. His soul was forever torn by the consequences of what he did not will and what he did not desire.

As an example, he often felt a strange urge to bury himself in the armpits of his horse trainer. He would have liked his little body to be swallowed by the firm muscles of his chest and to vanish in the musty damp animal smell like his horse's, that his body gave. Often, he would jump from the horseback to his strong shoulders and feel the sinews rippling under his little soft thighs, the boy's little penis rubbing at the back of the trainer's head, stiff. It was not desire and yet he needed this play to feel good.

He would get into skirmishes with his brothers for things he did not care for nor did his victories in fist fights with other children at school give him any joy. This conflict between need and want, between tenacity and enthusiasm, gave him a burning of the body, where he was unable to rest for days, constantly moving, constantly doing something.

When Thakur Rudra Pratap turned seven, he saw the trainer in the arms of one of the maids and their flesh a shiny sweaty messy knot like the horses after a long run. He decided to do something for the fevers and to empty his head of the contradictions that ran in his nerves. He went to the mango orchard where the heady smell of mango blossoms agitated him. He stripped to his skin and rode the horse among the trees. When he finished, he started again, spending the entire day like that. He was exhausted by evening and his will and desire, his restraint and his ache, remained feverish the entire night. The next day he began again. That summer he learned to withstand the furnace heat of the tropical sun which his skin absorbed and gave him a deep brown colour. His thighs burned with the bruises of riding the horse. When he could remember the number of each tree, he began planting mango seeds. He forgot his fever for those hours when he saw the infinite plants growing and his orchard expanding. The edges of his desire frayed, and the weight of his will dissolved in the flourishing of the mango trees. Only temporarily.

The father knew, as the watchmen of the orchards had told him the first day that Thakur Rudra Pratap rode naked in the sun. The father commanded, just observe but do not touch the boy. The boy would ride in the orchard and spend his entire day counting trees, climbing them, discovering the treasures of fruit and nests and insects. Sometimes monkeys descended on the orchards, and he chased them from one end to the other. He would talk to the trees as if they were his army and his conversations were authoritative. He took care to speak distinctly, loudly, and with power. Beneath these words he suppressed his desire for tender dampness of a human body, the husky voice of the maid wrapped to the horse trainer, the craving for a kiss that sucked his breath, or just some violence that proved he was in control. But nothing happened. The trees remained muted waving their leaves gently and the mangoes continued to grow and plump up. He would kiss the bark of the trees and they would reproach him with their roughness and dustiness. This agitated him, and he would let out a volley of curses. He would give in to the heat and intoxicating drowsiness under the thickest canopy.

That summer when he saw a horse mount a mare, he was fascinated by the bulk of the muscles and the sounds of neighing, and his fits of madness became more acute. His fever took a grip on him and overwhelmed him. His blooming nakedness became a threat and while he continued to ride on his horse naked in the sun, his sickness increased. His reason, will, desire all collapsed, and his daydreams became intense. At fifteen, he was a young man with deep brown muscles and lush pubic hair when he forced himself on the older maids made of velvet, sugar, and lullabies. Sometimes on the young men, who were farm hands made of rocks, ice, and silence. He would do his acts in the orchard beneath the moon or behind the canopy of leaves or the beneath the serene dusky wet skies of monsoon or beneath the blazing glory of the sun god. In all these acts his desire and will never came together. Sometimes he willed it with no desire and other times he desired these acts with no will. As a result, Thakur Rudra Pratap neither felt any contentment nor pleasure in his acts. Poverty and retribution brought about the silence of his victims. Some victims left and receded into oblivion while others who remained received him as the curse of fate.

When his actions turned prolific and his soliciting ingenious and salacious, the gossip and the rumours about him became folklore. He became famous as 'The Orchard Man'. His father worried about its impact on his workers and business and packed him off to a stringent boarding school in England. No one heard about him for the next twenty years.

A generation had been replaced in the town when Thakur Rudra Pratap returned to his father's deathbed to inherit all the mango orchards and the horse farm.

His desire had stratified under the surface of responsibility, and he had returned a learned man. He had studied criminal law and had learned about every possible act of crime and violence. He knew the destructibility of the human body and therefore no flesh, no smell, no skin held any fascination for him for he knew its fragility. He knew that all bodies manufacture the same shit, and rot or burn in the same way. Nothing stirred his heart. His will was not directed at anything. His desire lay frozen in his subcutaneous blood. He took the management of his orchards with rational detachment. He only came alive in his horse farm and would take his horse for a ride every morning in the early hours and in the late evenings when the silence imposed on the streets by men and women inside their homes suited him well. The people listened to the hooves of his horse either when they woke or when they were going to sleep. In between those hours, he took litigation cases for disadvantaged and marginalised native people for free, and looked after his orchards, always counting the trees and charging for the mangoes.

He was extremely good looking with a square jaw, large eyes, aquiline nose and dark hair and eyebrows. He had grown a handsome handlebar moustache that he waxed to upturned pointed ends. He was completely unattached, and no one dared to approach him amorously given his dignified contours and stoic façade. Not stiff but not supple either. Not stern but not friendly either. Not amicable but not amiable either. He enjoyed the solitude of the trees burning on the charred earth in the blazing sun. He was at peace with his cultivated damnation of solitude. Folks kept their distance as the folklore of his predatory sexual escapades as a teenager still reverberated in gossips and undertones.

One of those mornings, he crossed Alfie who was on his rounds of sanitation inspection in the cantonment. They were civil enough to acknowledge each other. They crossed each other many times after that but had never spoken, but always acknowledged each other.

And then he met you, Frieda. Through your roses.

It was your sister Sarah's wedding. You had made the bouquet of red roses and green ferns with morning glory. You had requested Badi Bai to deliver them a night before with instructions that they be put in water with a quarter teaspoon of sugar. As Badi Bai was walking with the bouquet, he crossed her. He was taken aback by the smell of the roses—a mix of red wine, burnt earth and a woman. He stopped his horse in front of Badi Bai blocking her way and she broke into cold sweat. She had heard the stories about the Orchard Man.

'May I have a flower from that?' Thakur Rudra Pratap demanded politely.

She extended the whole bouquet. He pulled one flower and smelled it.

'Who is the talent that made this?' He asked with sugar in his voice and a trance in his eyes.

'Frieda,' Badi Bai said, 'Alfie's wife.'

Badi Bai saw him transported to another world and she fled around the horse and ran towards your father's house. When she turned the corner, she looked back, and saw him in a state of ecstasy. Graceful tranquillity had beholden him. In his head, his will and desire were churning in strange calisthenics. When your father walked back Badi Bai that night, as she refused to come home alone, he was still there, standing like a statue, oblivious to the two of them walking past. As she turned to see him, she saw sparks over his head. It was just that, now, his will was firmly planted in his desire.

He made friends with Alfie the next morning as they crossed on their horse backs. The Orchard Man had done his homework for his object of desire and had an opponent to take care of now.

Badi Bai was afraid for you. Thakur Rudra Pratap was at Sarah's wedding with the red rose on his lapel. Badi Bai had noticed that his eyes were searching and following you everywhere that evening. He knew you were the gardener of the flowers and maker of the bouquet. When Alfie introduced you to him, he took your hand and pressed his lips to the lining of your flesh. You were shocked. However, it seemed like a gallant act without vulgarity or lust. Yet, everything stopped for him. A spectral stillness descended in his eyes and every movement was in abeyance. You pulled your hand, and his reverie was broken. A shy smile broke on his face, but Badi Bai noticed that waltz of his will and desire in his eyes and she knew the danger you were in. Alfie thought that it was just an innocuous whimsical act of an England-returned man.

In the evenings, Alfie would disappear around the bend in the road and meet his new friend, on his horse, erect and well dressed. They would either go to the bar at YMCA, whenever they wanted a quiet place, or to the Jackson Hotel in Civil Lines when they wanted to enjoy the live jazz band. The alcohol would warm them through the evening. They would spend time speaking less, daydreaming more. You would wait till Alfie returned. Almost always alone but occasionally, Thakur Rudra Pratap would drop him. And when he did that, he was civil, kept his distance and never met your eyes because there was no need for that as you were always on his mind.

Soon after Sarah's wedding, he invited both of you to the cockfight one late afternoon. That meant we could not meet that afternoon at Sheila Aunty's garden. He received you with courtesy at the gates of his orchard. The fighting pit had been created inside. He had invited the whole town and his orchard was festooned with colourful paper buntings and paper flywheels and everything was festive. The women were in silk and carried parasols and men in their best attires. The cocks were from two professional cockfighting clubs; one from Calcutta and one from Lucknow. One cock was bright yellow with red plumes like a rose on his head and the other was shining white with orange plumes like fire on his head. Both had sharp iron spurs tied to their legs.

When the referee gave the indication, the birds were introduced in the arena.

'Which one do you think will win?' Thakur Rudra Pratap asked Alfie, who stood together.

'The white, no doubt,' said Alfie. 'I am partial to white,' he added, smiling.

'Would you bet on that? I think it will be the yellow one with the rose,' he countered, looking at you.

Alfie laughed and did not say anything.

When the referee whistled, there was an explosion of colour and dust and movement and shouts. The two cocks were at each other, shivering, enraged and the crowd was excited taking sides and making bets and predictions. You did not like the brutality and moved away and went out of the circle of spectators to breathe. You saw me then. Of course, I had followed you. I drifted in the crowd from where I could see you. I cherished the time in the afternoons we spent together, and I was not letting the birds' fight take that time away from me. I found it exhilarating when you caught my eyes briefly a few times. You were nonchalant. We had agreed to not make our affair public.

The spectators were getting frenzied and intoxicated by blood, cries, cheers, and alcohol. He must have noticed your absence. The fight went on amidst the savagery, shrieks, and chaos. The roosters' movements were electric and quick. There was confusion of steam, blood, dust, and feathers. They would leap, arch back their necks and attack with their spurs and talons.

And somewhere there was you, hidden in the mind of Thakur Rudra Pratap.

The roosters flew and caught each other in the air like missiles and fell in a common mass of pulsating feathers in a crater of fine dust, bouncing it off the dry earth, building a cloud around the two birds as they trembled with excitement.

I looked at you.

His desire was rising in him, and his will was turning into wrought iron.

The roosters understood each other's power and were manoeuvring to gain the advantage. The yellow one was aggressive and strong, the muscles in thighs rippled while the white one was lean and craftier with a quick eye. They postured at each other with their beaks open and their eyes enlarged. The crowd was excited and shrieking and betting.

You stole a glance at me.

He wanted your body.

The roosters' attacks on each other were uninterrupted and the light was reflected like lightning from the shining spurs during attacks and swerves. After a while, they paused face to face, breathing steam. His mind was not on the game but searching you out in the mango orchard. He arose but Alfie pulled him down.

He looked at you.

He was excited by your presence and wanted to hold you to his animal bosom.

The yellow rooster managed to catch its opponent by the feathers in the top of the wing and dragged him down, thrusting and pinning him to the ground. The white bird croaked as it struggled, its talons flexing, catching air. When the yellow bird was tired, it released the white one and it ran around in circles disoriented as the yellow bird spit the white plumes that floated with dust and walked with graceful movements of its tail and head.

You were looking at me.

He was longing for your mouth.

The white rooster's wing was broken, and it ran with unbalanced strides. It was shivering. The yellow rooster leaped again. The white rooster stopped immediately and crouched down flattening itself in defence, unbalancing the act, and the yellow rooster landed away from him. It swerved and charged with ferocity breathing steam from his nostrils.

He followed your eyes and saw me.

His will wanted to possess your body.

The white bird lifted as the yellow rooster ran towards it. The latter missed the attack. They both slowed down. They paused and did a hysterical tap dance with their wings spread away from their bodies to cool down. Their talons left imprints on the dry dusty earth and the spurs shone ominously. Steam arose from their feathers and then they charged with their chests out, used their feet to push the ground and lifted in the air.

You had turned your face from the crowd.

He had an erection, and his burning was aflame.

There is another cloud of dust and feathers as they land. The white rooster, panting heavily, seems weakened but had the courage and continued to struggle against the opponent's attack. The yellow rooster clearly understood its strength and exuded angry confidence. The white seemed to be on the defensive. The yellow was clearly on the offensive.

I saw him look at you.

His desire wanted to enter your softness and warmth.

The yellow rooster's victory was imminent. The spectators were going wild. The sea of mouths in red lipsticks were shouting in excitement, the men were delirious with sweat running down their faces. The sweat, perfume, smoke and dust were an exhilarating combination. The yellow rooster accelerated its offensive pace to bring the fight to its conclusion but lost its guard.

His constant and insistent gaze followed you as you walked away.

Lift and thrust, rise and fall, in and out, he leched.

The birds danced around the perimeter, one following the other. They were tired but their aggression was alive. Suddenly, the white rooster in a burst of energy, leaped and grabbed one of the wings of the yellow bird, raised the other leg and stabbed it in the chest. A spray of blood gushed out like tiny red flowers from his heart. The smell of fresh blood arose with steam and dust.

Thakur Rudra Pratap closed his eyes.

His jaws clenched, he did not want to stop, further and deeper into you, more and more.

The yellow rooster was down. Quivering and shaking on the ground in the spasms of death it trembled on the ground struggling for breath, flapping its wings. The blood gushed forth and coloured his chest red. The white rooster had aimed for its heart. Steam, blood, and dust started settling around. The shrieks of the audience was like a crescendo.

His body tensed, and his eyes squeezed; the sweat had broken at his brow.

More! Faster! Deeper! Deeper!

Between the silence that followed the crescendo and the murmur that began in the crowd, a wet patch emerged on his bulging crotch. I had noticed the lust. The carcass of the dead bird was being removed. The white bird stood shivering in a daze.

He looked at me and smirked.

He turned to Alfie, 'Let us drink to that! Your cock's victory!'

You had stood in that orchard, amidst the trees that evening as the white cock won. The yellow lights had come on against a deep blue sky. There were fireflies in the bushes.

You had noticed that the cries of excitement, noises of joy, sighs of loss and sighs of winning had been released in the atmosphere. You felt a touch, a soft tender scraping on your belly. You were startled by its coolness and the hair on your arms stood at their end. It is only an evening breeze, you thought unconvincingly. You pulled the end of the saree tightly across.

You heard your name taken softly. It broke the calm and I saw you quiver as if a shiver had run down your spine.

I saw you standing there. Another woman, young with a translucent radiating skin had joined you. She was wearing a pastel silk saree and had pink pearls on her ears and hair. I could see the column of a blue evening between you as she stood perhaps six inches away from you. You both seemed animated. When she turned to look at me in the crowds, I noticed again her most beautiful eyes and red lips.

I had to greet Alfie. He had seen me in the crowd.

I went up to Alfie. 'Which one did you support?' I asked. And then without waiting, added, 'Of course, the white one!'

'How did you know?' he asked with mirth in his eyes.

We chatted a bit about the cock fight and then the heat.

'Would you drop Frieda home?' he said. He seemed happy. 'I have to go with him,' he pointed to the Orchard Man who was speaking with someone at a distance. The Orchard Man turned and looked at me. There were no expressions on his face, but his eyes drilled down into my soul. He then turned and looked at you. I knew then that he knew about us.

'Sure,' I replied.

'She is there,' he pointed in your direction. The beautiful woman was still with you.

'Ok, I will go and say hello to Frieda,' I spoke. This was my chance, and I took it.

As I navigated the crowd, I saw you were standing alone now.

I came and stood next to you in the place of that beautiful woman.

'Who was that beautiful woman?' I had asked lightly.

'No one,' you said, and the cold air vibrated between us.

'How are you feeling?' I asked. You were standing cocooned with your saree pulled tightly across.

'I feel there will be an explosion of rose blooms tomorrow morning,' you said, softly. I noticed the fireflies were surrounding you and enveloping you in a golden glow. I shall wait and watch this spectacle, I thought. You looked beautiful. And much as I wanted to kiss you, I would not dare to touch you in public.

Then, you, who smelled of roses and earth, said, 'You have taken root in me.'

'Like you have in me.' I spoke. And you looked at me, your eyes fixed with silence in them.

Thakur Rudra Pratap saw us standing together at the edge. The serpents must have risen in his chest and poisoned his desire and distorted his will for his face looked jealous and vulgar.

That night Alfie returned too drunk. The Orchard Man delivered him to the bungalow. You were waiting for him as you always did. Badi Bai had retired for the day.

When the reverberating sound of the car reached your ears and then stopped, you ran to the gate. The vast space of time in circles that made you anxious had come together at that point. You saw his very handsome face open the door and lift Alfie from the car. He walked to the veranda.

'He passed out.' He was breathing heavily with the strain of the weight in his arms.

'Leave him on the sofa in the drawing-room,' you said, anxiously.

Alfie stirred as he lay him on the sofa. You put his feet up. And gathered his right arm fallen to the floor and folded it on his chest.

'Thank you,' you said in gratitude.

He started to walk out, and you followed him. He suddenly turned and pulled you in his arms and put his tongue in your mouth greedily flicking it in and out like a snake's. His stiff handlebar moustache scratched your cheeks. You nearly passed out in fright. You slapped him, and he detached his wet drool dripping mouth and looked at you, hurt. 'Just once!' Thakur Rudra Pratap implored.

'Get out,' you hissed. He left.

You were shaking when you bolted the door. You were furious.

The next morning, you berated Alfie for his drunkenness and told him about the risk he put you in with the Orchard Man. 'That man is crazy, and you left me vulnerable with him.' You seethed. You did not speak to Alfie for a few days. He felt guilty about the misconduct by both him and Thakur Rudra Pratap. He avoided your eye contact. Alfie stopped coming home drunk. For a while at least.

A few days later at tea, he told you, 'The Orchard Man is dead.'

You turned white, and asked, 'How?'

'In an accident.'

You had become quiet those days and though we continued meeting at Sheila Aunty's garden, there were more silences than flowers. What love brings is more precious, you said each day. Those days we had stopped making love. You seemed scared but firm.

One afternoon you asked me, 'How did the Orchard Man die?'

'Alfie and he were racing their horses in his orchard. His horse stumbled frothing at its mouth and threw the rider who hit his head on a bark of the mango tree. Thakur Rudra Pratap's skull cracked open with a hiss and spilling blood streams ran around the orchard like red snakes. Fortunately, nothing happened to Alfie.'

'What happened to the horse?' Something was not adding up for you.

'The horse also died. Someone had poisoned the poor animal with Belladonna.' You turned pale and vomited.

Frieda, years passed by, and I can tell you now, what really happened. I did not tell you earlier as you were expecting then, and Alfie was my friend. While I did not know where I stood in all our relationships then, it could have destroyed you and the household that was just beginning to blossom. I gathered the pieces over a period from stewards at Jackson Hotel, from Alfie himself, from Badi Bai.

That night after the cock fight, he had told Alfie that his wife was extremely beautiful and that she was in love. He said, 'I noticed it in the way she looks, faraway, blissful and anticipating someone.' They had kept drinking. 'And that someone is not you!' he laughed. Alfie did not react, and he kept haranguing. 'I have my suspicion, but I will not say until you admit that your wife is having an affair.' Alfie did not believe him. He defended you and threatened him with grave consequences.

Many drinks had been consumed and then he finally challenged Alfie, 'I challenge you to a horse race. If I win, I will have your wife.' Alfie was humiliated that he was putting you at stake. He agreed in his intoxication, in his faith and in his belief in the vows he had taken in the church—of protecting and cherishing you. Alfie loved you and would have done anything to stop Thakur Rudra Pratap wagging his tongue and making advances towards you.

They continued to meet intermittently at the Jackson Hotel bar. Alfie in his fury with the Orchard Man had gone quiet. He would smoke and listen to jazz while Thakur Rudra Pratap drank. They would be civil to each other but hardly talked. The hotel stewards noticed the strange rendezvous evening after evening.

Badi Bai told me that she had given Alfie the Belladonna flowers around the same time. He wanted to feed them to a dog that was turning out to be a menace in the cantonment, which he had told her, when he asked for those. Badi Bai did not suspect anything.

When the race began a few weeks later, the Orchard Man was winning the race and whipping his horse hard to gain the lead. Alfie had calmly followed him a few paces behind. The workers at the orchard were all there as it was mid-morning. The sun was bright, and the breeze was light. The Orchard Man had an expression of glee and shine of an impending win when everybody saw the horse tumble.

It is all circumstantial, but I suspect Alfie had something to do with it. These things had happened so many years ago.

ALFIE GETS THE EVIDENCE

After a few days of the cock fight event, at breakfast, you told him, 'I have missed my period. I think I am expecting.' You became more splendid in your motherhood. The air of the house was firmly in ovation of your grandness. You looked dazzling when you went out with him on alternate Sundays to the movies, so much that you rarefied the crowds and he focused on you alone. You did not give away anything of your affair and it tormented Alfie with your capacity to create an illusion in his life.

Restless. Reckless. Relentless. That is what we were those days.

It so happened that when you came back from Sheila Aunty's place one evening, Alfie was waiting in a long loose white muslin kurta, sitting in the colonnaded veranda, smoking his Charminar cigarette. George Gershwin was playing on the turntable. Badi Bai had been sent to get the kebabs and roomali rotis from Bade Miya's shop.

In the courtyard, he removed the peacock silk saree from your body, the puff-sleeved blouse, then the rest of it. He removed his kurta. Animated and absorbed in your beauty, he looked at you with desire as the sun descended and turned your eyes from brown to golden. His body glowed in the penumbra of your shadow. He kissed you on the lips. He took you in his arms. You closed your eyes and rested your forehead on his chest. Alfie ran his fingers down the stones of your spine till the very end. He had his cigarette between his fingers as he did so. The smoke touched you and you could feel the thread of heat traversing down. He touched you lightly, pulling your chin up gently to look into your eyes. You looked up and saw his deep blue eyes aflame. He lay you down on the cold stone floor.

As he kissed you, he came down to your navel.

'What's that?' he asked noticing the bright red mark on your inguinal. I had left a mark of our passion there where I had kissed you.

'Oh that! I hit the corner of the table.' You lied. He looked at it and then in your eyes not believing you.

You suspected that he knew now. He wore his clothes and drove away to the Narmada Club. When Badi Bai came, you had showered and changed. She was surprised that Alfie was not there. You waited for Alfie for dinner.

He came at 4:30 in the morning. The dinner was still served at the dining table with nothing touched. He went and slept. He had his shoes on. There was a strong smell of alcohol permeating the room as he snored. He did not go to work the next day. He woke up at four in the evening, shaved, showered, and drove away to the club again.

You had not come to Sheila Aunty's that day because Alfie was home.

Then it became a pattern.

You stopped meeting me because you suspected that Alfie knew about the affair. This was nearly two months after the cock fight. You did not tell me about the pregnancy. It took only two days for you to realise how much you cherished the time in the afternoons with me at Sheila Aunty's. I was tolerant of your confusion and bewilderment at your married life even though nearly five years had passed. I cherished our conversations, which I know you found very noble and calming. Now you had found the rhythm to be tedious and lonely, even though Alfie was kind and understanding and nothing changed in his behaviour.

Alfie never spoke about what Thakur Rudra Pratap said to him in his wager. Alfie had started drinking heavily at the club and had started neglecting his home and work. But he knew that I was getting married in a few months. You were unaware of that fact since we had stopped meeting and Alfie hardly spoke much at home. You were in your first trimester and stayed home all the time with Badi Bai.

When a few days had passed, Badi Bai was away once again as you waited. You dressed in the finery that Alfie appreciated. You rubbed your neck with the perfume that he got for you a long time back. The sky was breaking in red streaks like your heart when he stumbled in. You went to him and held him in your arms. He stiffened and stood like that. You were not sure if he was sleeping or awake. You encircled your left hand around his waist and unbuttoned his shirt. You kissed him on his chest at the centre of his sternum. He smelled of smoke and alcohol. You decided to make love to him, nonetheless. You opened the buttons of his trousers and it fell to the floor. Still holding him with your left hand and with his face supported on your left shoulder, you undressed yourself. You kissed him on his lips and inhaled a stale breath. I will make you alive again, you thought and with a fierce passion, you kissed him all over his face, ears, eyes, nose and lips. You tasted the salt of his tears. His eyes were squeezed shut and his chin quivered but his body responded. You made love to him. It was a difficult love.

Now Alfie had stopped holding the cigarette in his right hand as he made reluctant love.

Alfie returned to his routine of not coming to the house at night.

You came to Sheila Aunty's garden again after a few days for the last time. You knew that I would be there. I spent every afternoon there despite you being absent. We did not speak much. We understood each other's difficulties. We knew that our tomorrows had become precarious and would fall off the edge. You said Alfie suspects and we cannot meet now. You extracted a promise from me that, we will revert to our respective roles of a wife and a friend to Alfie. I remember you said, 'I cannot do this to him.'

What was I to do? You fell in love with me after we became friends. We had conversations that you could never have with anyone else, not even Alfie. I found your conversations and thoughts attractive, and my feelings developed unconditionally, and you reciprocated. All this while as we were getting close, never once did I hear a complaint or a criticism of Alfie. You maintained his dignity and if anything, you spoke only good of him. I knew you had deep affection for your husband. And yet, you were attracted to me.

Your house had shadows creeping all over the corners. The order and structure seemed to be intact with the foundations lost in the quicksand. It was only a matter of time that everything collapsed.

Alfie had stopped coming home and stayed at the club. He had stopped going to work. Badi Bai would go to the club and implore Alfie to go to the office at least one day in a month and sign his attendance. That way he would be able to retain his job. He just looked at her blankly. Badi Bai called the peon from his office with the register, which was not supposed to be taken out of the office. He waited till 1 pm. Alfie was asleep. She asked him to bring it stealthily in the evening. When he came at 6 pm, Alfie was drunk and refused to sign. This happened a couple of times. When Badi Bai asked him after that, the peon implored that if he continues to steal the register, he would lose his job. He had seven mouths to feed. He stopped.

You waited for Alfie. You found care for him in your heart you had not felt so far. Your resentment at his coming forward to marry you and destroying your chances with DC and then his physical needs had clouded your relationship. Now his wallowing and vulnerability at your betrayal made you see him differently. Guilt stoked your tenderness towards him.

I had met Alfie a few times at the club and while my friendship had become uncertain, I wanted to know something about you from him. He did not say anything. He would be polite but quiet. He would be civil but not reveal anything.

It was about six months later; I was with Sheila Aunty when Badi Bai came. 'There is no money in the house,' she said. She gave her Rs 100. 'Come back when these finish.'

As she was leaving, I asked, 'How is Frieda?' Perhaps I had asked it too eagerly. She turned around and said crossly, 'You are Alfie's friend. You should ask after Alfie.' She was upset and had tears in her eyes. She knew. I was embarrassed and forlorn and in love. I felt the guilt that was contained between the two of us breaking free and becoming larger and larger.

'You must go and visit him at the club. He lives there now.' Little did she know that I had been seeing him, but we did not speak anymore!

He was terminated from his job shortly afterwards. The people from the club came and left him home one day. There were unpaid dues. Then the car was sold to pay those. He started taking the tonga to the club. When the tongawalla did not come, he would walk many miles to the club and not return till Badi Bai sent someone to fetch him. Debts kept mounting.

I had started sending the rations and fruits and vegetables again once a week through his office peon. You and Badi Bai knew where it came from. Alfie was oblivious.

Alfie moved around like an unanchored, rudderless boat sloshing in the winds at sea.

I did not have the courage to tell you that, oblivious to my affection for you, my family had accepted a proposal for me.

My mother was widowed when she was thirty. She had three sons and a daughter. I am the youngest born three months after my father had passed and therefore, she loved me more than the other three who were seven, ten and eleven years older than me.

The eldest is a lawyer and is married to a girl from Guntur. He has two daughters. The second one is a doctor and married to a doctor from Hyderabad. They have a daughter. My sister is married in Hyderabad. My youngest niece was one year old at the time.

'We have four daughters in our family and while I see all our goddesses in them—Lakshmi, Saraswati, Sita, and Durga; I want a son. I want a boy so that they also know what boys are like,' my mother would say.

'Vadina[1] is expecting. She will give you a grandson,' I said.

'I dreamed that you would have many sons,' she said.

'What if I do not marry?' I said thinking of you Frieda.

'But you must. Life has no meaning otherwise. You must love mentally and physically a person who will be your equal in every measure.' She said, then added, 'You are twenty-five now. This is the right age to marry.' I had stopped seeing you, Frieda, but thought of you constantly. I looked at the small puja mandir in my mother's room on the opposite wall as she spoke. We were sitting in her room, which was sparkling clean with white linen on her bed. She sat resting her back at the headboard with her legs crossed and I sat towards the other end facing her.

'Marriages are made in heaven,' she said. 'God has made someone for you also.' And your face flashed in my mind when she said that.

I looked at the affection on her face. I held her hand. She wore a thick gold bangle on her wrist. She wore no other jewellery. This was bought from my father's first earning, and he had extracted a promise from her that she would never remove it, even if he died and therefore, she never did. She wore white sarees.

---

[1] Elder sister-in-law.

'There is a girl from Vishakhapatnam who will be good for you.'

'Amma, I do not want to marry.'

She looked at my face searching. 'Do you like someone?'

'I don't know,' I said. I was willing to spend my life with you, Frieda, the way it was. Like a satellite around the sun. Moving around your life. Never getting absorbed in it. How else could it be?

'If you like someone, tell me. I will get your brothers to agree.'

'*Na* Amma, there is none,' I lied. I knew the impossibility of our situation.

'Then you should marry,' she said with an air of finality.

Alfie knew of your affair and had shared his doubt with me. I felt guilt but I felt love more. I had remained non-committal. Then you asked me not to meet. I was concerned about you and Alfie, but I did not think about the proposal. Four months had passed, and I had not met you, Frieda, after that silent afternoon at Sheila Aunty's place. My sister-in-law had a daughter, her second. While she was welcomed, my mother became insistent that I get married. She wanted a grandson.

'How can you know, Amma?'

'I dreamed that a girl emerged from the valley, she had curly black hair till her waist. I could not see her face as the sun was behind her. When she walked up, I noticed that she was carrying something. As she came closer, I looked into her eyes. They were rich brown and when I looked down, she was carrying a new-born son. That proves that you will have a son,' she told me animatedly.

'She could be anyone. That does not prove anything,' I said.

'But the child had the same face as you had when you were born!'

'Then you must have seen your younger self.' I made light of her dream.

'I have black eyes and my hair is straight. It cannot be me.' She spoke. I looked at her face. Thin skin. Lines growing in all directions. I felt affection for her.

'Give me time to think, Amma.' I stalled.

Badi Bai met me and asked me to meet Alfie at the club. 'Something is troubling Alfie, and he will not say anything. Can you please speak with him and find out?'

In the evening, I went to the club. I found him there and sat with him. 'I am sorry,' I said. 'But you should be at home with your wife.' He did not speak. He kept drinking at the bar. He just looked at the spot behind the counter, his eyes glazed and bloodshot. I asked him, 'Shall I take you home?' He remained silent. 'You have a young wife that YOU chose!' I spoke. He was silent. I recounted your wedding and told him how gallant he had been. He kept silent. I asked, 'Do you not love her?' I wanted to get a response. He echoed, 'Do you not love her?' After that it was my turn to be silent. Even though I loved you, Frieda, I did not want your marriage destroyed. The irony was, I did not want Alfie's marriage destroyed because of me. That would bring shame and dishonour to you. And I liked Alfie. I knew his past and how vulnerable he had been. If I could roll back time and retrieve all the mistakes. I was responsible for the situation Alfie and you were in. I wanted to help. That would be my redemption. You and I had not met for six months now. That was the best for everyone.

The suspicion of our affair left a throbbing loss in Alfie's heart. He experienced the cruelty of the situation not so much in the passage of time as he did in the imperceptible changes in your features. He observed you at the dining table in radiant splendour, smiling and exuding warmth in the words you spoke with him at the table. Your laughter exploded like a firework in thousand colours. He noticed the new earthy perfumes you had started wearing. His eyes laid a siege to your face. You still intermittently made love with him and it was more passionate than any other time. Yet, he suppressed his trembling at the thought of losing you to another man altogether.

At closing time, the bartender asked me to take him home. 'What do you do the other days?' I asked him.

'I ask around if someone wants to take him home and if no one does, then I leave him on the sofa in the corner. I have a quilt that I cover him with. He is safe here, otherwise he used to be found all over the town.'

'When did this start?'

'About six months ago... The club management is strict. I will lose my job if they find out.'

'Why do you do it then?'

'He got me this job. He has been good to me in the past. This is the least that I can do.'

'Are you not worried about your job?'

'No, not when it comes to him... You should have seen him in the days past when he was not drinking so much. He was a different person, full of charm and charisma. He used to be the life of parties.'

The bartender was tidying the place as we chatted with Alfie sitting beside me drunk.

'How did you meet him?' the bartender asked.

'I have known him for many years,' I said. 'We met when I took up the job as the Military Supply Contractor. I source dry and wet provisions for the Army. His job was to inspect my depot for cleanliness and hygiene. I liked him. He was objective and understanding. We would talk about how to keep the depot spic-and-span and he would advise gently. We would often have tea together at the Coffee House in Sadar after work. I learned to play snooker from him at the YMCA.'

'Then you must know that his wife is expecting.'

My face must have gone white. I did not know this. No one told me about it. Not Badi Bai, not Sheila Aunty! I took a few sips of water and composed myself.

'How do you know?' I asked, knowing that Alfie would never talk personal matters at the bar.

'Badi Bai came here a few times. She cares for him like a child. She wanted him to sign the office register, but he refused. She was berating him in frustration when she said that. I heard it then. From right here where I am standing.'

I sat there dumbfounded by the news of your pregnancy. I had no idea.

Then I stood up and put my arm around Alfie's waist to give him support and get him to walk beside me, he looked at me in the eyes and said, 'Why don't you get married, Mahesh Babu?' I knew the intensity of his wish. The pain and sadness were apparent. That was the solution.

He refused to come with me. When I deposited him to the sofa, his pants were wet with piss, and he had no idea where he was. The bartender closed the bar. I sat outside. The moon was bright and the night dark under the trees.

In the morning, I went to touch my mother's feet, like I did every morning. I consented to marry the girl from Vishakhapatnam.

The date was set for a month later.

The preparation was in full swing. I was the youngest. I was to be the bearer of sons. Everyone was excited.

However much I got excited, the name that escaped with my every breath was yours, Frieda. I could not tell you about the marriage. You were a wife. Then you were to be a mother. With my affection for you, I was destroying it all for you, for Alfie, and your unborn child.

I decided to plunge myself in the happiness of a married life that my mother wanted me to have. Yet, however much

I tried, I could not shake off the vacuum I carried. I kept a false façade. I felt like an imposter in my own marriage planning. I was lying to everyone, but the truth lay buried inside me, gnawing at me. And the truth was that I loved you.

I wanted to come and meet you. Just once. And tell you that while it was not fair, maybe my marriage was the only solution. My heart wanted to see you. My mind said that you are carrying a child and I have no right to destroy everything for you. And in that struggle, my wedding day arrived.

Our marriage was solemnised at around 5:30 am on 24 March 1940. I sat by the fire with Girija's hands in mine. I looked at them and noticed the henna and gold. I saw it as if I were outside the whole experience, as a spectator. One hand holding the other. We walked around the crackling fire. Shlokas were being chanted; the smiling faces of the family were engrossed. There was laughter and joy all around. I was empty inside. I saw affection in Girija's eyes and a softness that an imagination of sharing a life with someone brings. Girija was young at eighteen and beautiful with large eyes full of kajal. She had an endearing, innocent face that seemed to see no fault with the world. She smiled easily and had a sort of kindness in her.

After the ceremony, the shehnai-wala was playing raag Bageshri. We were seeking blessings from all. I saw the Gypsy. Half-naked and with ektara in his hand standing by the gate. He strummed the single wire in consonance with the shehnai. I looked at him and he beckoned me. I had not seen the Gypsy in a while. The way he waved his hands urgently, I knew you had sent him.

He closed his eyes as he strained to play synchronously with shehnai.

'She asked me to tell you, that your son is born,' he said.

I looked at his face. There was delight struggling to burst in my chest as I comprehended the message. I looked at his face to know more.

'Does Frieda know that I got married today?'

'No.' He was stoic. He squeezed my arm and left.

I was in a daze and elsewhere in my thoughts, thinking about you through the day. Everyone thought that my happiness was due to the marriage. When it grew dark, I walked around to your bungalow to catch a glimpse. I only heard the baby cry.

Girija was watching the fireworks when I went into the room. I closed my eyes and feigned sleep. I was uncertain about this marriage and could not touch her now after the Gypsy had told me about our son. She stood there. After a while, I could sense her gaze traversing my body. I lay still. I feigned sleep. I was awake the whole night. She had stood at the foot of the bed the whole night. Many times, I wanted to bring her to bed. She must have been tired, and I ached for her. But this marriage had been a huge mistake and nothing I could do now would reverse the fact. In the morning when my mother knocked at the door, I saw her turning at the foot of the bed to open the door.

The second night, I went to my room quite late. I saw her asleep. She was sitting near the head post on my side with her head rested on the post. She looked tired and beautiful. I did not disturb her.

The third night, my friends had decided to celebrate. Of all my friends, only Alfie was not there. I stayed out with them the whole night. I kept the celebration going as I was avoiding going to the bedroom. They took me over when the morning broke. That day Girija stopped putting kohl in her eyes.

The fourth night, I spent outside your window, watching the baby and you and Badi Bai. The next morning Girija gave up her beautiful Kanjivaram sarees. She adorned plain silks from that day. I felt guilty and frustrated but I could not do anything to change the situation.

The fifth night, I spent at the bar with Alfie. I told him that I had got married. He was so inebriated that he did not seem to have absorbed the information. When the sky broke into the deep blue, I went home. I did not have the courage to knock on the door. I just sat down at the door. I must have fallen asleep. I woke with the soft touch of her lips and saw her eyes aflame with gold and desire. The sun was just coming up and she was bent with her breath on my chin. She wore no jewellery except her mangalsutra. Shyly she sat beside me, her head on my shoulder. I could sense the weight of questions in her eyes.

On the sixth night, we sat beside each other. We did not speak. She kept her hand on mine. Then I told her about you. Only about you and nothing more. She did not ask me any questions. She just listened.

On the seventh night, I was alone. That morning, she had emerged radiant from the room in a simple cotton saree. After touching my mother's feet, she left with the few family members who had stayed behind. It was the custom for some families to stay back and help the bride adjust to the new home. I did not stop her. There was nothing I could do. All I knew was that she had become the debris of our storms.

That was my marriage that destroyed Girija.

I Will Not Leave Him

I had been disowned by my family for abandoning Girija, with strict instruction not to come back home. I took up a room at the YMCA. My business had suffered significantly in the last six months due to the turmoil I was in. I continued to meet Alfie at the club. His frequency of visits to the club had reduced and he seemed extremely happy with the new son in his life. He also reduced his drinking and was back to work.

Three months after the First Son was born, Alfie asked you if I may stay in the spare room in the annexe as I had been disowned by my family. 'It has a separate entrance, and he will not trespass our privacy.' Alfie was helping a friend in distress, tide over a crisis. You found it strange but was only too happy to oblige. This benevolence on Alfie's part changed his life forever. Now, I became a regular visitor. I would come and play with the First Born and run errands for the family when needed.

Alfie seemed to have forgotten about your affair.

One heart-breaking September twilight, he interrupted you amid cooking. That day Sheila Aunty had come for lunch, and she talked about the masks and said, 'Alfie, you poor man, you cannot look beyond masks.' And she had looked at you as you served food while the First Born slept in his crib near the dining table. Then she looked at the baby and smiled, 'This one does not look like you but he is so beautiful.' It may have been a passing remark but his feeling of suspicion surfaced with a vengeance.

Without any trace of harshness, he said, 'Frieda!' His voice did not betray that his heart wept. But he was not one to create a commotion. You were busy stirring the mutton in the pot and you said, 'Hmm'. In the heat of the kitchen, you had a shine of sweat. Badi Bai had gone to get roomali rotis from Bade Miyas.

'Look at me.'

You turned and looked at him through the fog of rising steam from the pot. He had a raging fire in his chest, but he kept calm.

'Is anything going on that you want to tell me about?' he asked.

'How would I know?' you said, feigning incomprehension, cognizant of what he wanted to know. 'Should I know something?' you asked and looked into Alfie's eyes with an impertinence, without blinking, chewing the silence in between. Alfie knew the fatality of love and its storminess. He realised that it will only worsen the situation if he persisted with you. He did not want you to leave him. He feared a finality of that sort. You saw his blue eyes getting wet, brimming. You changed your mind.

'I will tell you only because you are insisting. I wanted to wait for some more time,' you said smiling. Alfie went white. He stood tongue tied.

'I may be expecting again. But it's very early.' You said and hugged him. You could hear his heart hammering in his chest.

The imminent confrontation passed. Bliss returned.

Alfie met the French photographer at the club one day when you were seven months pregnant with the Second Son.

The French photographer was back in town. He came for two months each year and whoever wanted to get their photograph taken would queue up out his studio at the Russell Square.

A few days later, as the Frenchman sat at the bar at Narmada Club, Alfie joined him. They were acquainted ever since the Frenchman had started coming to town in the late 1920s. They started chatting and Alfie noticed a brown packet lying beside him.

'Those must be the pictures of the townsfolk,' Alfie said.

'Yes. I am taking these with me back to France. I am leaving tomorrow. But I will be back next year,' the photographer was garrulous.

'May I see them? I am fascinated how technology can capture the souls of people,' he said, light-heartedly. The Frenchman pushed the envelope in Alfie's direction with his left hand as he took the glass of brandy to his mouth with his right. Alfie moved his glass of gin and tonic and opened the envelope. He smiled as he browsed, and then blood drained from his face after flipping some.

'When did you take this one?' Alfie asked showing a photograph. It was a photograph of you and me.

'Maybe two or three years ago. They were a nice couple, very much in love!'

'How can you say that?'

'A Frenchman is a connoisseur of love. I knew it the moment they walked in. She was telling him about visiting my studio about 7–8 years back and the commotion it had created afterwards. They chatted and smiled and seemed very much in love.' He did not tell Alfie of the discretion he was asked to exercise.

He gossiped mischievously that we had come to his studio in the afternoon when the Frenchman usually shut it for his siesta. That I had met him earlier in the day and planned for the photographs to be taken in privacy and had agreed to pay him double his rates for the photographs.

Alfie was devastated. Now all his suspicions were confirmed. He suppressed his humiliation and continued drinking. That night he was smashed when he reached home.

The next morning, he came looking for me in the cantonment. He wanted to speak to me away from home. I was at the depot supervising the loading of provisions for the Army Canteen. I beamed a surprised smile at Alfie when I saw him. I noticed the confident gait with which Alfie walked towards me.

'Mahesh Babu, we need to talk,' Alfie said and while I extended my hand smiling. 'Man to man,' he added. That is when I realised the seriousness of his visit and turned green as a corpse and when we shook hands, I noticed how cold Alfie's hands were. I let myself be led by him.

Alfie led me to the car. He opened the passenger side door and I got in. Alfie sat in the driver's seat. He opened the glove compartment and extracted a hipflask. This is unusual, I thought. Alfie never drank in the morning. It was only 8 am. Alfie took a swig from the flask and offered it to me in curtsey knowing well that I was a teetotaller. 'You will need this,' Alfie insisted. I declined.

With a disarming sincerity, he said, 'Don't tarnish her reputation. I have come to request you to leave her.'

I was not expecting this. 'There is nothing. You are mistaken,' I lied.

'I saw your photographs from a few years back.' His lips quivered.

I did not know what I was going to say till the words spilled out, 'Have you spoken with her?' This was admission from me and now there was no turning back. Destiny was playing its game, and I did not want to compromise you in this game.

'That is between a man and his wife. It does not concern you,' Alfie said with a calm dignity.

'It's not dependent on me. She is the one who must decide.'

'How can that be? This is the matter between men to decide,' Alfie said.

'Like you decided on the day of your marriage,' I challenged.

'This is different,' Alfie countered with a strain in his voice.

'I want to know what her decision is. I cannot betray her,' I said with a calm resolution.

Alfie leaned his head back on the car seat and closed his eyes. His face reddened and flushed with repressed fury. His face dampened in a sheen of sweat, and his closed eyes moved in its orbits. The vein on the side of his head pulsed with a fervour.

'Then I will have to kill you, my friend,' Alfie said with a brittle coldness.

I trembled at his chilling declaration. I thought, 'What is written in our destinies will come to pass and no amount of human power could forestall that.'

'We will all lose something in this situation we are in. Kill me if you must but that will be no victory,' I said, defiantly.

Alfie knew the significance of my words very well. When he fell in love with you when he had seen you and your sisters leave the studio, it was not a victory. When he married you when DC had left you at the altar, it was not a victory. And now if he killed for your affection, it would still not be a victory.

'Son of a bitch!' Alfie said with a loathing rooted in desperation. 'Please leave my house immediately.'

Alfie had the knowledge of truth for some time, but he was afraid to confront it. He had expected a seismic tremor to pass through him and split his heart into two if confronted, but it was a calm firm blow that just crushed his soul. He knew it was unfair, but he did not have the strength to give it a label. An accusation would lead to suffering for you and for him and now there were children to think about.

After the euphoria of the wedding had passed, Alfie was not sure if it was love that he felt for you, Frieda. He had only thought of you often since he had seen you at Russel Square and then at the church when he accompanied DC. He had liked the determination on your face, the vanity in your features and importantly, he felt a flood of protectiveness when he saw you. He was smitten by your beauty. If he could, he would spend his entire day looking at the soft curve of your neck that started behind the ear and dissolved in your shoulder. He liked it exposed when you tied your hair in a bun. He knew he loved you. But love was something you both never spoke about. Many times, in his married life he had asked himself, 'Would I do this for love?' And it was the answer that guided him every time. Till the end, he was not sure if he could define the feeling as love but that feeling shaped his actions and he stayed with you, irrespective of your infidelity. He knew that he always had your loyalty. And in the context of his family, your pregnancy, the honour, that loyalty was more important than your fidelity.

Alfie had confined himself to his room after that. He seldom came out. One night when you heard him sob in his room as you passed by it, you decided to speak with me. You knew that Alfie had been drinking in his room and that he was not sleeping. He had started missing work and had acquired a haggard look. He was not eating properly. Even Badi Bai was concerned. You and I had discussed the possibility that sooner or later we would have to confront the aftermath of our passion which would break the delicate equilibrium of our relationships. It could endanger your marriage, it would have repercussions in your family and then there were the children, one born and the second on the way. We, who knew the strength of our passion, agreed that the time to take a decision had come. I agreed to leave.

'You cannot leave,' you said. 'We can be together if we continue to give the children Alfie's name. I want children and I know Alfie cannot have children. We did not have for the first five years when it was only Alfie and I.'

'It's an incredibly significant thing you are asking!' I was thunderstruck.

'They will carry your blood. They will carry his name and I will carry them in my womb. We will share!'

I was drenched in perspiration as if I had stepped out of a shower.

'I will offer you what is beyond infidelity for I deserve honour and security and love. In that order. It is the only way. I am willing to go to the ends of the world with you but not without these.'

In a small town such as ours, it was impossible to hide an affair like this. The solution that you had put forth became a matter of hell for me. I knew the risks of a scandal, and the impact it would have on all our lives. Yet, I was not ready to lose you, Frieda.

My days were filled with unbearable uncertainty and longing. I had the fear of losing you. I was so anguished with the impossibility of this promise, that I could not swallow a morsel and I started losing weight. I pretended to sleep but could not. I was losing focus at work and the business was going downhill. It would be a cost of betraying Alfie's confidence. I was feverish with anxiety and when I went to the doctor, he told me that there was nothing wrong physically. I was strong as a mule. At night I woke up breaking into sweat and gasping for breath. I felt my heart miss a beat or two at times. I was going insane with the terror of abdicating my sons, at the terror of forsaking you, at the terror of continuing to humiliate Alfie if I stayed.

In the delirium of passion, I eventually accepted it. It may have broken my heart, but my soul was at peace. I knew that from now on, I would have to accept shame, anger, injustice, and humiliation for the sake of what was important in our tiny universe of a handful of people.

Alfie took to alcohol like fish to water; water that was an ocean in colossal emotional tempest.

Alfie Loved You. So, Did I

Alfie loved you, he who had no family and no responsibility till he got married. He was fun-loving and good-natured, and always there for his friends. He was the life of the parties. Never judged anyone. Always appreciated by people. With his friends, he was always willing to share a drink, a game of pool, or a game of bridge. If his heart so desired, he would go hunting or trekking. Snooker was his favourite sport, and he would play at the YMCA often.

Affairs were a different matter. With women, his interactions were innocuous flirting and infatuations. The women soon realised that his relationships and networks are wide, not deep. He was in love with everyone and therefore no one. He was committed to many and therefore couldn't commit to one.

My friendship with Alfie started at our work and then moved to personal time. One evening, he offered to teach me snooker. I was terrible at snooker with the balls flying all over and the cue stick digging in the green felt. He was initially amused and then was in splits at my gaucheness. My lack of control of the strikes was amusing to both of us and he resolved to make me an expert. We met every day in the evening for an hour after work to play and my game improved. Sometimes DC would also join us. He would often go to the club after our games for a few drinks. I am not given to drinking or smoking as you know, but I would give him company. In my family, it was considered unacceptable to indulge in drinking and smoking. Those are the sanskars[1] we have bequeathed our sons too. I often rescued Alfie from drunken soirees to bring him home. Badi Bai knew I was dependable, and she and I had a pact that I would ensure that he does not drink too much and

[1] Culture or manners.

reach him home safely and that she would treat me to gulab jamuns every weekend.

Alfie loved you. We had heard much about you from DC because of his friendship with us. Alfie one day told me about the ride you and your sisters had on Russell Square when your dupatta flew away and that he heard you say, 'How can I marry one of these men? They can't even save my dupatta!' The spirited way he spoke about it. I realised he was in love with you even before he had been introduced to you. I realised that he went to church only to see you there. It was an impetuous act when he agreed to marry you. Everyone was surprised by his action. I think in his heart he was just doing the right thing by marrying the one he loved. You were oblivious of his existence, and mine for that matter. And then his distraught girlfriend came to your wedding and hysterically began kissing him. You saw me take her away. That incident sent ripples in the society and yet, he stood by your side. It was a guilty evening for him for more reasons than one; usurping a friend's fiancée, the presence of a girlfriend, and then later getting smashed on alcohol.

Alfie loved you. He grew distant from his friends and pensive after his marriage. We always asked him how his new bride was, and he would always light up and hide the shadows lurking in his heart. He would talk about you affectionately. We noticed that now he was cordial with his women friends, and never crossed a line of propriety given that he was a married man. He would not flirt anymore. If at all, he got more engrossed with hunting and his outdoor pursuits. He was running away from something.

Alfie loved you. He forged a great relationship with your family despite your mother. Your mother never spoke to him. After he had stopped her from slapping you, she had taken that as a challenge to her authority. She despised him as much as she disliked you. Hannah and your father came to your house regularly. Your sisters had started getting married. It had been three years of your marriage. When Sarah got married, he organised everything. I organised the catering for her wedding dinner like I had done for yours at his request. As an Army Supply Contractor, I had the network to organise these events. Do you know DC had asked me to organise the catering for his wedding? That's why I was there supervising the preparations for the dinner service at your wedding.

We had started meeting in Sheila Aunty's garden. When I saw him look at you when you were dancing in a yellow saree at Sarah's Haldi ceremony[2], I could not but admire his love for you. Such affection. Such joy in his eyes. I was happy for you both. But the question that I suppressed was, so where do I stand with you? You lived with Alfie, but you loved me. Or did you? Or was I just a distraction to fade away with time? You had never once said anything about the state of your marriage or against Alfie. Therefore, was I just for conversations and companionship?

Alfie loved you. But that was not enough for you. You both had civility and a distance. He would affectionately buy a gajra[3] of jasmines for you each evening and you would put it in your hair. He would put Manna Dey or Geeta Dutt's songs on the gramophone for you. You served him dinner. You would both eat in silence. You were welcoming to his friends, and they all admired you. It had been a few years with no children to bind you, no common interests and a sense of betrayal persisted in your heart despite the civility and co-habitation.

Alfie loved you. So, did I. Therefore, when the Gypsy told me that our son was born, I left home. It took me seven days to do that and only after Girija left. All she told my family was that there is someone else in his life. My brothers were

---

[2] A pre-wedding ritual where the bride and groom are smeared with turmeric paste, both for good luck and to even out the skin tone.

[3] A flower hair garland traditionally worn by South Asian women.

upset for bringing shame and disrespect to the family, and they asked me not to return. I took a room at Jackson Hotel and lived there. I continued to meet Alfie and keep my pact with Badi Bai. When I told Alfie one evening that I had been disowned by my family and that very soon I would need a place to stay as Jackson Hotel was expensive, he asked Badi Bai to clean the spare room in the annexe for me. I could not resist the offer to be close to you. Alfie was generous. I was his friend. I was your lover.

HOW FAR WILL HE GO

And then he walked…

After our third son was born, the mid-wife came in the night bearing the news that the child was born with a birthmark that covers his entire body like a sheet except for his face. I remember the house had smelled of iron for the nine months that he was inside you. When I held the baby, the mid-wife said this is what happens when the child is conceived when the woman is on her period.

Just after that Alfie started walking around his room incessantly. Inebriated.

Initially, he walked with a pattern, five steps forward, three steps right, five steps again, three steps left, five steps forward, three steps right, five steps again, three steps left, repeat, repeat, repeat, repeat…and when the room seemed to be crowding in and folding in on him, he started walking in the courtyard in circles, head bent down looking at his feet as if wondering why they don't stop.

You would come and put your arms around his shoulder and walk with him speaking softly. I saw affection in your cajoling. I watched you from the terrace. I don't think he heard it too because his feet had taken his ears. After some time, you would stand in the middle of the circle, and he would spin like a spindle with his face towards you as he circled the courtyard. Sometimes the end of your saree would ruffle, and it would try and catch him or flap against him, but he was oblivious. Sometimes you would put the hand of the First Born, now nearly five, in his and he would walk with him. Sometimes you would put the new-born in the centre of the courtyard, and he would walk around the baby, ignoring his red skin completely.

I lived in the room in the annexe. Badi Bai gave me food. Alfie was my friend. I loved his wife. I looked at the faces of the children and lived. They were the fruits of my guilt, but they carried Alfie's name. Alfie knew. You knew. Badi Bai knew. And I lived a culpable life of delinquent love with no status except a tenant in a room in your home.

Then one day I came in and stood at the centre of the courtyard. I wanted to apologise. That day he walked out of the courtyard and started circling the cluster of houses that formed our neighbourhood. He walked past the houses, the courtyards, the front gardens, the wells, the front gates. He would not look in the eyes of the people but would walk in circles. People started noticing. What was inside the four walls of your home had now started walking in the neighbourhood. People thought that he had gone out of his mind. He did not speak but just looked at his feet and walked. They would offer him water and food and he would accept the water but not food. All this while, rumours flew past him like little birds, as he walked.

For his meals every morning and evening, he would sit on the chair with a small table under the guava tree in the courtyard. That was his usual place. You would serve him the first serving from the kitchen. He had stopped sitting at the dining table. You gave him the respect of being the head of the family. Never once did the family eat before him. I do not remember when or how it started but after he had eaten, I would remove his plate and rinse it and eat from it. He noticed that with his blue eyes but never said anything.

Then one day, the children of the neighbourhood tied a cord to his trousers and put a string of crackers at the end of it. They lighted it and it burst but he kept walking looking at his feet. Left. Right. Left. Right. He was shaking but he kept walking. When they told you, you felt humiliated. You came running out, shouted at them and wiped your tears. You put your arms around his waist and took him out of the neighbourhood and that day you two walked the streets and the roads of the town and the city in those moments of shared embarrassment. From then on, the city roads became his companion and the roads moved beneath his feet while he stood looking at his feet. Left. Right. Left. Right. Left. Right. Left. Right.

While you two walked, a darkness hammered in my chest. If only I could set it right.

Badi Bai and I would be home, waiting and looking after the children. Badi Bai never accused me of anything, and her dignity gnawed at me. If only she had given me a good shouting or berated me, but she was cold and not unkind. She was distressed with Alfie's condition, but she distracted herself with the children, the kitchen, and the chores of the house.

You had always found it difficult to converse with Alfie, given the difference of age, perspectives, upbringing. Your relationship had become like a courtyard robbed of its sunlight, where only sombre silence and echoes of an unhappy past existed. With each adult grappling with their own gale of emotions, none in the household spoke those days. We lived without words, without colours, and without sounds...just the motion of the feet and a bewildered mind that held the secret in the quietude. The silence and motion seemed to be swallowing up our lives.

Alfie now thought that he had lost you irretrievably. His world had shrivelled into that single thought; restless, black, and malignant. Every look and every touch pierced his soul. Every word drilled a hole in his soul. Love had turned bad and curdled.

As he walked each day I wondered, how far will he go and how will he know his way back home. His pain bled. It bled into the streets and into the paths he took. It left a solitary trail of sadness behind. He walked like an unleashed open question.

He walked on dry leaves in autumn, on cold earth and frost in winter, on fallen flowers in springs, on dry dusty roads in summer, and in puddles in the monsoon. But inside his mind there was only a dry rustle, and his breath a dry wheeze devoid of moisture of affection. In burning sunshine. In calm moonlight. In rain. In hot Loo winds. He walked till his body elongated but the shadow remained the same. His feet hit and struck the earth raising a small cloud of dust. Or is it the earth that arches and curves to fill his soles, as if having waited from the time man was born.

You stopped going after him after some time. You had conceived the fourth son. Your heart drummed with anxiety as he walked. Your blood pounded with worry, but he walked. Spoons, clocks, mirrors, chairs in your home all foretold... you had promised, you had taken a vow to go to the end of the world with him but not this when millimetres were insurmountable.

Sometimes when the burden of loss was unbearable, he walked with hummm, hummm that came from the pit of his diaphragm...and sometimes there was a swarm of wasps' buzz that drilled holes in his brain. He would strike his head with his palm as if dislodging memories stuck to the side of his skull, but he walked. The chilling cold of your absence came to singe his limbs. He walked. Now seeing, now remembering, now crossing through the hell. Dark silence. Dark silence.

Like the cycle of life, things are born, they live, and they die. But his grief born of the loss of love was stuck in time. It neither grew old nor got erased with time. It renewed afresh every morning and it squatted there in his head. There was an incomprehensible fury of all that was robbed from him.

He walked long distances and went far. Now he was walking along the Narmada. You sent the Gypsy to follow him from a distance. Later when the fourth son as a young man, would leave home to circumnavigate the Narmada, you said that while he was in the womb, Alfie walked the Narmada and you continuously thought about it. That's why he got it in him to do that from the time he was in the womb. Then again the Gypsy would follow the fourth son.

The dust of memory rose from the earth sometimes as he walked looking at his feet. You kneading the flour, you smiling by the Narmada, you looking at old photographs and wondering and then glowing up with something that you noticed therein, you looking at our sons as they played with a sense of pride and remorse, you asleep with the upturned book rising and falling on your stomach with your breathing, you sitting at the dining table engrossed in cutting and decorating the salad, the way you walked into a room like small waves of grace and freshness. The way your long wavy hair sometimes caught the collar button of his shirt as you dressed him each morning; yes, you had started doing that! And then you would be trapped. You were trapped as the voice that echoed in his ears and mind, long after you were silent. He remembered how sometimes you paused in the middle of the sentence like the words had evaporated and that there was nothing more to it there. He would just nod at those sentences hanging loose on the strings of air. Sometimes he remembered how he had watched the embers that burnt in your eyes in the moonlight and when you looked so beautiful...since then he learned to look at all things of beauty twice, once to remember and once to forget.

Sometimes he felt as if his heart would stop...there were just shadows and mist walking with those two feet. Left. Right. Left. Right. Sometimes as he walked, the town would be gradually emptied of all sounds, colours, sights and the roads would be white with two feet traversing the infinity of a mind. Left. Right. Left. Right. His walk was full of desolation, deaf, mute, flat, with no wails, no answers, and no love. Just Left. Right. Left. Right. He walked neither awake nor asleep, just walking and attempting to lose his sadness, his fervour, his secrets, his volition, his burning, his lust. Left. Right. Left. Right. As he paused sometimes to inhale, to breathe, the air would burn his lungs and licking the lips would leave the taste of your name, a tingle of life, a shard of memory and it cut and chafed his lips. Every so often a tremor would pass through the rhythm of left right left right! His body would just not stand still, it pushed him, forward, onward, on and on like he was going on the journey to netherworld. Left. Right. Left. Right.

His spirit lingered in the white spaces between the words till he burnt the words one by one in the cigarettes he smoked. All he wanted was to convey the reason of his loss. None came.

Silence was his new language of grief.

We All Keep Secrets

We all keep secrets.

Things had started arriving when we had had five sons. One day at a time. It started in the season when the winds turn the sheet music of rain, and the breeze gets trapped in the branches of the trees.

It soon seemed clear to everyone that this arrival of things will take time to culminate.

The first thing came in a parcel tightly wrapped in white cotton and tied across with twine thread. The address was smudged in blue ink that had become black on the edges with a red lacquer seal. It was a damaru[1]. You said, this is a deranged fragment of someone's imagination that has escaped logical thought. And you consigned it to the storeroom after throwing away the packaging. Later the Gypsy sold it for two rupees.

Then came a silver birdcage, which had no birds in it. Then came a bolt of cloth made of fine cotton. It must have been expensive. Then came a sitting stool made of sandalwood. As you opened the package, the fragrance—soft and unsettling like a buried struggling memory, wafted in the house. You kept this one in the parlour. That was the only thing there. We had lost a lot to the pawnbrokers given the condition of our household. It was either the Gypsy or Badi Bai who mediated the selling.

Initially we suspected it was from Sheila Aunty, who had left India after the Fourth Son was born, to marry the American she had met at one of her art retreats in Shimla. She never wrote

[1] An hourglass-shaped pellet drum.

us a letter but she knew our financial situation and maybe this was her way to help.

Badi Bai was more than seventy years old now. She had developed a tick and was sleeping a lot. When you asked her if she was well, she said, I want to collect as many dreams as possible. The waking world is worthless. She made mistakes like sleeping in your bed or putting her head in Alfie's lap and snoring. Suddenly she started dressing in a red saree, applying lipstick, and taking her umbrella to go for a walk in the night. To protect myself from the moonlight, she would say when the children inquired. One day she mentioned how she was not fond of red colour. And you had asked, so why do you wear the red saree then. She said that the day she picked up Alfie as a three-month-old baby, her cream-coloured saree had turned red with the osmosis. There was his parents' blood on the floor. 'It was like an ocean of blood that I had waded through,' she said. 'The red colour became my covenant with Alfie.' She may not have liked the red colour, but it kept her connected with Alfie and by extension to all of us.

Soon after Badi Bai had developed these behaviours, came the book. A bound version of *Amar Chitra Katha*. You gave it to the eldest, who gave it to the second son, who gave it to the third son who refused to part with it. Then came a marble statue of a cow and a calf. You looked at it for some time and then Badi Bai gave it to the Gypsy with a syllogism, I have loved calves but never enjoyed walking. Then came five balls of wool each in an assortment of colours and sizes.

One day, you put together the packs and observed the handwriting and said, this is not Sheila Aunty's writing. I thought whoever sends these must know that there are five sons in the house. And I checked the postal stamps' seal imprinted on these parcels. These things were coming from all over India. It was not one place. But the hand that wrote the address was the same.

Then came a triptych in kantha work. It was a forest scene with all kinds of animals and birds in colourful stitches pinned to the coarse cotton fabric. You folded it and kept it away. This too would be sold off by the Gypsy for three rupees. Then came three wooden wheels, all same size about six inches in diameter. The Gypsy and I made a wooden scooter with a T-bar and a board for the younger boys. Then came a railway map of India and as we turned the pages, an old used ticket fell out so smudged that its letters were consigned to oblivion.

Then it all stopped. For a while.

And you said ruminating, 'The person who sent all this must be a woman.' I had the same feeling.

'Why do you say that?' I asked.

'Look at the care with which everything is packed,' you said. 'And the handwriting is delicate.'

My suspicion arose from the fact that whoever was sending these seemed to know us well. How appropriate each item was.

And now when the nights turn moonlight into pearls on grass, the postman started coming again. We were expecting our sixth son.

A dictionary of Hindi idioms, two LPs of Suraiya and Amir Khan, a volume of Jane Austen containing *Pride and Prejudice, Emma* and *Sense and Sensibility*, six bushes of roses with a note—one for each of the boys, a bottle of honey—it mentioned home-made, a string of 54 beads of rudraksha, a four-metre square silk durrie in white and blue with Himalayan prints, set of ten clay mynas, which you promptly gave to Alfie and who put it on a thin long shelf in his room and where sometimes it was difficult to distinguish a real myna from the clay myna, now that Alfie had become some sort of a myna whisperer, the house was full of those birds.

Then the postman stopped coming for some time. All had become so used to the postman knocking at the door and delivering a mystery each time, that when the entire day passed without his knocking, there was a perceptible disorientation as if the day had been denied its due. Badi Bai announced daily the item that was delivered and when she did not, an inordinate slowness descended in the courtyard. She played the radio incessantly those days and when anyone shut the radio, she would say it gets cold when you turn off the radio. And she would switch it back on. She liked to hear the static more than the news or music or plays that were broadcast. She said it was the voice of God.

In summer, when you were ostracised by the church, the postman came again with a letter for Alfie. This was in a different handwriting. Badi Bai gave it to him discretely. Following Saturday Alfie was sober and was home. We were surprised. He sat and observed the sons playing in the evening and then he had dinner with us all after many years. On Sunday, Alfie came to the church to fetch you. Later that year, the sixth was born.

The things continued to come. After the seventh was born, then came the letter. It caused a happy bewilderment in the family.

Mahesh Babu,

I will not use any endearments or politeness. We did not have time enough to develop those adjectives between us.

I come to you with an offer from my heart. Would you consider coming and staying with me. We cannot live as man and wife. Bring your children and their mother. Bring Alfred.

I am not afraid to admit that I am lonely. I have tried to search for love in God and have reached a stage where nomenclature of relationships is meaningless. I have become accustomed to the gap that was created by our marriage or the lack of it. No man, who is cherished, is enough by himself to obliterate the ruinous power of his absence. It will be enough to have you near me without any claims on you. I also understand that what I am asking may not be possible. With all the goodness of my soul, give me the opportunity to take care of your sons. They deserve a good life. I can give you that. It is not my duty, but I will feel privileged to take care of you all. At least, it will give me some atonement for what life has presented me.

I admire Frieda. Tell her that. What she has, I don't. She will get all my respect, should you decide to take up my offer. I can understand what she must be going through. We, women are all one and the same except that we come with different faces.

Girija

I was surprised. I had not thought about her in the last fifteen years. 'It's from a creditor,' I lied and a collective sigh escaped from those gathered around.

Later you were in the kitchen chopping onions. Badi Bai was dozing off on a chair near the door. 'How bad is it?' you asked. I looked at Badi Bai and then at you. 'She won't hear a thing,' you said, 'she is asleep.'

I sat on the chair, shifting my weight from side to side. This is a letter from Girija.

'Who?' you asked. You had not yet dismantled the peace from your face. You did not know Girija. I had never told you neither had the Gypsy. You continued chopping the onions.

'I have not been totally honest with you,' I said. I saw the calm dissolving slowly from your face. 'The items that we have been receiving are from Girija.'

'Who is she and why is she sending those to us from all over the country?' You could portend the seriousness of the subject. With these words your lips quivered just slightly.

Then I told you about my marriage, about Gypsy conveying me the news of the birth of our first son on the night of my wedding and about my resolve of coming back to you.

You remained silent. You had tears in your eyes. You had continued chopping the onions.

'If I had known that you were getting married, I would never have sent Gypsy to tell you the truth about the First Born.'

'Does it matter? That was a long time ago,' I had said.

'It does. I am guilty of destroying a woman's life. And can't you see, she is still tied to you!'

'And I am tied to you. It does not matter that my position is undefined.' I had said with a heavy heart.

Then you said crying, 'Men are all the same except that they come with different faces. Men create us women, and then they destroy us.' I felt something crack open somewhere inside you. It was your delicate heart breaking. Again. This time for Girija.

You did not allow yourself to indulge in the culpability. You had taken the decision. When you looked up, I could see the determination on your face refining your splendour.

Then as a matter of elegance, you slowly and carefully woke up Badi Bai. She said, is it tomorrow yet because I have a suspicion it is yesterday still chasing us.

I was afraid for you and as I put my fears in chronological order, starting from the beginning. You said, 'Badi Bai, we must do much today. Come.' You both left. I sat rooted. The kitchen was empty. The chopped onions lay glistening and pink on the countertop burning the eyes with their aroma. The emptiness did not seem pitiful. Only irreparable.

In the afternoon, when the heat vaporised dreams and liquified horizons, there lay bric-a-brac of items in the courtyard, like precocious fragments of some disaster. You had a steely expression, and your ferocity and innocence were indistinguishable.

'What are you doing?' I took your hands in mine and asked nervously.

You took the hand away and sat on the sandalwood stool extricated from the foyer. With your gaze fixed on the pile of items delivered by post, you said, 'I am trying to put the world in order. A small portion of it, which is assigned to me.' You spoke with crisp tranquillity.

When everything was collected, you said, 'Send this back.' Your composure and humiliation were palpable. I did not know where to return those items. There never was any return address on any package. When you saw my confusion, you understood and said, 'Burn them then!'

With the lucidity of a dream, I put a light to the pile, and it all went up in flames.

With your skin shining with sweat and reflecting the golden light of the fire, you said, 'This is your home. You are the father of my sons, and you will not go anywhere. We will not go anywhere.' The smell of burning sandalwood rose and inhabited the courtyard, the rooms, the kitchen and rose high up towards the yellow sun. You had finally claimed me.

YOU HAVE MEN LIVING IN YOUR HOUSE

It started as a susurration and then it gathered amplitude as time passed and became a loud reprimand from society. People said you are a prostitute. You have men living in your house.

You had abandoned your faith after your marriage with Alfie. But after the First Son was born, your faith returned, and you started going to the church every Sunday. You believed in the communion but not in the congregation. And you avoided your mother whenever she seemed to be there. Initially Alfie came with you but when his troubles started, he stopped. You may have been poor, but you dressed immaculately in the few good sarees you had, to attend the church. You were courteous with people but not effervescent. You kept your distance and dignity.

That day you stood outside the church with your five sons. Eldest was ten and youngest in your lap. You were pregnant with the sixth son. You were not allowed to enter the church. You had ignored the hurricane you had felt gathering. While people knew that you were married to Alfie and that I lived in your home, they had never been too righteous about it. There were whispers and banter about I being the father but never had anyone said anything openly or ridiculed us.

There was unacknowledged pain and unbridled fear in your eyes.

You had refused to let out the rooms on the terrace to a respectable member of the church who wanted to rent that for a young woman whose relationship was questionable with that member. The assumption for such a proposition was that in our home it would be a perfectly acceptable situation.

In the eyes of my God, I have not sinned. You thought. Why else would He bless me with five sons and place the sixth in by womb? You stood and pleaded to your God and His community for acceptance. The service continued. When the communion started, you left your youngest in the lap of the eldest and went in to take the communion. The priest passed you without giving you the communion.

'God does not differentiate,' you mentioned as the pastor passed you for the communion. Your protest was drowned by Psalms 51 that the organ started to play. You felt a heavy blow like someone punched you in the heart and a veil of darkness descended in your eyes. The congregation stood up. As you walked back, you could hear the hissing of gossip. *Loose woman. Hussy. Whore.* You flew out with humiliation and tears in your eyes.

You stood there thinking why must I accept this excommunication? The church is a place for all. It's the abode of God. I should be welcomed. You trembled with shame.

When the service ended, the people walked past you, most did not look in your eyes. Those that did, accused you of being a prostitute. When the first gob of spit splashed in front of you, it crashed your ear drums and tears surfaced in your eyes. It was the church women who had turned against you. You stood with tears streaming as you clutched a child to your bosom and others clinging around you.

When the second spit gob landed on your sandals and the eldest one took the handkerchief from his pocket and bent to clean it, your heart broke. It was like he was cleaning your sin. You resolved that you will not be the face of shame. You wiped your tears and stood with dignity despite the trauma that each spit gob built. Till the last person left the church.

When the pastor locked the church, you were still there with your five sons. 'Go home,' he said as he passed you.

At home, Badi Bai had kept hot lunch ready. You served Alfie first. Then washed the children and served them. Then you went to the toilet and shame and hurt spilled out of your guts. You retched and vomited till there was nothing left. They had given you a heavy cloak of humiliation that Sunday.

You are a prostitute. You have men living in your house. They judged.

You took men as boarders in spare rooms on the terrace, who would pay the rent. They had a separate entrance, and they never crossed your courtyard. We needed the money. My business had completely wrapped up by then, my political career was nascent, and I had no income. Alfie continued to drink and there was nothing he would bring home except debts from the liquor shop, debts from acquaintances and relatives. You had to find means to support the children.

You stood outside the church every Sunday. You had your five sons and a swelling belly. You knew that you had not left your God and that He would not leave you. Whatever morning a Sunday enfolded; wet, misty, grey, bright, scorching you would be there before the congregation arrived and you would stand till the pastor left.

The children would want to go in the cool interior of the church. They asked you why we stood outside, while everyone else was inside. You said we are waiting for God to come to us.

I would wait at the corner from the church with the bicycle to take you back. Parched mouth, dry eyes and swollen feet, you would walk beside me. We no longer had the car. Alfie's debtors had taken it long ago. I would have one child on the front bar, two at the back rack. The eldest would walk with us. The youngest would be in your arms.

However angry I felt against the church and the congregation, I could not dare to enter it. That would have tarnished you further. We had no formal relationship in the eyes of the community.

That Sunday, the sun was bright, and spring was in the air. It was March. When we were coming back from the church, the eldest asked, 'Who is our father?' You said, 'My husband, Alfie. He is your father.' I felt a stab in my chest. Frieda, you were married to Alfie and all the children carried his name. 'Then who is he?' He asked indicating to me. You said, 'He is Uncle, our everything.' Such affection. I wanted to kiss your forehead, but we had never crossed the line of propriety outside our bedroom.

Next Sunday, you stood outside the church again with your five sons. As the service progressed, you heard the hymns. You were tired, nearly eight months pregnant. Alfie came and took you by the hand and you looked up. He had come to the church after an awfully long time. He had spent the last evening with the family, which was an irregular thing for him to do. For the last so many years he drank alcohol every evening. He looked so handsome that day and so confident. Not a trace of alcohol. Clean shaven and in his light blue linen suit. He took you inside. The congregation was stunned, the hymn stopped after a few discordant notes. All eyes were on the seven of you walking in a single file. Alfie in the front, followed by you, then the eldest son and so on till the youngest fifth son who had just started walking a few weeks ago, followed all at a certain distance.

'This church married us,' he said when he stood in front of the congregation. 'She is my wife. These are my children. Do they not carry my name? If Jesus saw no fault in Mary Magdalene, who are you to judge this woman? The church is the bride of Christ. There are all kinds of sinners here. Yet, you are accepted. Why is it difficult for you to accept a woman who has no fault except following her destiny? This church has the audacity to mock its own faith. One of you gave a note to my eldest that his father is a holy ghost. How dare you? Not one of you can disprove that he is not my son. Is this your faith? I have believed that Christianity is a faith of love. Show some love to this woman. You will realise that she has a heart of gold.'

Then you saw Sarah walking and running in, worry and sadness written on her face. She came and embraced you and buried her face in your shoulder and cried. She whispered fiercely. 'Come, let us go, my sister. These are cruel people. Let us go.' She wanted to protect you. Alfie had sent her a telegram.

The youngest one who had run away from the cluster was picked up an old woman, her skin serrated with time. She came forward with an unbalanced gait, left him close by and she went on to touch your arm with her knotted old fingers. 'Women are like earth. They nurture whatever seed is planted in them. God be with you,' she said and walked out of the church.

As you all walked out, Alfie said, 'This church may abandon her, I will not. In good times and bad times, in love and in ill health, in prosperity and in poverty…I had promised. I will never abandon her.'

I saw it all standing at the door of the church.

Then that sad entourage of ours walked back home.

After that day in the church, Alfie went back to drinking. Our Sixth Son was due. I remember that it was monsoons, and it was raining heavily. The morning was a grey sheet stretching with dampness and gloom. Alfie slipped and fell in the courtyard. You asked that no one touch him and that everyone go back to their rooms. You sat down next to him, held his hands, and closed your eyes. You cried and you prayed. There were vibrations, which kept reverberating in the house. You sat there as the rain fell on both of you. He had blood running from his head mixing with rainwater. He had hit his head while falling. Exhausted, you fell next to him with your head on his chest. Badi Bai and I lifted you and took you to your room. I was worried about you and the child in your womb. You were nearly full term then. Badi Bai helped in changing your wet clothes and warming you up with a cup of tea.

I knew that you had used your second prayer!

I picked up Alfie and took him to his room. I changed him and bandaged his head. He slept and I left him to rest. You forbade anyone to disturb him. Alfie did not wake up for seven days. He felt tired and weak the day he got up. He was quiet the entire day. He did not ask for alcohol that evening. Or any other evening after that. Ever.

The financial situation at home did not change. We tried to be self-sufficient in many ways. We had a cow to provide milk. We had chicken to provide eggs. We hardly ate meat. The fisherwoman was kind to give us fish on credit knowing well that she would never recover her dues. We ran credit everywhere—with the cloth merchant, the grocer, the stationery shop—it was becoming a mountain.

Now, when you went to the church, the pastor gave you the communion. Alfie had changed.

I came from the annexe that Sunday evening and combed the house looking for Alfie. I found him in the brine of his own isolation, on the sofa in the drawing-room, with a fine tendril of white smoke from the cigarette held between his fingers, his hand hanging beyond the armrest. The sofa was strangely placed, like it had been added to correct the empty spaces. Like the lies that fill empty marriages. I lifted a chair and placed it close without making a sound. I sat down near with my head full of thoughts or motives. I spoke to Alfie in a low voice, affectionately. I felt more affection for him now than at any other time. 'I am willing to disappear. I have given you the sons. Frieda wanted them to carry your name. I am inconsequential to interpret this game of fate. But if it is possible to put your world in order by my disappearance, I will accept it as a privilege on behalf of our friendship and on behalf of the love that I have for Frieda. I am helpless to change anything else. Perhaps my disappearance will bring the harmony and etiquette in your marriage ultimately.' I twisted my hands together as I spoke, a nervous gesture that was also pleading for an answer. 'Perhaps I will undertake a pilgrimage.' Alfie did not move. His eyes were closed while I waited.

Alfie's hand moved and he sucked hungrily at the cigarette. When he exhaled, it darted off in my direction. Behind the curtain of smoke, Alfie said, 'I don't understand. Did you ask me when you entered Frieda's life?'

We both sat silently.

'Then why ask me now?' Alfie said after a while as he put the cigarette out on the brass ashtray on the table. 'Marriages follow a path set by two people over time. The signposts and traces that convention and emotions place for them to follow, were obliterated or confused in our case. No wonder we are lost in this fog. Our marriage has disappeared, only its façade remains. I am not sure if your disappearance will solve anything.'

I only saw Alfie's dignity in the open landscape of his distress.

'My life is broken, and I can't put the pieces back together. I do not feel anything as my mind and my hands are getting colder and colder. I have not been able to feel anything for a long time. The only person who can give you any answer is Frieda.'

MOTHER'S GIFT

One afternoon as I sat for dinner you said, 'Amma ji wants to meet you.'

'How do you know?' I asked. And you said that you had a dream. 'There was a child being chased by wolves. There was dust and growling and feet of wolves and the feet of the child. In one momentary flash I saw the face and it was brown eyes and black hair with fair skin. I could not see very clearly, it all happened so quickly but I knew it was you. And as you ran, I saw a small white dot that increased as you ran towards it and it was flowing in the wind and as you ran closer to it followed by the grey cloud and bared wolves' teeth, it enveloped you. When you emerged from that thin white cotton screen, you were smiling.'

I smiled and wondered how you interpreted that Amma wants to meet me. I had not seen her in a long time.

The sweet song of the myna played with ektara woke me from the siesta. We were used to mynas singing in the house now that Alfie had a few of them around. The Gypsy hovered in the courtyard playing his ektara. He never came beyond the courtyard. He was so integral to our lives, yet he never crossed that threshold. The Gypsy would go away in search of his mysterious beau but would be there miraculously whenever he was needed. When not needed, he would come on his own and spend time with the children or sit and sing folk songs in accompaniment with his ektara. I had seen him sit at the top step, chat with you, and tell you stories as you and Badi Bai worked in the kitchen. You mentioned that his stories were strange and intriguing. When you had orders for making the flower bouquets, he helped you with cutting the flowers, pruning their stems, and keeping them in water carefully till they were delivered. Either Badi Bai or he would deliver and collect the money for those.

I knew there was something brewing in his head that day. I could see the thoughts blooming and vaporising.

'Bauji, I have a message for you from the Baada[1]. Amma ji wants to meet you,' he said.

Was it a co-incidence?

'But you never go to the Baada. Who told you?' I asked. Frieda, you knew of the discomfort that the mention of you or of the sons or of anyone close to you caused at the Baada. It so happened, once I had to go to Nagpur with a team of party members and the person whom I had asked to deliver my message to you did not do that and you sent the Gypsy to the Baada to find if I was there. My brothers were upset and politely asked him not to come back ever for any reason except to give them the news of when I was dead.

'Your mother had sent a servant from the Baada.' He spoke. 'I met him on the street waiting for you. He declined to come to the house.'

He looked distinctly uncomfortable and squirmed.

'There is more…' I persisted.

'Someone on the street called Frieda a prostitute!' he said sotto voce, after a long pause.

'And what do you think?' I was angry.

'I don't think anything,' he said looking into my eyes directly holding my gaze. He too was hurt. Then, 'She is just a woman in a trouble called love. I have known her since she was born. She does not have a vile bone in her!'

I stepped forward and patted his shoulder. 'That's true.' I said and added, 'Now run along. Tell her I will meet her Tuesday afternoon.'

---

[1] A cluster of houses within a common boundary.

The heat made me sweat. I had covered my head and face with a cotton gamcha[2]. I entered the Baada around 1 pm. The Baada was a cluster of houses within the same premises. My mother lived with my eldest brother in the first house. She had a small garden outside her door. The May sun beat down ferociously, and everything was stunned in its glare. My brothers had explicitly asked me in the past not to come to the Baada anymore after I came to live with you. I entered her garden and even before I could knock, I noticed that the door was left ajar, and I entered stealthily. It was a cave of cool darkness inside. It took me some time to adjust my sight. My mother wrapped me in her arms. She had been waiting. Her knuckled fingers and old palms on my back pressed me into her. The hot skin and the wet cool shirt sent down tiny shivers. She felt soft and smaller than before.

'Sit, Mahesh, sit,' she said in a whisper releasing me. She closed the door of her room that connected it to the rest of the house. I removed the gamcha. She poured me water from an earthen surahi in her room.

I sat on the chair near her bed. After giving me the water, she sat on her bed and held my hand. I drank it with my other hand. The coolness of the water descended twirling in my oesophagus. It felt nice.

'You seem to have lost weight,' she said.

I laughed silently, 'Amma, you always say that. Ever since I was a child.'

'But you have. I heard things are difficult for you.'

'Yes, they are but we manage.'

'Does Frieda look after you?' she asked, affectionately.

'Above everyone else,' I said. And she tightened her grip on my hand.

---

[2] Towel.

However men may grow up and whatever they may become, they always feel their own preciousness with their mothers. Mothers have the art of making men feel more than what they are.

'I believe Girija wrote to you.'

I nodded.

'And?'

'How is that possible, Amma? Frieda is too proud a woman to even consider that.'

'But what do you think?'

'Amma, I don't know Girija. I knew her for those few hours only. I cannot exploit her magnanimity,' I said.

'But she is your wife…'

'I have not done right by her… Every day I ask for forgiveness for the injustice, of my betrayal of her.'

'She does not think like that.'

'How can you say, Amma?' I said.

'She has been writing to me.' I was surprised at that.

'Since when?'

'All the while.'

'That's good. I am glad.'

Then she told me all about her.

'Girija was heartbroken after she left. She felt humiliated after you told her about Frieda. For many days after she did not speak with anyone. She lost a lot of weight. You know her father was a landlord, rich and well known and a patriarch to the local temple. The old temple pujari, Aduri would come late mornings after his temple duties were done for the morning and spend time in their veranda, talking about agriculture, about the people of the village, about the water problem and other issues in the village. Once when he was sitting and singing a Thirumurai hymn, Girija came and stood behind the door listening to him. That was the first reaction she had shown after a long time and her father was grateful to Aduri. Now he would come and sing a new hymn every day.

"What are these hymns?" she asked one day.

"These are from Thirumurai, for the bhakti of Lord Shiva."

"For Lord Shiva?"

"Yes. These hymns were written by 27 different poets in the Pallava period…though these were written in Tamil, I sing them in Telugu."

"Will you teach me?"

"Ask your Appa[3]… If he says yes, I will."

When she asked her father, he agreed. He even encouraged it by getting the Aduri to spend more time in his house and to keep teaching her in a systematic way. He was glad that Girija was showing interest in something after the debacle of her marriage.

In a few years she learned not only all the Thirumurais but also Veerabhadra Vijayamu by Bammera Potanaamtaya, Sivaratri Mahatyam by Srinatha, Sri Kalahasteeshwara Mahatyam and Sri Kalahasteeshwara Shatakam by Pedda Dhurjali, Basava Purana by Palkuriki Somantha and many others. Now she is a Shaivite devotee while her family members are Vaishnavas.

You know she had no brothers, only an old father and mother. In a few years they died one after the other, and she started looking after all the fields and agriculture. She has many cousins who help her.

The other day she wrote to me about the puja she did for the blessings of Lord Shiva before sowing the paddy. On the day they were ready to sow paddy, she picked five rocks from

[3] Father.

around her fields, which are a few hectares and then she washed them with the water of the Godavari and painted them white with rice flour. She then applied vermilion and turmeric on these rocks. After placing them at a corner of the field that is readied for sowing paddy, she put paddy sprouts and flowers near these rocks and offered prayers to Lord Shiva. She sowed the few sprouts first and then her farmers commenced the sowing of sprouts. She called it Lingalaku Pettadam. It is a village tradition. You are a city boy. You will not know these traditions of our villages. I vaguely remember we also used to do this when I was a little girl back in Andhra.

Once I asked her what does she do when she is not learning and tending to the fields.

She told me she gets up before sunrise and takes a bath from the well from which she fetches the water herself. She has servants, but she does it on her own. Then with wet hair she goes and plucks the flowers from the garden and thereafter visits the temple where she worships Lord Shiva and returns with the ash on her forehead. She starts the day by supervising the farm workers and giving instructions and then has her breakfast which she cooks herself. She then spends time reading and learning literature. She meets the farm workers again in the evening and tutors the children and women or watches the folk performers like Oggu Katha or Perini who pass her village. Most of the folk artistes perform from Shiva Purana or sing from Shaivite literature because she likes only those. She cooks dinner and eats before sundown.

On Mondays, the day of Lord Shiva, she distributes milk and grains to the poor. The people of her village love her. I wanted to send her some clothes, but she said that she only wears white sarees now and has put away all her jewellery. Even her mangalsutram for she did not want to carry that humiliation around her neck.'

I listened to the destruction I had caused. I had made her an ascetic.

And then Amma said, 'Do you ever think about her? Do you want to know about her?'

'It does not matter, Amma. She is not happy. And I will always be guilty of erasing happiness from her life.'

'I asked her the same question once. Do you think about Mahesh? Do you know what she replied? That her devotion to Lord Shiva and her busy life with fields and people depending on her, she has learnt to forgive you. In that forgiveness, she has also learned to forget you.'

'Why all those parcels and this offer now?'

'She has the means, and she would have done that for any other destitute. She has risen above the compulsions and duties that relationships impose. Your marriage does not mean anything to her now.'

'It was a disastrous mistake.' It was all I could say.

'So, what will you do now?'

'Nothing. But Amma, next time you write, please tell her that what she offers is generous but not possible to accept. Do express my gratitude and seek her forgiveness for me.'

'I agree that what you did was wrong. It was not fair for her. She has diverted her mind towards God.'

'Has she? It is Lord Shiva...my namesake. If nothing, she has raised me further in her mind and I feel wretched about it.'

'But think of those children. Your brothers say they are yours. You will be able to secure their future. Here they will just struggle every day.'

'Amma, I am trying. I will do something.'

She sat holding my hand looking at my face thinking. I could see thoughts passing in her mind reflected in her deep-set, old eyes. She heard the ruffling of clothes and tinkling of jewellery behind the door connecting her room to the rest of the house. She indicated that I go and hide under her bed, and she lay down. Then there was a knock.

'Amma, are you okay? I think I heard someone speaking…' that was my eldest sister-in-law.

'I am fine. I was dreaming and must have been mumbling.'

'Open the door, Amma, I have got some coconut water for you.'

My mother got up from bed and groaning she opened the door.

My sister-in-law came in and I saw the hem of a mauve-coloured saree with a thin golden zari border from under the bed. I saw her bare feet with her toe rings, the traditional symbols of a married women. She placed the brass tumbler of coconut water on her bed side. And turned and stopped at the door.

'You must ventilate your room in the evening, Amma, it smells of sweat.'

'What time is it?' my mother asked as she stood by the door.

'It's nearly 3 pm. Do you not have a clock in your room? You want me to get one?' she asked, respectfully.

'I have a clock on the table. But it is dark here and my eyes don't see too well. That's why I asked.'

'Amma, let me know if you need anything. I will come by again in some time.'

'You are a blessing.' My mother said and closed the door after her. I came out and sat on the bed.

She held my hand. 'How is Frieda?'

'She is expecting again. The seventh one.'

'Ask her to give this child your name. You have given her husband your six sons.'

'How is that possible? What has been rumours and conjectures will be confirmed! Who knows what new shame will befall us then?'

'No no... Nothing will happen. You deserve to have one son carry your name. For your moksha.'

We sat like that for a few minutes, she looked at me imploring.

Then she opened the wooden cupboard in her room with a key from among a bunch tied to the corner end of her saree. I saw her frail bent back that looked like it was falling in love with gravity and felt a rush of affection. Such a tiny woman with such huge sons. I knew I was loved the most by her. Very quietly she turned. She had a plain wooden chest in her hands. It was locked. She gave it to me. 'Take this. I have kept this for you and your children,' she said.

'What's this?' I said taking it. It was heavy. She took a key from her ring of keys, gave it to me and said, 'Now run. This time of the afternoon, everyone is inside. No one will see you.' She handed me the key. Once again, I felt like a little boy who was secretly being given sweets by his mother. As I wrapped the gamcha, she pulled out a small square piece of cotton cloth and tied the wooden chest which was about a foot long with nine inches height and width. 'This way nobody will know what is inside. Take this carefully.' Then she nudged me gently to the door.

When we opened it that evening, Frieda, you were so shocked. With your trembling hands you shut it immediately.

ALFIE'S ILLUSION

The Seventh Son had been born. Now, Sundays came with fresh energy. There would be rows of polished shoes near the door, a pair increased every few years as a new child came and was ready to walk. There were seven shirts of different sizes that would be ironed and hung in the children's rooms. There were some trousers and some half pants that were paired with the shirts for each son depending on their size. After breakfast they would line up in Alfie's room where he would comb their hair. You cajoled him to start doing that. The children need their father's touch and attention, you said. He would put Brylcreem in their hair and then place the comb in a straight line that extended from the tip of the nose and the centre of left eye till it touched the hairline. At that point he would part the hair. He parted the hair so neatly that a straight line of the scalp was visible. The boys liked the ritual. They would examine each other's parting and ratify its perfection and feel smug. This was the only thing that Alfie did for them now in the entire week and the boys looked forward to it. Later, in their lives, this would be one habit that none of them would lose. The straight line of hair parting.

While the boys' hair was being groomed, you would put on your saree and sandals. You would put a rose in your hair above your right ear and a apply a light lipstick and kajal. I had requested you to wear a tiny dot on your forehead as a sign of a married woman. You had said, 'I don't like it.' And I had said, 'Wear it for me.' Since then, you wore it every Sunday. Alfie went to the church only on Easter. Rest of the time, I would walk you all to the church but wait outside.

When the sermons were prolonged, the children would get restless and daydream about morbid things. They would dangle their legs as they sat on the church benches, and you would get the most restless ones to sit close to you. The fourth son and the sixth son sat next to you. The First Born usually sat with the seventh. When the prayers were long, they would look distracted by the stained-glass windows, or outside at the trees and the birds. Sometimes they would smile and giggle by making gestures but without saying anything. They had a language of silent humour which only they understood. The First Born always waited in anticipation for one of the withered oldies in the church to fold on themselves like a hymn book with a thud and then be carried out with a wave of distress before a pious hush descended. Then the chants from the Psalms would rise from the choir. The Sixth Born often saw the woman with the pink saree in the front pew at the corner near the vestry. She looked back at him and smiled. She always unsettled him and yet he kept observing her.

After the service ended, you would meet your sisters and friends. Your mother still avoided you conspicuously. The children would stand in a huddle refusing to play with other children and then they would return with me, their Mahesh Uncle. Sometimes while returning you would ask them about the sermon, just to check if they were paying attention. Often, they did not remember anything.

Then on Sundays, when Alfie joined them for lunch at the dining table, the boys would be cheerful.

Alfie had followed a routine even through his mists of sadness. It was the predictability of his actions that rooted him in the day. It was necessary after the turbulence of the first twenty years of your marriage. Frieda, you had aligned yourself and the household to his routine with a fine balance. You were the first one to get up in the house. After a warm bath, you would sit and say your prayers for about thirty minutes asking your God for peace, hope and happiness. You prayed for each son and for Alfie and for me. Every day you asked for His forgiveness.

Till Badi Bai could manage it, she would be up and ready, by the time you finished your prayers, and she would bring you a glass of warm water, a bud of garlic and a clove, two cups of tea and biscuits. You would take this to Alfie and give him the garlic pod and clove to chew properly, and then drink the warm water. It is good for your heart, you would say. The two of you would drink your morning tea after that. Frieda, you would sit beside him and speak with him softly and tell him about what you planned for the day. Mostly the newspaper would be delivered by then and you would read a few headlines.

When Alfie went for his bath and ablutions, you would help Badi Bai in preparing the breakfast as the house stirred with the boys waking up and getting ready for school. When the boys were small, Alfie used to walk them to school and later when it was not possible for Alfie to do that, it was the elder ones who walked the younger ones. After the boys left in the morning, you would spend an hour with Alfie. You would have breakfast together. Alfie hardly spoke but you spoke to him about the sons, your sisters, the church, the neighbours, and anything that would keep Alfie engaged. You would try and read in his large blue eyes what went through his mind. Sometimes he smiled and sometimes he appeared to not understand and you would explain again. Sometimes he would nod if you asked him something. You left him magazines and the paper to read and would put on the radio to BBC world news that he was fond of listening to.

In the meantime, Badi Bai would serve breakfast to me. Every day I would come to Alfie's room where he and you were, and I would inform you both that I was leaving for work or an errand. I would have bathed, oiled my hair, and would often be dressed in white cotton kurta with a Nehru jacket, pyjamas and leather jootis. We, the two men, looked in each other's eyes for a moment and something transpired there that you could never fathom. Was it an understanding? Was it a dare? Was it confirming each other's place in this house? You would never know. For me, it was a sense of gratitude and a promise to be there for him, for you and for the sons, come what may. It was important for me to reinforce that every day to him.

The fresh flowers would have come by then. It was the Gypsy's responsibility to get fresh flowers either from your garden or the market. You would have told him the previous evening what you needed based on your client's' requests. When there were no bouquet orders, Frieda, you embroidered flowers on the sheets and pillowcases for the home and sometimes for your sisters as gifts.

At noon you would serve lunch to Alfie and sit with him at the dining table as he ate. Badi Bai would sit with you both and you would chat. Alfie would then have a siesta in his room with the cries of the vendors on the street, with the sounds of the traffic filtering through the courtyard and the curtains, with the chatter of children returning from school, with the songs of the beggars passing by, with the chirping of birds on the guava tree. You would wait for me to return home for lunch and then the two of us would eat together and then retire to your room. These were the only private moments we had in the house full of children and responsibilities. It was in these moments we planned the household budget, we discussed about the sons and when the words were depleted, we sought solace in each other's bodies.

The boys returned from school by 3 pm. They would be served tea and hot snacks in thirty minutes after they were changed and freshened up. The time from then till 6 pm was spent with the children, chatting and playing, and you preparing dinner. I would return to the courtyard from wherever I was and would help the boys with their homework. In the summers, Alfie would sit in the veranda and watch his family. The First Born always sat beside him, and they chatted. Only the First Born had the key to his words. This was the only time that Alfie spoke with anyone. At seven, I would serve Alfie his dinner and sit with him as he ate. Then you, Badi Bai, the boys and I would have dinner. The boys would take turns saying the grace before dinner. I would also close my eyes respectfully.

After dinner, the sons would congregate at Alfie's room, while I retired to my room in the annexe. You would all say a short family prayer and then the boys would go to their rooms. Badi Bai would go and supervise the kitchen maids to tidy up. Frieda, you would remain to tidy Alfie's room and chat. You would tuck him in by 9 pm and lie in with him. You would listen to jazz on his gramophone playing softly. You would pat either his head or his upper arm. Sometimes Alfie would want songs that you liked. This was the hour you both simmered in the warm broth of memories. It was the solace that preceded his nocturnal terrors, where flowers withered and walls corroded, where ageing made his brain a putrefying swamp of mistakes and regrets, where mad winds of his imagination blew away the roof off his home and carried away the boys by the string of their blood. Alfie would create an illusion of slumber and you would leave only after Alfie had fallen asleep. No matter how late you got.

THE SUN-BREASTED WOMAN OF THE GYPSY

She sold breasts.

At the evening mela, the tall man with a braided and beaded beard, saw her through the kohl-lined eyes shaded by a broad multi-coloured turban. She sat with a straight back covered with three layers of moonlight. One layer covered her head, one covered her eyes and one her breasts. Her upper body shined like smooth marble.

Men died to touch a breast of their choice with their lips. Only lips. No hands. And only once. For half a minute. In return for money. That was the deal.

Some went for the soft tissue. Some went for the under-curve. Some for the areola. Some pecked. Some licked and some took a mouthful. Their beauty was such that any thought of violence to them evaporated at their sight. She ceased to exist for those moments when men were intrigued by her organs. She stood outside watching her breasts intoxicate men.

He removed her turban and put it near her feet. He had swirls of thick hair dropping to his shoulders, matted at the ends. Giving off a smell of sweat, tobacco and testosterone. With bronze shining skin, tempered with wind and sunshine, tightly stretched on high cheekbones, he sat in front of her with a straight back, emulating her posture. He observed the objects of his interest. He then looked in her eyelashes braided with moonlight. She had closed her eyes. As if in meditation. The thin eyelids on occipital space could not conceal the lights that burned in those eyes.

He moved his gaze down. The skin of her breasts shone like hallucinations. His left hand pulled the money out from his pocket. He laid it all at her feet.

He bent at his waist and brought his mouth close to her left breast. He stopped a few millimetres from it. His breath warmed the cool moonlight and blood rushed to it. He looked up and all he could see was her flawless skin disappearing at the curve of the shoulder and the elegant trunk of the neck rising on that sweet glowing landscape. He then saw the curved shadow that the moonlight cast under her right breast. She smelled of cloves and cinnamon.

He took the areola gently in his mouth and kissed, with his lips enveloping it firmly. Soon he felt her cardiac tissue lodge in his throat. He choked and lost his breath. All his energy drained, and he released her as he gasped. All it took was less than fifteen seconds. She had broken in pearls of sweat.

'What you are! What you could be! What you will never be!' She whispered as she pulled away his head by the hair.

He raised his eyes and filled them with her colour and moonlight. She was covering herself. He sat dazed as she picked up her money and left. From now on she would never trade her left breast. It had been marked like a black sun with blue and purple lines radiating from the centre to the periphery.

He returned every day thereafter. He enquired and asked about her. They always said that she was in another place. He went to that other place. She had gone to another. His actions of describing her trade, the breasts and terms made him a laughing stock. He remained fervent. A hundred years passed. And she had become a myth. No one knew about her now.

Doubt crept in whether that had happened at all. He had imagined it for sure. Yet, the smell of cinnamon and cloves was real. Eyelashes braided in moonlight were real. That feeling of the sweetest heart beating in his mouth was real. Even the gap that he felt in his soul was real.

It was during one of these haunted meanderings that he helped your mother with your birth. And that is why you were always so special to him all your life. He knew your mother would never like you and so he came intermittently to see how you were doing. He would bring his ektara and sit outside and play. You would sit with him when you were a little girl. He would tell you stories. No one knew where he lived. Your mother's anxiety and anger mellowed when he was around.

As the pale jaundiced lights of a tired day hit the water, his heart started palpitating. He was undressing to take a bath in the Narmada. It had been seven years since he had encountered her. Maybe it is the memory that fibrillates his heart. This is it, he thought. 'My heart is giving up on me.' There was a dull ache and a deep breath escaped him. With last of the sunbeams coruscating on the waves, she emerged from the river. He noticed the black sun on the left breast. The evening sun had emblazoned her into liquid gold. Age had wrapped her in more beauty.

He swam to her. Touched her on her shoulder. 'You must tell me what took you so long,' she asked. It took him three nights to tell her everything.

After he finished telling her, that night they lay naked, he on his right side and she on her left, his bronze skin, and her pale skin merging, drawing out a cartography of desire. Their eyes shining, their hair tracing their faces, he pulled her close, tightly, inundating his chest with her breasts. His leg between hers feeling her soft down on his stomach, she moved lower, and he felt it on his thighs. He kissed her mouth slowly. Leisurely. Both feeling the pleasure that warm bodies provide. Breathing softly and heavily. Silently. Like the beginning, similarly, there was only silence and not the words. Words had no place there. His right-hand fingers caressed her satin skin on the cheeks. He moved down. Tracing the length of her neck with his tongue, he brought his luscious, shining lips to the aureole. Kissed the fabulous soft breasts. First, the right one. Then the left one. With the sweetness and roughness of his mouth, the pink nipples hardened between his lips. One after the other. Blood kept rushing there, embarrassing the tips to turn red with delight. She placed her hand on the thick mop at the back of his head and pressed his handsome face further into her breasts to gorge on the desire they felt. The harder he kissed the more she arched her back. His own erection stuck somewhere between their feverish bodies. When he brought his left hand down between her legs, her muscles broke like a wave one after the other. Her skin drenched with moisture like in a monsoon rain. Her retina had light disintegrating behind the eyelids.

He had tears in his eyes. It made her shiver. His intensity.

Her mouth the colour of roses. This is sin. She said, 'Is it possible to forgive?'

'If I believed in God, I would believe in sin. I am only human. This sin is my destiny,' he said. He read fear as love in her bright gracious eyes. Her fragility terrified him.

Salty and sweet, sticky and bitter, vulgar and delicious. He had penetrated her wanting to fill himself with her. He had groaned like he was singing the aria and she moved like she was shifting the oceans. The waves sweeping everything, tearing, and crushing everything, their entrails, their defences. Streaked with crimson blood, a million suns exploded in their visceral sanctum sanctorum. Outside there was a shower of meteors near the Narmada. Those that slept saw it behind their eyelids. That hamlet on the riverside was engulfed with the strong music of cinnamon and leather and tobacco and jasmine and the air sparkled like it was infested with fireflies. People tried to capture it in glass bottles and those who did savoured it for a long time. They traced that spine of music from that house in the hamlet where the Gypsy slept to the bank of the Narmada where a boat had left in the black-blue misty twilight of early morning.

When he woke up with orange knives of light cutting the room and bleeding dust particles to the floor, she was gone. Everything metamorphosed. Narmada's white marble into water. Blue sky into grey ribbons. Clouds stuck into the trees.

Wind into whispering whine. Two into one. Heart in many little pieces.

The rest has been a memory.

He went searching for her. There are rumours that a sun-breasted woman makes earthen lights for the temples sprinkled on the banks of Narmada. The Gypsy is still looking for her.

The Gypsy will survive all but disappear the day Frieda will be buried. He never changed in his appearance. Always smooth skinned, bronze coloured with honey and tobacco voice.

ALFIE'S LIFE OF BIRDS

One for Sorrow!

The parakeets were boisterous and noisy each morning and evening, visiting the guava trees swelling up with fruits. It was Holi. We were a strange family, neither Christians nor Hindus. But Frieda, you believed in Indian traditions and before each Holi, you would send the Gypsy to collect the red flowers from the Palash trees near Dumna forest and Sita Pahari. The Gypsy would get the tonga and I would ride with him for six days. We would come back in the evenings with rattan baskets full of red and orange flowers. Red was from Dumna and orange were from Sita Pahari. I would sit mesmerised by the six fires that the Gypsy built in the courtyard and placed large vats with water to boil the petals. The petals bled their colour for a few hours. The coloured water was then cooled and drained with a cotton sheet and rested. This will be used on Holi as colours in the pichkaris[1].

One vat was kept on fire with the coloured water till all of it evaporated, thereafter, depositing a dark red powder at the bottom. The Gypsy would scrape that and collect it in an earthen bowl and leave outside your door, Frieda, after midnight before Holi morning.

Alfie would sit with doom pressing his shoulders. He lived days that are not registered in the ledger of the living. He wrestled with defeat in the silence of the nights and came back at the crack of dawn to see the faces of the sons. There are seven now, the smallest amongst them is three. I know our children are strange. All parents damage their children, some more than the others. He sits and observe the damage done by us. We confused their blood—mine and their names—Alfie's.

---

[1] Water pistols.

Next morning, you would dress in a pastel saree with a red border, put frangipani flowers in your hair that was oiled and tied in a tight bun at the nape of your neck; you applied kajal that accentuated your black eyes, and you decorated a thali with flowers, sweets, and the red powder that Gypsy had left outside your door. You would take the end of your saree across the blouse and the bosom and tuck it at the waist, showing the fair skin in the sides of your torso. After my bath, I waited in the chair I usually used in the corner of the courtyard. I remember your gait as you walked to me, your hips swaying like a young girl's and joy dripping with each step your naked feet took.

I would stand up. Put my right hand on the head and left on my heart. You made the tilak on my forehead with rice and haldi[2]. You put some sweets in my mouth. Showered a few petals on me. That year as you dipped your hand in the earthen bowl with red powder, all hell broke loose.

A swarm of parakeets descended in a cacophony attacking a myna who was terrified with all the claws and beaks attacking her. The myna landed in the earthen bowl. A red dust cloud exploded as you pulled back your hand reflexively. You and I fought the parakeets to disperse the attack. As the parakeets flew away, all that was left were a few feathers, a red dust cloud and a few petals floating in air. The myna breathing heavily with its beak open sat in the bowl drenched in red powder.

Alfie walked up and picked the myna. Frieda, you stood there trembling and I stood astonished. As he walked away, he picked a sweet that had fallen to the ground and sat down. You smeared the red powder on my face, first the right cheek and then the left. I put my right hand on your head and smeared your forehead with the red powder. *Holi ki subhkamnaye*[3], I said, affectionately.

---

[2] Turmeric.

[3] Best wishes on Holi.

Alfie saw that the myna had a broken leg with her claws curled up. The bird sat shivering with a racing heartbeat in the cup of his palms.

As he removed red dust from her feathers, the boys came with their friends to play Holi. 'One for sorrow. One for sorrow.' They shouted and jumped and pointed at the bird.

Two for joy!

Alfie put a tiny splint on the right leg of the myna. But that leg dried out and she chewed off the dead leg. All that remained was a delicate stub. He didn't know if it was a male or a female myna.

While he lived in abeyance, the myna took care of him. It came and sat across him and he fed her. Peas. Slices of fruits. Shreds of chicken. Caterpillars occasionally. It hops on one leg in the courtyard. It nods its head sometimes and digs its yellow beak in its chest and looks at him. Sometimes it fluffs its feathers and spreads its tail. It makes different sounds chirr-chirr- chirr, then krr-krr-krr, sometimes hee-hee-hee and others. It seems happy.

These days Alfie feels unwell. One day, as he lay with the dead weight of his limbs and torso on a reclining chair, he heard a melodious singing on his window ledge and saw a tail bobbing. He was pleasantly surprised in his stupor. And then it dived in. He raised his heavy eyelids slowly and saw two of them. He thought he was hallucinating about the singing and seeing two of the mynas. He felt good.

So much bird shit in your room. He heard you behind sheets of sleep filled barrier, muffled and reproaching. He felt you pressing his hand. That felt good too. Then he sensed someone scraping the floor and cleaning the room, dusting the surfaces, and changing the sheets. He felt the breeze descending from the ceiling. Shut the fan. Please. He said into a dark tunnel. The bird will get killed. The breeze stopped, and he was drenched in sweat. He smelled foul and fetid and did not care.

In the evening he felt a little better but there was still no life in his bones. He heard the boys crying, 'Two for joy!' 'Two for joy!' 'Two for joy!' I was with the boys, standing there smiling with pride.

Whenever he sees me, he experiences an attack of betrayal and inferiority. That sense of inferiority will stay with him. He had accepted my presence in the house, but he could never resolve that feeling of inferiority. That feeling came from my having made a space in your life, mind, and heart, which would never be his. I had given you the sons which he could not. But he also realised that without you, Frieda, his existence would be worthless. This truth stunned him. That's when he had started walking in confusion, maybe to get away as far as possible. But he could not. He always came back to you and the sons and the situation we were in. Alcohol was not a palliative and memory became a disease that mutated with the birth of each son. He doesn't drink anymore. But the only reason he lives now is to see the faces of the sons who carry his name.

He drags himself to the courtyard and sits down in his usual chair. He saw that his myna had a companion now.

Three for friends!

He has good days, and he has bad days.

He is not a companion to anyone. Even the myna. It had to find its own kind. Perhaps you and I are of the same kind.

On his good days he notices things. He notices that the second myna whistles and sings. It is frisky and hops and turns this way and that on the guava tree, in the courtyard, the window and in my room. And they both seem together all the time. Sometimes they both sing a duet, each bowing before singing. They make melodious sounds alternatively. Sometimes they stand opposite each other, with beaks open and touching while crouching. They seem like kissing each other. They bow frequently to each other. Sometimes they preen each other on the head and face.

Their behaviour is pleasing and beautiful, and it brings tears to his eyes.

He suspects, that the crippled one is a male. Why else would he bring gifts of strings, grass and caterpillars and lay it at the new bird's feet. They are building a nest at the top of his almirah. He does not say anything about it lest you remove it.

April is ending now. All the beds are laid out in the courtyard. Mine. Then yours. Then Alfie's. Then four more beds, three with two boys each and the eldest son has his own bed. At the far end is Gypsy's, whenever he stays the night here. One morning, when he opened his eyes, he heard the sweetest music by the mynas. The beds are gone. Folded and tidied up. The sun was rising but his bed was in the shadow of the house and the guava tree. He saw the two mynas playing on the guava branches. There was a nest up in the branches.

The complete one would step back and forth, then stop, raise its tail, and crouch shivering. The lame one would puff and bow a couple of times and then they would frolic. They repeated this a few times while making all sorts of noises. Then suddenly the legless one flew up behind and sat on the back of the other one while balancing on its wings. The mystery was solved. The legless one was the male. They did this a few times and both flew away in synchronicity.

Alfie's mind felt devoid of thoughts and feelings. Lifeless like his muscles and bones. Instead of warmth in the blood there was only an odd coldness in his veins now. Sometimes in the nights, he hears sweet whispers, never sure whether it was the mynas or you. Only sometimes when the mynas would shriek with a shrill voice, I would get up and chase them away. I knew the Gypsy told stories to the older boys, and it was his voice with a regular tone and soft inflections that brought sleep to his eyes.

When the rains came that year, there were three mynas. The pair had laid three eggs and only one had survived. Now the children shouted, 'Three for friends!' I wondered if they were talking about us…

Four for letter

He sits alone on Sunday mornings. After he is done with grooming the sons, everyone leaves for the church.

That morning, the eldest one had stood under the guava tree and looked up and said, 'Four for letter.' He looked up and noticed that the younger bird had acquired a mate.

No letter came. But he was reminded of the one that had come some years back.

> *Dear Alfie,*
>
> *Your wife and children stand outside the church in the patio every Sunday. The priest refuses communion to them. People spit at them. It is claimed that she has acquired many lovers in her marriage like a prostitute. They say your children are bastards!*
>
> *Anonymous*

He had sat with that piece of paper in hand. The effect of alcohol had drained like water. He had sat still, trying to fathom your humiliation. And its impact on the five sons then. Frieda, you were heavily pregnant with our sixth child. They never said anything to him, who was so lost to alcohol.

I remember, it was Saturday. The next day and he spent the entire day with the children. He sat at the dining table with his gut churning at imagining their insult and with his blood demanding alcohol. He did not sleep that night. When the epiphany of a question emerged, 'What would I do for love and not for anything else?' he knew the answer. They needed his loyalty.

Five for silver

I had started spending time with Alfie. I sat and told him stories.

Alfie did not speak much. Silence is the distance that had accumulated. You had stopped being accessible in his sentiments as a wife. You had become a place called home, that he held on to in order not to escape to oblivion. He couldn't summon a memory when he had desired you desperately, devastatingly, deeply. At times, in his solitude, he tried to dig a memory of a gesture, or a word said endearingly. It restored his spell called Frieda for a moment but then brought the feeling that his life had become exceedingly mythical and inexorably literary. Any woman, specially the one who is loved dearly, is enough by herself to defeat a man by the destructive power of her emotional absence. Yet, he lived life within the perimeters, which had been marked by two bodies, unassailable by the anomaly of emotions, harmless, necessary, and invincible for the names of our sons who are not his blood.

He tries to focus on what I was saying. I was telling him how the mynas got pretty feet. Long time ago a myna and a peacock became friends. The peacock had beautiful feet and the myna had ugly feet. When the monsoons arrived, they were both incredibly happy and frolicked in the rain. The trouble was that when the peacock danced, he looked at his feet mesmerised and forgot to spread its beautiful tail. The myna, poor at dancing, said, lend me your feet and perhaps I will dance. The peacock lent his feet, and the myna flew away with them. That's why the peacock now has ugly feet and cries every time he looks at his feet while the myna prances around in pretty feet.

I am that peacock, he thought. He was not one to show emotions and kept quiet.

I pressed his hand as it rested on the steps. We were sitting on the steps from the veranda to the courtyard.

Frieda, when you bore the seventh son, all your hair turned silver. You told him that you have named the last son after me in gratitude.

That evening he had sat numb. He had lost all his bargaining chips the day he had come forward to marry you without your consent. Consent was not something that was either solicited or promised in your marriage. Only loyalty.

The eldest son now spends his evenings with him specially after Alfie told him that he is his son as we had walked back from the church after he had challenged your excommunication. In any case, he loves him the most since his childhood. Sometimes, they both sit in silence. It's comforting to observe that.

He sat in the courtyard in the evenings and observed the household. He was old. When you brought him tea one evening, he saw that your white hair had lost their sheen from bright silver to dull aluminium. But your eyes shone the same they did thirty-four years ago when he had married you. You started wearing only cotton sarees and put a red dot on your forehead. He never asked but he knew that it was my influence. When you got up and went to get him a napkin, you tripped at the small step at the veranda and almost fell. You just said 'ufff', stabilised yourself and went in. When he saw you stumble, he had a kind of presentiment then. He would be the first one to die. He was older than you. He thought it reasonable that whom he loved the most be the one to lead him to the end of life and help him reach the other side. He thought about the life, and how he had lived with this woman who came as a flash one evening at the church when her groom could not make it. He never felt shame or regret even for a moment for your presence in his life. He had always maintained a solemn dignity and while his love had me involved, it did not shake his affection for you. Yes, it was a thunderbolt and a torment, but he had accepted the truth a long time back. All relationships become platonic when the fire of the bones melt away with time. He had waited very long for that and now we all were like three old friends without malice. We had too many secrets to let any malice creep in and destroy the peace.

'How many mynas are there on the guava tree today?' he asked the First Son.

The First Son looked keenly and said. 'Five.' Alfie looked at his face. How youthful and handsome and troubled he looked.

'Five for silver,' he said as Alfie waited for him to finish. Alfie remembered your silver hair and closed his eyes.

Six for Gold

As the mynas had increased in the house, the money too improved. I started working, and the Gypsy stopped selling things from the house. The kitchen fires kept going.

In the evening, Alfie heard Gypsy tell this story to the younger children. It is the one Shiva tells Parvati in Padma Purana. A brahmin was telling a story to his wife who was constantly distracted by her myna whom she loved. She failed to answer a question he asked as she continued to play with her myna. The brahmin cursed her to become a myna herself. Now that she became a myna, the brahmin regretted it and adopted her as his own and called her Muni Kanya. The myna was sharp and intelligent and could talk. When the brahmin recited it, she learned the vibhuti yoga that Krishna explains to Arjun in the Gita, and she recited it all the time. The gods became happy, and she was born an apsara in her next birth.

However, the three of us have no redemption, Alfie thought.

He had lived with an exquisite emptiness without purpose or direction, exiled for his past actions and incapable of any future without you, whom he shared with me and the children. It was our affair that made him expel himself from the world of the living. He had begun translating the intolerable distance that existed between you and him and summated it into a metaphor of defeat by confining himself to this great solitude. It took a lot of courage for him to stay intact with all the cracks in his heart and soul. It took his sustained silence to build solid defences against the insults of life.

The day the eldest one spotted the sixth myna that stayed back and said, 'Six for Gold', you told him that we would sell and move from this house to a bigger one away from this place.

Then Badi Bai told him that my mother had given me the inheritance, a box of gold a few years back before the seventh son was born, that Frieda had kept safely.

The Muslims were still leaving for Pakistan. It was after the communal riots of 1961. A decent Muslim family was migrating, and they sold the house to us. It was a haveli. 'The boys are growing, and they need separate rooms now,' you had said. You loved guavas and this house had a lot of guava trees, a mango tree and a plot at the back and a garden in the front for your flowers. It had everything you wanted. Frieda, you sold half the gold to buy the old red brick haveli near a mosque. Alfie took the six mynas with him when we moved.

Seven for a Secret

Those days Alfie walked without a thought, without will, without direction early in the mornings. That's when he had met her.

When she told him she waited for him, he did not recognise her. She said she became a prostitute because of him. He did not recognise her. There was too much makeup.

She said…

'That day I waited for you in my best saree, with thoughts like birds, bright and coloured, flying all over the sky. You had promised to come. You said that you would take me to DC's wedding. I was delighted because ours would follow soon after. It had to. We had been together only for a few months, but we were close. You had explored the topography of my body as I had done of yours.

I had taken care of you after your horse-riding accident. You lay naked in my bedroom as you had injuries to the scrotum and perineum from the cantle edge of your hard saddle. I had witnessed your vulnerability. I took care of you after the doctor had stitched you up. I thought you were still recovering but you disappeared. I found out what you had done after you had taken the vows with her that day. My destiny changed forever in those few hours.

Alfie, what has become of you? You have destroyed yourself for your bastards! Come to me and I will mend you.'

He did not say anything. There was nothing to say.

They knew each other in their youth. There was no love lost between her and me and now we made efforts to be civil in each other's presence. She knew that all the children were mine.

She came and visited him on Sunday mornings when there was no one home for an hour. She said, 'Alfie, your situation is pathetic. You should come with me. We can still live like we used to before you married impetuously. I still love you.'

Alfie never said anything. There was nothing to say. Badi Bai knew her and everything about her and therefore her lips were sealed. She was as discreet in her dislikes as she was exuberant of her likes. Alfie had little memory. He was totally consumed by you, Frieda, and what had become of him in his relationship with you.

She brought Alfie the seventh myna after we moved to this new house.

The boys were no longer excited by the mynas. The eldest one still gave him company in the evenings. When Alfie showed him the seventh myna the First Born bantered, 'Seven for a secret...what's your secret, Daddy?'

Very soon, Alfie's secret will no longer be a secret but a salacious gossip and an embarrassment for you, Frieda.

Eight for a wish

When the seventh myna came with a partner after a few months, the First Born got married and Alfie wished them a happy life. He wished that the First Born receive all the affection that was rightfully his. He also wished that he would get the companionship that a man deserves from his partner.

The bride's mother came to Alfie and said, 'I am giving you your daughter finally.' Meeting her, Alfie always had a feeling that she had been hiding something from him when she had surfaced out of the blue.

Frieda, you were not happy about the wedding. 'She is a prostitute and is a daughter of one.' Alfie said, 'Now she is our daughter-in-law. The past is past.'

And the Gypsy said, 'She will be the cause of your death.' You both looked at him without understanding who he was speaking to. To you or Alfie.

Next evening when Alfie sat in the courtyard, the First Born came and sat next to him. His bride followed with henna designs on her hand. They sat on either side of him. Alfie felt good about that.

The eldest said, 'Daddy, now there are eight mynas.'

The bride said, 'Eight for a wish.' He looked at her face, translucent skin, large brown eyes and a few strands of hair quivering across her forehead in the breeze.

Alfie said, 'My wish has come true in you.'

He noticed that the myna with the broken leg was getting slow. It had been seven years since it first came. The lame bird had learned to whistle and called him 'Daddy'. Alfie still fed him every day and he shared his food with the other seven.

Frieda, you did not like the mynas. You kept complaining they shat too much. And Alfie said, their shit made your roses redder.

Nine for a kiss!

As he sat with the broken legged myna in his lap, the others came and sat. On his shoulders, on his arms, around him and in his lap too. There were nine mynas.

And when one Sunday the mother of the bride kissed Alfie, he remembered her kiss on your wedding day.

In his youth, she had wanted to marry him, but he had thought the whole idea to be absurd. She was not the woman he loved but she said that no one in the world was perfect. She would provide him with happiness and cherish him with all her soul. She said it would be enough to make him learn to love her and be eternally happy as he'd always dreamt of since his parentless childhood and that she would build a solid household of dreams with the one who loved him and live out the countless days in the warm glow of happiness and when she told him that she would leave it all behind, all her lovers, Alfie thought that this woman was good and when she repeated it for a hundred days every evening, he agreed to get married. They had made love before but now it had a new meaning. A meaning that ensconced in its permanence, a commitment, and loyalty. When she removed her clothes, he realised how petite she was, tightly muscled but full of soft contours. He reminded himself that he would learn to love this body and would be happy. When he bundled her in his arms and they squeezed together in the cold of the night, submerged in the layers of sheets, he felt nothing. They made love many nights and he waited for the flowers of love to blossom in his heart. He would say, 'You are an exceptionally beautiful woman, the best, look at you,' and she would feel proud. He felt nothing, just a waiting for some attachment to emerge. He would be affected by the smooth line of the soft fabric of the nightdress on her buttocks and would say that she was pretty. But he was not alone. He knew the way her looks affected the men on the roads and streets, and the way they looked at her as if she was standing naked in front of them. He had seen their lust-laden looks, but he was impervious to all that because now she was his woman, and he was the man who would eventually fall in love with her.

Then he had the accident. He had gone hunting and his foot was stuck in the stirrup and the horse sped away from a snake in Sita Pahar. His perineum and scrotum had lacerations. The doctors stitched him up at the Military Hospital. When Alfie was discharged, she took him to her place.

When the night plucked out the stars from the sky, the animal would enter her breathing with the same rhythm and dance to the lost music of the night and would leave its contented entrails on the topography of her body. Her lovers would come and go, and he would see it all like a voyeur with a stitched perineum. Naked bodies entwined like snakes, slithering and spouting saliva and noises of vulgar lust. He would lie there and feel that transitory doom. She would sleep till late as the days brought regular light and seasons. Alfie was well taken care of, and his perineum healed. But not in his heart. Those were the nights when he decided that he could not build his love on other men's desire.

Now she visited as our First Born's mother-in-law People called her Your-Highness. One day as he sat alone in the morning in the courtyard she came and sat beside him. She said she had a secret as she kissed him on his old mouth with her tongue flicking inside like a viper. Alfie pushed her and walked away.

I saw that you had gone white as you saw them from the kitchen window.

Your-Highness followed him to the room. She stood at the door with a smirk on her face. 'She is your daughter,' she spoke. 'I was waiting to tell you that day when you did not come. And next I knew you were marrying Frieda.' There was no emotion on her face as she said that. She locked his eyes for a few moments. Then said, 'I know he is not your son. None of them are. You had suffered a severe damage in your accident and your seminal vesicles were irreparably damaged. The doctors told me that you would never have children even though your sexual organs would function perfectly after some time. But I was not worried as I had conceived before your accident.' She paused as she went on to read his face, then turned and went away.

THE ENDING...

TEN FOR A BIRD, YOU MUST NOT MISS

It was your thirty-fifth wedding anniversary. You had sent Alfie a lemonade around five in the evening. The cassette player was playing the songs of *Pakeezah*. He was sitting near the March guava tree. The tree was full of fruits. You were busy preparing a celebratory dinner. But Alfie was not himself of late. He walked around memoryless. He would stand in the corridor expressionless trying to figure to what purpose did he come here or what is he to do next. The days were warm, and he was near the guava tree since afternoon sitting there with a faraway look, with a foreboding. His face had reddened with the glow of the slanting sun.

The noisy mynas were busy nibbling at the fruits and dropping bits of crushed fruits. Under the tree it smelled sickly sweet of guavas. There were flies all over.

The First Born had sat with him as he did every evening. He decided to go and fetch the Gypsy that evening. You had asked for him earlier as you wanted him to come and help you remove the fruits and prune the trees. There were too many mynas and parrots in the mornings and evenings, and it was becoming a nuisance.

Urja sat with Alfie. She looked at the blue eyes of the unassuming man sitting facing her, hands in his lap, fingers entwined. She noticed for the first time, his spectacular ability to hide his strength in his silences, the illusion he was capable of, the ambitious devotion in keeping his sons together. She saw in him the character of a gambler who had won in his defeat. She liked that solitude of the evening alone with Alfie, just the two of them. When she realised that he would not stop staring at his hands as he sat there quietly, she got up and went to sit next to him. She leaned her head on his shoulder and thought, 'This is my father.' As she felt his warmth on her cheek, she thought, 'It's only bodies that dictate life; the rest is only a result to contend with.' There was nothing complex there. It is always written in our bodies, the instincts, the fire. The thought or analysis comes after out of convention or weariness. Having lived in the brothel she was aware of this truth. She realised that the same truth weaved the destinies of this family. The same truth that led Alfie to abandon her mother and marry Frieda. The same truth that is elegant and primitive and threaded in the blood of the sons. It was neither humiliating nor marvellous. Just memorable.

Jamuna, the betrothed of the second son and Rewa, the betrothed of the fourth son, were there in the kitchen with you. Urja went to her room. Alfie's reverie was broken when he noticed the shrieks of his one-legged myna. It was stuck on the tree on the cable that held a naked bulb. The bird was hanging upside down. Quietly he went and pulled the bamboo ladder from behind the garage and brought it with effort. Thereafter, he leaned it against the sturdiest branch.

He stepped on the first rung, balanced himself and looked up. The bird was far up there. He climbed the second rung easily, holding the sides of the ladder firmly. The bird kept shrieking at the risk of losing the other leg. He then climbed the third, fourth, fifth step and the sixth step slowly. Now he was in the canopy of guava leaves and the fruits. Only the lower part of his pants and sandal-clad feet on the ladder were visible to you from the kitchen as you tasted the kheer you were making. You must stop him, you thought. He held on to the ladder with his left hand and extended the right. One more and he would reach the bird. Urja saw him from her window. She ran out. 'Daddy, come down,' she scolded, ordered and shouted all at the same time.

Alfie was on the seventh step, and he extended his hands and caught the bird. He looked at her triumphantly. The ladder slipped. For that instance, when he was in the air, he realised that this was the end. There was no time for goodbyes at 5:24 pm that March evening. Thud!

Urja shrieked in horror. The birds flew away from the guava tree. The eldest and the Gypsy entered the courtyard running. Someone stopped the cassette player. You dropped the pot of kheer. As you came with a hammering heart, you saw him lying on the ground among the leaves and guavas. His body was lifeless, but his eyes were open defying death. He recognised you as his eyes shone when he saw you. There were tears in his eyes in sorrow as if he was breaking the promise, he had made in the church so many years ago. You sat beside him and held his left hand. He looked at you intently, with more dazzle in those eyes, with more grief in them, with more gratitude in them and most of all, with abundant love brimming over. He managed to say, 'I have only loved you so!' You kissed him on his forehead.

You still had hope in you. 'Get the doctor!' you shouted at no one in particular. After all his eyes were open and radiant as you looked in them. You prayed, 'If this be my last prayer, let him live.' But all your prayers were exhausted. You wanted to reverse time and begin all over again. Differently. You were submerged with rage at yourself and the world and the life you had chosen. The doubts and the un-love you began with. This man had kept all the vows he had taken, maybe impetuously but you had not. Your fragile peace that you had so delicately balanced with the mundane discipline of predictable activity was broken. Yet, you saw his death as a betrayal. When you searched for his other hand, like you always did, to cup it with yours, there was a dead bird in it.

Mynas descended nosily, and sat all over his body. There were others in the guava tree perched like spectators in a stadium. Then began their lament of the birds that was heard miles away in the town that day. People knew that death had arrived for someone.

I noticed. The Gypsy noticed. The First Born noticed. He said, 'Ten for a bird, you must not miss.' There were but ten mynas sitting on his body and singing the lament.

At Alfie's funeral, Your-Highness came. She cried and wailed like a professional mourner. Her dirge was upsetting and the First Born was inconsolable. Urja sat quietly without shedding a tear next to her husband, our First Born.

In her lament, Your-Highness reminisced about the time she had with him. That she was innocent and in love when she gave her body to him. She cared for him when she nurtured him from his accident. And yet, it was not to be that she be his bride. She wailed that she should have been in place of Frieda mourning him rather than as a visitor. She broke her glass bangles melodramatically like a new widow was supposed to do.

She wailed that she had finally given him his daughter as his first daughter-in-law and that when he had a bad accident many years ago, she had nursed him back to health. That her dream of a happy family was completely lost with his passing away and she started beating her bosom and tearing her hair. The more she lamented, the more the townspeople's jaws dropped. They had in any case come in droves because of Your-Highness, following her ranting, from near the river and gathering through the town and welling up like a sea wave in the house. She was revealing secrets in her requiem and people were always curious for some good gossip. You noticed. The silent, wide eyes and the open mouth of a town. Alfie lay dead in his coffin in the courtyard. Even the First Born was looking at her stunned. The only other noise was that made by the mynas in the guava tree.

You were seething with anger and humiliation but gently gathered her and took her inside. As soon as you closed the door behind and picked a glass of water to offer her, she wiped her tears and tidied her face and hair and smiled. You paused.

'I felt the same humiliation the day he married you out of the blue.' She spoke.

You extended the glass of water to her. She drank it too quickly, dribbling it from the sides of her mouth.

'I was carrying his child then.' She revealed.

'Please leave,' you said with dignity and steel in your voice. 'The dead belong only to the family.'

Before the funeral departed for the graveyard, you went to the coffin and kissed Alfie on his cold lips and said, 'My love was late in blossoming, but I loved you. Why else would I give you so many sons to carry forth your name?' You looked at his face sadly. Alfie lay there in his wedding suit. You had put a rose on his lapel from your garden. In the graveyard, you signed the papers from the cemetery warden to reserve a plot of grave next to Alfie's for yourself. Only then you dropped a handful of dirt on the coffin lowered six feet under.

Something shifted in Urja's heart after Alfie's death. She became your nemesis.

On the third day, you came back and planted the rose cuttings from your garden near the head of the grave.

After Alfie's death, age became tedious, and you found memory draining away from your body. You felt that death had brought about an infinite distance between you and Alfie. Sorrow had made your face pale like dull alabaster. Your eyes lost their brightness. Yet, you walked erect with self-respect and determination, something that you never abandoned. Though you retained your elegance, you felt that Alfie's death was an insult. You wondered if the partner that is sadder in a marriage dies before the other partner. After all, Alfie had absorbed all the insults and pain and had stuck with you. You missed spending the hour in the evening when you would speak to him about the sons and the events in their lives and he would give his opinion in a few words. You realised the strength of those few words now, which had guided you all along. You remembered how over time Alfie had changed from an amorous husband with his masculine whims to being a certainty of presence in the house with his consuming need to keep the family together. You understood him better now, his yearning for love and his commitment to your marriage. He had stopped searching for happiness for the sake of stability in your marriage.

Frieda, you were angry with death and with Alfie. He did things you could never anticipate. You felt a rancour towards death for having left you bereft. Every memory of his made you cry, the way he liked his eggs, the way he held your hands when you tucked him at night, the way he would listen to you with intent big blue liquid eyes in his last days, the memories of him walking naked in the house in his youth, his dashing handsome face when he would get ready for work, the odour of his aftershave and the smell of his skin after you had made love, his slippers, his towel still hanging on the hook. The memories and images came inadvertently, and you would stop in the middle of whatever you were doing and would slap your forehead because you remembered something important that you had forgotten to tell him. You remembered how he was in a bad mood for days after the dog culling event.

Those days you would walk around with a lump in your throat. Your memory of Alfie had accentuated his goodness and you remembered his bad with sympathy. You would not sleep well and complain in the morning that the dripping tap resounded with the absence of Alfie the whole night. You had taken your parents' death as a practical culmination of old age and had thought of death as something that happened elsewhere to other people. Alfie's death brought home the fact that you too were disappearing gradually and that you too would turn into memory for others till oblivion absorbed you completely.

One evening, when you went to his room like you did in the evenings, you touched his absence on the bed and found the hollow the shape of his body on the mattress beneath the taut sheet. You followed the contours with your fingers and your eyes welled up. You missed him at the dinner table.

Frieda, you were besieged by solitude, and you found that time had suddenly expanded after Alfie's passing and you squandered it aimlessly by walking from room to room and tidying things that were already tidy. You now disliked sitting at the dining table. It reminded you of Alfie's absence. You said your evening prayers as a matter of routine without meditating and without meaning any of it.

You did not touch a thing is Alfie's room for a year. Then you cleaned his wardrobe and trunks with bitter gusts of camphor mothballs. You piled them all in the backyard and condemned them to fire. You stood sadly stoic while ninety-year-old Badi Bai sat sleeping in the chair and the glowing flames shining the tears that wet her cheeks. Frieda, you had thought that consigning his things to the fire would assuage his memory. But memories turned out to be fire resistant. And the more you tried to forget, the more you remembered. It was worse that you remembered the strength of your feelings but not the details.

You remembered the early days with him. Things like when he had accidentally walked into the bathroom as you were showering and the tremor that ran through you before he apologised and stepped out and shut the door. You remembered the gushing sound of him urinating in the pot in the silence of the night and you thought that it was the first time you had heard a man relieving himself and you found the sound vulgar and uncivil. You remembered that he asked you to soap his back once a week which invariably led him to end up making love to you in soap spuds. You remembered one new year's when you were coming back from the party at YMCA and as the firework started, he stopped the car in the middle of the football field in the cantonment and made uninhibited love with the marvellous explosions in the sky. You wondered if despite all the lovemaking, you were happy with him then. In public you seemed a happy couple, but you knew the misery you carried within. You were already getting tired of putting up a facade of harmony and happiness with him when you had met me. I had rejuvenated a spark in you.

One night after DC had come for the last time asking for his letters, you confronted Alfie, demanding why he had come forward and obliged you to marry him. You cried and argued bitterly and raged about the loss of possibilities until the light cracked in the window. Alfie, groggy with so much talk, exhausted without sleep and tired with so much weeping, got ready, brought you tea and said, 'Frieda, my love, let's start today. We will build the love that two married people build one day at a time. You will see yourself sitting on top of a mountain of love by the time we finish.' He said it so firmly that Frieda, you could not tell him that you had found love in me.

You got the guava tree cut to its roots. You removed all the guava trees from the house and forbade anyone to bring guavas in the house. The mynas were gone. Only Urja made sure she ate a guava every day at her window in full view of everyone. The family learned to be civil in ignoring her defiance.

The only thing you kept was his gramophone and all the records. You would play his jazz records at odd hours, and I would tell others to not disturb you. 'She is on the road in the past. It will bring her relief. She will return. Let her be.' I knew that the only person who would dare to challenge us both would be Urja. I would sit at the door guarding your reverie. Every evening when I sat down for tea with you, your sadness filled my marrows with a painful foam but there was nothing I could do except be present. I, who never prayed, said a prayer like an amateur and wished that your sadness would pass. We had broken conversations without meaning, the sentences suspended mid-air, the commas, and full stops out of place. It was our way of not speaking about things we both did not dare approach and were avoiding. Things like guilt, things like betrayal and things like death. We both struggled to define what we were doing so far away in time from Sheila Aunty's garden and how we reached here from all the pleasure and bliss we had experienced. Sometimes when you looked at me, your grief seared your soul and you found it difficult to breathe. That is when I would hold your hands and then the roses in our garden reminded us of coffins and cemetery.

After Alfie's death, Urja had become quiet. What she felt was a seething anger for you for destroying her life. In Alfie she had found her father that she did not have her entire life and now he was gone. Her mother's dirge at Alfie's funeral revealed secrets about which she wanted to get even with you. She targeted me with her anger. One evening, when everyone was in the courtyard to get some respite from the fire breathing walls of summer, she asked you, 'What is Mahesh Uncle to you, mother-in-law?' Silence descended like a shadow of death.

You just smiled as I held your hand. You were trembling with indignation. You knew someone would ask you this question one day and while you had thought about it many times, there was no answer that you could give that would be socially acceptable. Tears welled in your eyes, but you did not say anything. You let me continue to hold your hand.

With vehemence, she persisted. 'Tell us your secret?'

The Second Son who was sitting with Jamuna, now heavily pregnant with her second child, stood in front of Urja and said, 'Stop it.'

'What will you do if I do not stop?' Urja challenged. Her body was taut with adrenalin, and she seemed to be hunting for blood.

The Second Son simply lifted her from her chair and before the First Born could do anything, he took her to her room and deposited her roughly on her bed. Then he locked the door from outside.

'I will open the door, only when the devil in you is pacified,' he said behind the door. The First Born was at his heels, flustered and unable to do anything. 'Bhai, you will not open the door till she is ready to apologise to mother.'

When the Second Born left, the First Born opened the door and locked it from inside. The two did not come out till the next day. When they came out during dinner time, Frieda, you were gone.

NOTHING WILL HAPPEN TO ME

At four o'clock in the evening, after tea, you called the Gypsy, who was playing his ektara in the courtyard.

'Please get me a rickshaw,' you said.

'Where to?' he asked.

'I don't know.'

'As you wish,' he said and disappeared.

You then went to the Last Son's room and told him, 'I want to go away for some time.' He understood.

With one suitcase, you ascended the rickshaw and said, 'I will give you ten rupees. Just take me around.' You sat erect and we all saw you ride away. I called the Gypsy as soon as you disappeared. 'Follow them at a distance. Ensure she is safe.' And the Gypsy jumped on a cycle. I knew you had left in grief and would be back.

You passed streets with poignant names, houses with guavas and papayas ripening in the heat, silent facades, uneven roofs, bicycles, indifferent humans, curves on the tree-lined roads, corner shops, playgrounds with young men, street cricket with torn balls and makeshift wickets.

The grief had brought a wave of nostalgia and you wanted to return to old places. You told the rickshaw driver to take you to your childhood house in the cantonment. You remembered the roads and your school journeys. The happy unwanted child that you were, only cherished by your meek father and Hannah. You remembered your angry mother. It was only her anger that you remembered and nothing else. You started crying. You wiped off your tears as you reached the house only to find a dilapidated structure with cows and dogs. The place seemed smaller than you had remembered. Then you asked the rickshaw driver to take you to the bungalow, DC's house. As you passed the bungalows made by the British, with arched corridors and circular columns, you remembered your father who tended to the gardens of these bungalows as he worked with the army horticulture department. It was here you had been fascinated by the white ladies learning the dances to waltzes emanating from the turntable in the dark gloom of the salons. You stopped outside DC's bungalow, and something dawned upon you. You got down as the rickshaw driver drank from his glass bottle. You opened the gate and walked to the old mango tree with a hollow which seemed to have nearly closed. You could penetrate it with your fingers and feel a metallic box inside. Your hand would not go in. You rang the bell, and a young Indian Army officer came out. He did not know you.

'I used to live in this bungalow for a short while a long time ago. As a young woman I had put a metallic box in the hollow of the tree. It's still there but the hollow seems to have become smaller. Could you help me extract that?'

The young officer was amused. He asked the orderly to extract the box and asked you to come inside and wait. He offered you a lemonade which you accepted. When the orderly came back, you took the box eagerly, and the officer was intrigued.

'In the 1930s, I was in love with the District Collector who lived here. We were to marry but destiny had other plans. He went back to England.' The young officer was kind and he listened to you with humility. You had this look of nostalgia. It was when the DC had taken you and Noa home and you had worked on your saree. You used to write to him every day but never had the courage to hand him over those letters. It was gratitude and shyness that you did not give him those letters. Noa knew and she was the one who suggested that you leave it with him in this tree trunk. That way it will be with him forever.

'I now have seven sons.' You said with pride as you held the box in your hand.

'What made you remember?' he asked.

'My husband passed away last year.'

The next you asked the rickshaw-wala to take you to the church where you were married. You only felt regret there and did not stop. It was an old church now and you never came back to it after your wedding. You passed the deserted football grounds and evening streets. This road had become better with a thick canopy of trees on the sides. The yellow lamps had started glowing in a very blue evening. You thought of your sister Hannah in heaven now and how she cared for you. You remembered your sister Noa who was now married to an actor in Bombay.

Only when you saw the Narmada Club, did you take out your handkerchief and wiped a tear. You were entering the cantonment area where Alfie had worked.

A policeman on motorcycle stopped your rickshaw. 'You should not be on this lonely road at this time. There are robbers and thieves who do the rounds here. Not to mention the drunkards,' the policeman said. He was polite and concerned.

'I know. Nothing will happen to me,' you said, sternly.

You told the rickshaw-wala to take you to your Niece's. You were disappointed at the unrecognizability of the world and depressed by what you had seen so far. You took no pleasure in this ride and observed with a blank mind the gwalas[1] milking the cows and the others bathing naked at the municipal tap where the water comes only for an hour or so in the evening. You saw the plumes of smoke from the earthen fire stoves that stood outside the tight knit houses for the fire to catch strength

[1] Milkmen.

so that the women could cook dinners. You heard the temple bells and the evening azaan.

In the night you reached the Niece's house in the periphery of town and knocked at the door. You almost fainted when you saw her. She was thin and old, unlike what you had remembered her to be. There were a couple of poorly clad but healthy children playing about.

'I have come to stay with you,' you said.

Your sister, Sarah, had got her daughter, your Niece, married to the first man who had proposed. He was a poor clerk in the municipality, and the Niece had not recovered from her lost love. Though the Niece held you responsible for damaging that alliance and her subsequent misery, she respected you and loved you enough to welcome you.

You recovered from your initial shock of grief in a few days in the new home. The food was frugal but nourishing. The Niece had given you the children's bedroom and you had your comfort and privacy. You refused to go to the church with them and enjoyed the few hours of solitude every Sunday.

Every night she came to your room with a cup of warm milk and you both sat there and chatted. The children would be asleep, and the husband who worked another job to substantiate his income, never returned home before midnight. Sometimes she made your hair and tied two braids other times you made her hair.

One day affectionately you said, 'Remember the time you spent with us? You were the first among the family to come and stay with me. I liked you staying with us.'

'Did I have a choice? I was only eight years old.'

'I already had four sons and the youngest was one year old. But I took care of you.'

'How two people remember the same thing differently,' she said.

'Weren't you happy?' you asked, surprised.

'I felt abandoned all the time without Mama and Papa. I remember playing behind the house, under the tamarind tree the whole day. Badi Bai would look after the bigger boys and you were busy with the smallest. Only Alfie Uncle gave me company. While I played under the tamarind tree, he would sit and keep a watch without ever saying a word. In the afternoons you and Mahesh Uncle would retire to have siesta and the hot sun, the tamarind tree and Alfie Uncle would be by mates. I had made a rag doll out of the undershirt Alfie Uncle gave me and I would speak with her. My face and clothes were unwashed for days and only sometimes you would notice and ask Badi Bai to give me a bath. I was almost invisible in your house.' She was crying. You held her to your bosom and cried with her.

'Don't cry over the time that is past.' You patted her back.

Then the other day she asked, 'Aunty, did you ever love me?'

'Why do you ask?' you asked.

'Because I am not sure.'

'Of course, I love you. But I could never love you more than my sons.'

After a pause the Niece said, 'I understand. I could not love you more than my Mama.'

You had been there at her place for more than three weeks when the Niece asked, 'Aunty, do you like my home? I know it is humble and it has its troubles.'

You affectionately said, 'See, I have not missed my home for so long. I am glad I came to you.'

'Does it make you happy?'

'I love your warmth.'

'And the misery?'

You knew it would end up to this. Acts of the past catch up sometime.

'It was not my fault.'

'But it was, I had confided in you. I was only eighteen.'

'I had seen so much humiliation and disrespect because I had loved men and I did not want you to go through that.'

'Do you think my humiliation now happens to be any lesser?'

'Who is to say?' you sighed. You knew what you had done. When you saw that the Niece, a beautiful, young woman was getting happiness and fulfilment from her life, that demon rose for a few moments in your heart. Deliberately you had spoken about it to the few women at church and it had become a scandal. You had spoken about her affair with the young doctor, half Muslim, half Christian, who wanted to marry her. You had also told Sarah, that his family has members who suffer from tuberculosis and that it will create problems for the Niece all her life. Sarah had refused to meet the doctor and got aggravated, 'I have three other daughters. If she elopes and defames the family, who will marry my other two?' It was déjà vu for you. She had spoken like your mother.

The Niece did not marry the man she loved. Sarah had got her married off with the first man who brought a formal proposal.

That night you were sad and could not sleep.

The next day when the Niece brought the milk, you held her wrist and said, 'Sit down, I want to talk to you.'

She took the enamel comb and stood near the headboard and gathered your hair. As she combed you said, 'My biggest regret is to have two men in my life. I loved your Alfie Uncle though it came late. But I have loved Mahesh too. When I became pregnant with the First Son, I had resolved to stop meeting Mahesh. My ambition to be a mother was fulfilled. I was prepared to live my life with Alfie alone. But then Alfie brought Mahesh home and gave him the annexe to live in. That proximity broke barriers between him and me.'

She continued to comb your hair.

'Life would be worse without Mahesh. I would eventually learn to love Alfie because of the love that Mahesh showered on me. In the beginning, I would be angry with him all the time and there was a feud in my mind that I fought with him for coming forth to marry me in the church. I found that humiliating as that obliterated my choice in the matter. Only much later after the children were born did I realise that my life would be destroyed had Alfie not come forward that day. My internal feuds with him vanished over the course of time and I did not know when love emerged. In fact, my love came wrapped with my fault and guilt and I decided to never forsake him.

I knew that the children lived with the pain and strangeness of the adult relationships in my home. They developed an imprecise sadness and a deep sense of lack of normalcy of a regular family. The First Born always reminds me of Alfie, the way he speaks, the way he eats and in his behaviour. The youngest reminds me of Mahesh mainly because he is a spitting copy of him.

They say you feel it in your bones first. I felt that for Mahesh when he came with the hordes of children to retrieve the kite fallen in my garden. A thought flashed across my mind like lightning; he will bring children with him. That thought yet incompletely formed shocked me. I destroyed that thought as soon as it emerged. That was no way to think for me. I was married to Alfie.

When the impetuousness of passion has passed, when the brutal expectation from hope has passed, when the ghosts of illusion have passed, only a weariness of living is left behind. Love remains love but like clots in clusters of memories, that become heavy in old age. The old age smells strange with the odour of fermentation of muscles with each breath. When

I do the arithmetic of my life, there were more difficulties than pleasure, more humiliation than honour, more anger than empathy, more responsibilities than leisure. I have tried to remain happy during my squabbles with days and nights, during my difficult balancing act of emotions with two men in my life, during nurturing seven sons who all had developed their own way of dealing with the complexities of our lives. In all of that, I did not pay much attention to how difficult love can be. Now when I think about it as I am ambushed with old age, love was ephemeral. It passed quickly and seems like an unreality of a dream. But sometimes one beat echoes with the silvery resonance of that vibration, that memory and brings back the yearning in the heart which this tired body struggles to register and savour.

'I took respectability from Alfie, and I took fertility from Mahesh Babu. I was the wife of one and the lover of another. I drove Alfie to his alcoholism and gave Mahesh Babu no legal status. Even his children call him Uncle. When I gave Alfie six sons, Mahesh Babu demanded the last one. That was his fight for recognition. I could not say no. So, in my house there is always a struggle between the blood and the name. I had been excommunicated by the church and my children have been called bastards. The whole world has been the audience of my situation for years. We are a whispered saga of the society. Now I have four daughters-in-law and sometimes I see questions in their eyes. The eldest one has no respect for me. She mocks me and questions me about who Uncle is. So, darling, I bless you that you have strength and that you have honour that I never had. I wanted to live my life with honour, but it has eluded me so far.'

The Niece had bent and hugged you and kissed you on your soft old cheeks.

Then you said, 'I did all this by destroying the lives of two women—Girija, the one Mahesh married and Your-Highness, Urja's mother, whom Alfie should have married.

My home is built on the carcasses of many. I will never be absolved of the destruction that my need to have children caused in so many lives. I have remembered this as my guilt and have tried doing good by others so that I may be vindicated. But Urja comes as a retribution of all those accumulated wrongs. I understand this. Yet, I am unable to bear the humiliation now when the dusk is settling in my bones and twilight in my breath.' You were crying. The Niece held you tightly to her bosom.

One day, you took out an old, folded paper and asked the Niece to read. She read a few lines and looked at you and smiled.

'This is "Bright Star" by John Keats. I didn't know you read poetry,' the Niece said, affectionately.

'This was given to me by DC. It came in one of his letters. I did not understand much of it in the first instance, and he would explain it to me in subsequent letters. It was also an excuse for him to write to me. This poem brings warmth in my heart. Go on, read it aloud. I want to hear it.'

You sat mesmerised listening as the Niece read the poem. Over the last fifty years, you had read it so many times that you remembered it by heart. Every time you would read it, you would imagine someone who could love you like that. The faces changed from DC to Mahesh to Alfie, and it would bring back your faith when you found life difficult.

'I have framed a copy of this poem and it hangs in my bedroom.' You told her shyly like a schoolgirl after she had read it twice for you.

When a month passed, I knew that your inability to return was not because of the unwillingness but because of the inability to come around the humiliation by Urja. The Gypsy had followed you the day you had left, and we knew where you were. We were relieved that you had chosen to go to the Niece's house. So, without notifying, exactly after one month,

I knocked at her door precisely at 11 am. The sons and I missed you and it was time for you to come home.

When you saw me, you thought you would die of joy, but you remained stoic. 'Thank God,' you thought. I followed you into the kitchen and sat opposite you. You continued stuffing the bitter gourd that you were preparing for lunch.

'You have come uninvited. Who told you I was here?' you asked. 'I would have taken a bath and made my hair and dressed properly had I known you were coming…,' you said.

'The Gypsy followed you here the other day,' I said.

You finished making the lunch. 'They are at work and the children are at school.' You told me about the Niece's family. Then you wiped your hands on the apron and left me waiting at the table in the kitchen. You came back after your shower, looking clean and well arranged. We had lunch together and when it was exactly 2 pm, the Niece arrived with her two children.

'Lovely to see you, Uncle,' she said as she hugged me. She was genuinely affectionate and happy to see me despite her tiring day at work.

'I hope you had lunch. I guess you have come for Aunty?'

'Yes, we have missed her. We will leave shortly. Let her gather her things.'

'Shall I make lemonade for you before you leave?'

'No no…we are fine.' I had said patting her arms.

As we left, I tucked some money in the children's hands. 'This is for you to buy chocolates,' I said.

And you kissed the children and hugged the Niece. 'Keep our conversations as a gift that I bequeath you. Keep my confidence and dignity. I hope the secrets of my lifetime will be safe with you.'

With your head held high, back straight, shining eyes and a demeanour of control and grace, you came with me. I felt the same relief that you felt at coming back home in the sigh you made in the rickshaw.

LOOK, SHE DOES NOT CAST A SHADOW

When that woman in pink saree entered the house one day, a few months after Alfie's death, the whole household was transfixed with her beauty. Her splendour was so magnificent that everyone wondered what she desired in our house.

The door opened without creaking and Urja, who saw her first, quivered at the sight of so ethereal a woman. The light radiated from her skin with the texture of youth. She wore a pastel pink saree with pearls in her ears. Her midriff looked soft and the way she had tied her saree far below her navel, sent butterflies in the stomach of the sons when they saw her.

She came without an escort and smelled of tuberoses and spices. Her power was apparent in the confidence with which she carried herself and her manner demanded that she be obeyed.

'I have come to meet Frieda.' She announced.

It was mid-morning and Jamuna and Rewa were still tidying the house. The Gypsy stopped playing his ektara in the courtyard. Everybody sensed a change in an invisible energy that swept the house like a wave.

'Please wait, I will call her,' Urja said.

She smiled. The crimson lips with velvet on them seemed like in a dream and revealed the pearls of teeth fresh from the oysters. That smile wounded the women with its beauty and the men felt doomed deep in their viscera. You walked in with your apron on and spots of turmeric in your fingers. As you wiped your fingers on the apron, you were taken aback by that strange, beautiful woman who stood before you. You turned pale. You recognised the smell. It was the same smell of nutmeg, cloves and rose water that you smelled each time you had used your three prayers. You felt a stirring that dropped your heart into the pit of your stomach.

'I want a bouquet full of colours. Make it as large as you can make it. I cannot tell you the occasion.'

She gave an envelope with money. She touched the cheeks of Urja lightly with her lips and turned to leave. The Sixth Son came out of his bath and was still wrapped in only a towel when he saw her cross the courtyard.

'What is she doing here?' he thought as he crossed her. Then said, 'Look, she does not cast a shadow.' Before anyone could spot the shadow, she was gone.

That night Badi Bai died in her sleep. She was ninety years old.

Something else happened that day. The First Daughter-in-Law started hissing. Her words, so far dipped in defiance and sarcasm, were now coated with viscous vitriol. And as we tried to catch those words, it left a brown burning on the skin from where her words ricocheted. The First Born looked helplessly.

After Badi Bai's funeral, you became busy with flowers. Flowers of all colours. Intense to pastels to white. Your room was full of fragrance. The trellis of your eyelashes was usually covered with pollen, and you isolated yourself with the flowers. You were losing interest in the world around you. The only person you spoke with now was the Gypsy and only when it was necessary.

Another thing happened after Badi Bai's funeral. Urja found the box you had given Badi Bai to destroy after DC had visited you nearly fifty years ago. It was found tucked away in the corner of an iron box, which was locked. It had the letters from DC and the pearls he had given you. Urja read each letter. And re-read them. Her colour changed to pale blue as she read those letters, like she was imbibing poison.

You created the bouquet in a most magnificent design and colours. Any angle you looked at it, it told a story in light and sparkle. Uneasy till it was deciphered. You knew the woman would be able to understand. It was completed in ten days.

In the meantime, the First Born had his hands burnt deep brown in a few days. The rest of the family avoided Urja.

On the eleventh day, when the woman in pink saree returned, it seemed as if she had not left. The Sixth Son opened the door. She looked the same. He felt a soft chill as he led her to your room. She quivered in front of the bouquet, like a mirage quivering in the desert. She gasped at the magnificence in front of her and some of her arrogance dissolved in the fragrance of the bouquet. The flowers reflected their colours on her complexion, and she seemed pink and blue and purple and yellow and orange and red and white and ochre and green and all the shades in between. She moved in a trance. Thoughts were suspended in the air as she moved around, and agonies found home in the bones. Her astonishment also changed colours. She touched a flower and it turned black. The whole synergy was lost. The harmony and balance got disfigured. Then she pulled a rose by the pinch of her thumb and the first finger, and the mystery of cohesion was broken and the whole bouquet came apart. All the flowers wilted and fell. It reminded you of your wedding when the flowers tucked to your blouse had wilted and the butterflies from your crown had flown away. A drop of nervousness rolled down your spine as a bead of sweat.

She raised her chin satisfied and said, 'This is very delicate and precarious. Please make me another.'

You knew your art. You had never failed before.

You said, 'I need a strand of hair and an object from the person you want to give this.'

She smiled and said, 'I'll make a deal.' And she pulled a strand of her hair, the colour of light and gave you. Then she said, 'Use something of yours.' She left like a breeze. You turned pale.

You asked the Gypsy to dig a grave in the backyard and bury those flowers.

The Sixth Son came to me that night. He said, 'We must prepare now.'

'For what, son?' I asked.

'Don't you see her soul is camouflaged in the flowers? Our mother wants to go on a journey.'

'I don't understand,' I said.

'She will tell you soon.'

That night you sat numb and broken hearted with your shadow brittle and shattered in the little yellow light.

The next day, powerless, driven by an unseen force, you started the work again with an obsession in which you forgot to eat and drink. The First Born came with dinner on the third day and stayed back as you required help to sort the flowers. It was midnight when Urja's voice was heard resounding the courtyard.

'What are you doing with that prostitute mother of yours?' You were struck like someone had pierced a bullet in your chest. You clutched your heart and fell. I ran to pick you.

The First Born slapped Urja with a force.

'My hands burn with your words. I will douse this fire before it burns the house down.' I had never seen him angry in my life. She did not stop.

She clutched her cheek and seemed devil incarnate. 'Why is Uncle picking her up? What is he to her? She betrayed my father all her life shamelessly. Poor man died with a broken heart. She keeps two men and is respected. Mummy this, Mummy that. She calls my mother a prostitute, she abhors her, whose place she took in Daddy's life. But who knows how many men she has had? What difference does it make if it's two or twenty?' She was in flames ready to burn the house down.

'Please leave my house.' The First Born said with a restrained seething anger.

'And make your children prostitutes like Daddy Alfie did his women?'

'Stop, all of you! Son, take her to your room. And forgive her,' you said with sweat and pain running through your body.

You were in pain and yet you called the Gypsy. You told him something sotto voce.

In the morning when you did not come out of your room, I came to look for you. I was shocked to see you lying in the coffin in the middle of the room. Sunlight fell on your face but there was peace. Your breathing was slight. I called the doctor. You had slipped into coma. Your sugar level was remarkably high, he informed us. The Gypsy was adamant that you not be moved to the hospital because that was your wish.

Since then, you have laid in this coffin, and I spend my entire time telling you stories. The doctor said you can hear but that you will not respond.

I Have Stopped Climbing Stairs

The Sixth Son is standing fixed in the far corner of the room like taxidermy art. Everything is still. The large windows are open, and flood of warm sunlight falls on you. I, who is protective and alert, did not notice her nor feel her presence till I saw her near the head of the casket. The same pastel saree, the same luminous skin and the same out of this world, dazzling beauty. She did not have the shadow even though she was standing against the sun. She kept looking at your face smiling and stroking your forehead with utmost gentleness.

The Sixth Son came alive with that smile and rushed to you. The visitor held him by the back of his neck and slid her tongue into his mouth. 'How you have wanted this since you were six!' the red lips quivered, and she gave him a passionate kiss. She licked his face and bit his earlobe. Heat rose through his body, and I could see the colour rising on his face. I was rooted to my chair and could not even move. And then she was gone.

'She sniffed my soul and her lips tasted like honey,' the Sixth Son said as we all sat in the courtyard that evening. 'She is just doing what she does. We must say our goodbyes, tonight she will descend like a wave on the stones and take our mother away.'

Frieda, all the men are worshippers. Specially yours. We stood with reverence and affection. The seven sons, me and the Gypsy. Each of us loved you in our own way. Each kissed you one last time.

Then Jamuna and Rewa came one after the other and kissed you. Urja refused. Koel came later and she also kissed you on your hands.

In the morning twilight before sunrise, the woman with the pink pastel saree and luminous skin, smelling of tuberoses and spices, came with the most beautiful bouquet and swallowed your soul with a kiss. At the funeral, the Sixth Born saw her fizzle and dissipate in smoke as the mourners threw earth at your casket in your grave. The world became quiet, and the flowers deserted our garden. The house was taken aback by your absence and till today the roses do not bloom in the bushes you had planted.

Now I am the only one remaining. I smell silver oaks, mango, frangipani as I walk to your grave. The gravel crunches under my feet and there are birds singing in the graveyard. I come to your grave and wipe the dust with my hands. I light the candle and incense and sit near your grave. The rose bush planted from cuttings from your garden are growing profusely here. They smell like you. Alfie and your graves can be spotted from anywhere in the cemetery. The rose bushes have covered the headstones of your graves with such intensity and with such authority that they are known as the Graves of the Roses.

I sit there and ponder about our lives. The seeds we sow do not bring life until the seeds die and are consumed. Our bodies are seeds, perishable but what comes from it is utterly imperishable. Look at our sons and their children. They who come through us will live and grow and we will live in them. With our love, our aberration, our understanding, and our madness. I do not ignore Alfie who is buried next to you. He was my friend, perhaps the greatest one there ever was.

Frieda, you had saved the last cigarettes of Alfie. Now dry and brittle, they were found in your lingerie drawer tucked under your clothes. Reminder of a love that Alfie made with a cigarette in his fingers. They also found an old bottle of cedar and cinnamon aftershave that belonged to Alfie. The remnants of love were being discovered as treasures. What remains strictly private, when a person is alive, becomes public after the dignity of life is stripped away by death. There was nothing of mine that you had saved. Perhaps because my gifts are the seven sons!

When the Last Born showed me these things, I remembered Alfie. I admired Alfie. I liked his elegance, the fluidity and precision of his words, the cinnamon and cedar smell of his aftershave, easy personal charm, total absence of spite and the suave way he spoke made his conversations engaging. He was full of charisma and smiled easily when we were young. I saw him change and wilt like the flowers in your bridal blouse the day you got married. I have carried the burden of guilt. It becomes heavier as I grow old. One thing about old age is that there is no redemption from it. It is never kind to anyone.

As much as I was possessed by your love, I found it impossible to have you to myself completely. The best part in a day were the few hours we spent together. I learnt to live with the leftover hours, like discarded morsels you could give me after you had cared for the sons, for Alfie and after you had spent hours in the kitchen or planning for the smooth running of the household. Sometimes a few extra hours brought joys of togetherness when they were least expected because you had finished a task early or Badi Bai had taken over or the Gypsy had discharged the errand that I was supposed to do. Frieda, you enjoyed spending time with the sons. You made sure you spent half an hour with one son individually once a week and with seven sons you had time for every son that way. You solicited their counsel and got them involved in the family affairs however distracted they were or however small the resources in the house were. Sometimes I was frustrated that you were the efficient queen of your empire, and I was just an outpost territory. But this thought could never find home in my heart. I knew I was important for you and that was enough for me to carry on. Because Alfie depended on you completely, whenever you would ask about the dinner menu or guest list or what you should wear for a party, he would say, 'Whatever you wish! I am sure it will be wonderful!' He was telling the truth. This would get you worked up. All flustered, you would then speak with me about it. I would ask questions and give considered suggestions and ideas. I would tell you what combinations of dishes you should plan for, what combinations of colours would suit you in sarees, and you would feel nurtured and important. I was interested in your small domestic conundrums. I found them charming and liberating, helping normalise a life that was tarnished in the eyes of society. Among the three of us, our relationship acquired a naturalness and a rhythm where each of us managed within the physical and emotional boundaries that were established over time as we put on weight and as the slowness of age descended on us. Together we would battle the world outside our home, overcome the societal incomprehension, react little to the nastiness and hatred. We had arrived at a balance when the physical attraction had faded, and mutual dependence has acquired a flavour of affection that each of us basked in without excess and hurry.

I have stopped climbing stairs after what happened to Alfie. I know, it was a ladder and not stairs but with old age, one minor fall brings the embrace of death. My misfortune came in the form of a stroke. 'Don't do this to me,' I prayed to God. It reversed my role with the children. They gave me care and courage to carry on. My lucidity became clouded. I needed to sleep all the time then.

The Sixth Son takes care of me. He married Koel, the singing girl. In marrying her, our house became the house of crows.

He helps me bathe and change my clothes. I cannot control the muscles and he helps me move my limbs and he cleans my drool as I do not realise that it escapes my mouth and soils my clothes. He has started putting a bib on me, like you do for a child. He gives me enemas, holds the chamber pot at intervals, he applies compresses on my bedsores and gives me massages to keep the circulation healthy. He recognises my sadness. He has shifted into my room. He makes sure that my immobility does not create more severe ailments. He talks to me affectionately and sometimes Koel comes and sings in my room. I find it calming and sometimes I sleep as she sings softly. He has also brought the old gramophone that belonged to Alfie, in my room and plays it softly in the afternoons. The songs that you liked, Frieda. So, in a way, my time with you in the afternoons continue. Although now it's with your memory in Sheila Aunty's garden.

The Last Son has proposed to the levitating dancer. You remember, he stole all her tutus for many days. Till there were no more tutus to be found in the city. When she decided in the strangeness of missing tutus, to pack and leave, his temperature started rising. He could not bear the thought of her leaving and he picked one tutu and gave it to her saying he found it under the pile of other clothes. She was ecstatic. She put it on and started pirouetting. His temperature started dropping. Then when she was leaving for her performance, she kissed him on his cheeks. Her lips burned and tingled and that gave it a nice red hue.

So, every day he would give her a new tutu and hide away the old one and every day she would give him a kiss to take away the rouge on her lips.

One day when a kiss was just not enough, she put her tongue in his mouth. Though hot in the beginning, his mouth started to cool down after a while. As he stood bare-chested drying the laundry, she touched his chest with her palms and that area cooled. She removed her clothes and stood skin to skin with him. The places her skin touched his, he cooled on those spots. He felt sensations of hot and cold that he had never felt before and it was exhilarating for him. When they made love, he did not scald her uterus.

And that is how the dancing, levitating woman with red lips entered our household after you were gone.

They have put photographs on the mantle. Of Alfie and you, on your wedding day. You can see the lack of affection in your pursed lips and the way you look out of the frame, and he has a smile full of doubt. There is another photograph of Alfie and me, both with warm smiles and looking straight at the camera. There are seven photographs of each of the sons when they are six months old, taken in the same studio. There are wedding day photos of the first, second, fourth and sixth sons and their brides. The seventh will join this echelon soon. His photograph is yet to come from the studio.

I remember, after WWII ended, I took a part time job at the local Congress branch. I could find work but that would have required me to be away the entire day. The only time with you that I could get was the afternoons and I was not willing to sacrifice that. So, whatever little I could make with my nascent political work, I would bring home.

In 1956 after the States reorganisation, Congress Party agreed to give me the ticket for contesting the municipal elections. First Son was sixteen and had started working part time at the film theatre as an usher. Second Son was fifteen and he was besotted by Jamuna. Third Son was always reading and when not reading, he was helping you. Others were small then. I won the elections. I started getting a small salary. Corruption was rampant, but I stayed clean. You and I had discussed this many times that my public life will be for the good of the people I represent. That will be my redemption.

Alfie had become the myna whisperer.

You remember in the 1961 elections, they made me responsible for public works. I started staying away for inspections and for the political work that I was doing. Urja came a year later into our home when India and China went to war. She disliked you and hated me. The First Born was besotted and she was good to him. I had spoken to an old friend of mine who was a General Manager in the defence factory to get our First Son the job of a sub-foreman. He had started earning a regular salary now. The Second Son was jobless and spent all his time at home waiting for Jamuna. The Third Son continued to remain in his feverish world of imaginary women. The Fourth Son was often absconding from school and in the river swimming. The others were still small.

Then four years later, the Fourth Son left home in search of Rewa. Alfie agreed. You sent Gypsy each month to find out how and where he was. Nothing changed with the Second Son. You wanted him settled but he refused to marry. The Third Son started working in the Municipal Library as a librarian. He refused to marry. The women were not as attractive as in his imagination. He continued to search for the one that could match his imagination. This son of ours was destined to always remain a bachelor.

It was that time when the Fifth Son nearly died from the glass shards that he stabbed himself with. You used your third and final prayer then.

In the 1967 elections, I wanted to run for the Legislative Assembly, but was not given the ticket. I was told that the stakes were high, and that the opposition will bring up my personal life. I was politely refused the ticket due to personal conduct. I was livid, but you calmed me down and said there is so much to do at home.

Alfie and I had become amicable to one another, and we spent the evenings together. I talked politics most of the time and he listened. The Hindi film music played in the background.

The boys had all grown up and were doing their own things. The Sixth was doing his BA then but spending a lot of time with Aslam. The Last Born was hiding tutus those days.

Then Alfie passed away. Then Badi Bai passed away.

Badi Bai died of a broken heart. She had taken care of Alfie all her life and with him passing away, she lost the will to live. While you were still dealing with your grief, you gave Badi Bai proper last rites in accordance with the practices of Islam. Then Urja found the box you had given to Badi Bai many years ago. It contained letters from DC and the pearls and the wedding saree he brought you. It was the ammunition Urja needed to berate and humiliate you. All hell broke loose.

Then you left the house for an entire month.

When you came back, the Sixth Son brought the singing girl to give her refuge in our home. Now it was the turn of the intermittent crows after the persistent mynas.

When you were here in the casket preparing to die, only the Gypsy and I remained. I, in this room telling you about our life and the Gypsy, outside playing his ektara.

The First Born comes and sits with me each evening after work as he used to do with Alfie. He does not speak much but I like his presence. Urja does not come. She despises me. The other sons also come and visit me. The Last Son reminds me of myself at twenty-four. That was when I had met you, Frieda. He ensures that I am well nourished. He has brought the old radio also in my room and I listen to the news. The first news that I listened after you passed was that India and Pakistan had entered into war over East Pakistan. The last news that I listened to was about Mrs. Gandhi lifting the Emergency.

Between the last two news and the sons, nearly seven years have passed. I am well taken care of.

I miss my brothers. They don't come. They still think that I am a blot on the family name. I have sent word to them many times through the Gypsy. All they say is they will come. I know they will come. They will be here for my dead body.

ALL IS SAID AND DONE AND MORE

Desires ran so deep, that I threw my life into it. Never to emerge on the other side. Death has been experienced with others. But it is the experience that matters. It's not love that matters anymore. All is said and done and more.

How do I begin after you? I saw the burning bush. The sun arose from its roots. Burning the air around. No covenants. No commandments. Days swept under the demands of living and loving. I loved Alfie as my brother. For his graciousness in destruction.

Demanding me to feel it! I have rolled in the days. Like a drum. Worshipped the only Goddess I knew. Every day. No dogma just circumstances. That's the world we ever lived in. Everything was spectacular. Happiness was a concept. Guilt was real.

So much has been taken. So much has been given. Traces left behind.

Stay with me. Hold me. Be mine. You said. Not like an autumn leaf full of colours and dying. Ambitions, fear, religion, music were all the perils of youth. Paths had run awry. Heads turned in different directions.

Give me something the world cannot give. Peace. I will not crawl down from the heady heights of your breath on my neck. Not that I dislike altitude. I wanted to fly. With you to the heavens. Where can I go by myself? Without you, I will always be the same. Lost, rudderless, like a kite cut from its strings that I had come to retrieve so many years ago. You recognised it in your bones. What am I supposed to do now?

So much has been taken. So much has been given. Traces left behind.

Things did not make sense. When you asked me to move into your home. Never have, yet I waited for an epiphany, for a sign that it was love and not lust. Truly. And that damnation I felt when I came across Alfie each day. Pieces of life never coming together. I keep thinking. A new start will make the difference. So many new starts. Each son a new hope. I had become a wanderer. Travelling inside my mind.

I have wreaked havoc on people I have loved. By confounding them about my place in the world. What does anyone want from me anymore? Seven sons that carry my blood but not my name. Except one.

You said, I could give you a dream. You may close to live in it. Look at my eyes. Touch my face. I have done what you asked.

So much has been taken. So much has been given. Traces left behind.

Remember the burn. The whispering. Each person a guide to God. Strange life of a pilgrim. Finding the way. From darkness to light. From mind to the heart. Hands on the bed. I rock back and forth. Only there remains no movement. Except in the head.

I am scared. Fifty years. I have been giving life. Or just ruining it. Carefully, diligently, day by day. For others and me. I can't remember the man I wanted to be. What makes a man? A woman when she holds him night after night. It was a troublesome existence.

So much has been taken. So much has been given. Traces left behind.

I have lived a fantasy. Everyday. Being what I wanted to be. A saint or a sinner. A father or a lover. There is no forever. Forever is an instant that is burned in your mind.

Sometimes I think I knew more about the world, about love, about you. Long ago I used endorphins to ignite my days. It opened the windows of instantaneous truths. Built a world full of colours and visions. I saw things from the annexe that other people did not. I was a permanent observer in the household from the distance of a garden.

So much has been taken. So much has been given. Traces left behind.

How do I stay there? How do I get out of the cloud of confetti days and sparkling nights? Let humanity kick in... Breathe. Breathe!

My mind is a bioscope that you and I made, Frieda. I sit back and watch it. Dream it as a new dream. My mind is a gramophone. A new music each day. What makes me happy? Being in love with one woman all my life. Prosperity and fame or poverty and disgrace? Here, take anything you want. It can be yours, Life said. I chose liberty with a key in the bosom. Called it a covenant of love and blood.

So much has been taken. So much has been given. Traces left behind.

How did I reach you? Found my way to be there with you? Fireworks, a bright morn, I relinquished all with a bride by my side. I parched her earth and scratched her days. Am I guilty I loved you? Are you guilty that you robbed your sons of their real names?

Utopia is rare. Only few find it. We paid attention to the moments. Everything in there is perfect and complete. Just as it should be. White walls, orange tree, red roses that do not bloom anymore. Why are you so quiet, Frieda? People dream of those gone away. You dreamt of those that were yet to come. I don't dream but feel your constant presence. A sense of waiting had crept into me. Waiting to find a path to reach you again.

So much has been taken. So much has been given. Traces left behind.

I am the only one left behind. To burn on the path. Like tears in canals. Like rails on the tracks. How do I begin now? I walk on the barren land bereft of dreams, lacking in air. Lord, give me courage, strength and gratitude. Let it be the way, you supposed it to be. Let thy will be done!

Bamboo trellis fence. A bright star in the sky. Cars on the road. Children playing and chattering and laughing. Guide me on my way. The light above. And the light within. Speak with each other and push me. Breathe. Breathe! Do not die, Mahesh!

You are beautiful and desirable. I am still drawn to you. To your surreal presence I give up this marvel of life. To eternity. For your voice and its timber. I will wait to reach you after I am gone.

So much has been taken. So much has been given. Traces left behind.

EPILOGUE

I knew.

Lying on the ground feet towards the south, I knew. They tied my toes. But it was not over yet.

The world floats, shimmering and quivering, with whitewashed whispers, a spring light catching my eyes, I regard my departure. I am repeated in an echo, its Rig Veda that is being read. In a horizon bound in smoke, I emerge with half profile of sweetness and fragrance and the other half of sorrow. The gold and ochre, the music of silence throbbing, giving wings to my heart. The language consequently fell silent and has fallen off my body. They have descended in a swoop and will take me to the house I was born. My brothers are here. I hear them in silver muffled whispers that turn to iron when they speak to the First Born. They asked him to take a bath and now he is in a white dhoti. They extracted the fire from the kitchen. Dead Frieda's kitchen.

I am content to watch. It is my body that is being cleaned with ghee and turmeric. I do not make a sound lest it break the mourning. Everything is exaggerated, and the silk hued extravagance amazes me. The randomly traced lines of the bamboo annex my body. First Born has tears. Frieda's kitchen fire sits covered in a pot near my head. I feel its warmth like Frieda's breath.

I feel alone and bewildered and need succour in the face of this spasm. I still do not know if it's the gods or the devil that bewilder me and makes me see what should be unseen. This is neither life nor a dream but the fear of epiphany, of knowledge that my soul does not know yet. It is a miracle of tenderness as my life and its meaning, my struggles and its penury, my affections and its aftermath have ended. I am now no more what I was or what I seemed. Now it seems that love is nothing but something other than what is hidden inside it. Though I have transgressed, I am yet to meet my Maker and become one with His vastness.

They have invoked Rudra. The First Born beseeches that my body be submitted to my Maker in its glory and splendour. He is protecting me from the evil and devils that may devour my body on this journey to eternity and he provides the ablution of tears as he puts rice on my mouth. They have untied my toes. I do not feel the flames as the fire baptises me. It's spectacular how Agni takes my body limb after limb, fibre after fibre and embraces it. I cease to exist. The *kapaal kriya* hurts, even though there is nothing but emptiness in there.

I find myself without a body, without a forehead, without the silence of your eyes, without the vision of your parting lips verged on revealing to me your love. I am now on a voyage. Yet, they hold me in a stone. Prashanam. They take my ashes and touch it with milk. The First Born with his back to Narmada, empties me in the river. I float and swim.

The First Born is commanded to stay at the Baada for thirteen days. You are his First Born and you should do your kartavya[1]. His head is shaved but a small island of hair remain at the top. He takes bath with cold water and stays in the room with Prashanam. He keeps an offering of water and sesame every day. He is given food once a day. There is a burning lamp and a framed picture of my youth. I stay with the First Born. He loved Alfie the most but now he knows. That it is my blood that nourishes his bones. In his aloneness, people come in white. They sit in front of the photo and the lamp. When they speak, the vowels are heavy as lead, and the sentences drag themselves, sinuous, like a reptile's tail. They speak spitting words and maps and histories. They speak with immaculate flesh and sharply edged mouths. Dizzy, they speak of games

[1] Duty.

of chance, puddles of piss and sentimental historic quagmire. They accuse him of being the First Born.

On the third day, an old woman comes. She touches his face and sits looking at the First Born. Then she says, you look just like him. The First Born does not know her. They sit quietly. You should have been born of my womb, but Frieda took you. I feel guilt that cannot be absolved. It is a very live feeling. I kept waiting for him and kept myself from living. The First Born does not understand. I am Girija. He married me a long time ago. The First Born touches her feet. And she says, you should have been born out of my body. Then she leaves like an ancient regret.

On the tenth day, the Prashanam is destroyed. Grief has reduced and wilted the First Born. Sanskrit chants of the Rig Veda waft from the earth as things become smaller and smaller. First the people, then the houses, then the trees then the earth.

I meet the ancestors, in spirit, on the twelfth day as the First Born brings the rice pinds[2] together. The hymns and bells are sweet and the flowers blooming and beautiful. The sky is streaked with colours of the rainbow as rain washes over me. There is an umbrella, a gold coin, rice and ghee that are given to the brahmin.

The light has burst with the songs of the bugles. The wind has begun its symphony in the forest. I glance at the world and hold it all with its seas and the mountains dangling in the air, with the oceans rising to wave a goodbye, with light filtered through agate clouds. I am all light, leaping from one cloud to another, each beckoning me to take me faster and closer to Almighty.

It is the thirteenth day. As the Gita is recited, the First Born still in his dhoti and bare chest, serves food to the brahmins

---

[2] Rice balls.

and family. He gives the gift of a white cow to the temple. The living have moved on. In the night, they bring back the First Born. You are nothing to us. Only half-blood. Do not come to the Baada again. I stand with the First Born and we watch them disappear in the corner of the street. Like a course of a river that turns, and doubles back and then flows again coming a full circle, like a single wave built by waves and waves after it, I move.

I travel through the galleries of memories, through echoing presences, through the festoons of milk coloured gratitude, through the domain of salt and birds and multiple moons. No shadow falls from my forehead. The path is filled with flowers, soft, fragrant and colourful. The canopy of fireflies are stars crowding the sky. I travel at the edge of thoughts, through the chaos of smiles and past the corridors of remembrance. My path of decentred circumferences, each step an intersection of a thousand suns, each point a thousand existence, I reach.

My search has come to an end. I am in Vaikuntha. I have the majestic, glorious Lord in front of me, sitting on His gilded throne with the poise of the Almighty.

Did you gain what you wanted from life? He asked. Affection and tenderness in his voice.

Your grace, I did.

And what was it that you wanted?

Just to be loved by her.

ACKNOWLEDGEMENTS

With deepest gratitude for:

Abhishek Kothari—you started this by connecting me to Dipankar

Tara Khandelwal and Bound India (www.boundindia.com)—where this manuscript was first read and feedback given

Rama Krishna Reddy—for being kind enough to connect me to Sarada

Sarada—for giving me insights of the culture of Andhra Pradesh/Telangana

Aruna Vasudevan—we missed the chance to work together but your feedback in structuring the manuscript was invaluable

Anil Menon—for an encouraging feedback on the manuscript

Mythrey Mukund— for an honest feedback and kind words

Indrani Ganguly—for being my gracious editor and for breathing soul into this manuscript

Dipankar Mukherjee—for being kind enough to accept this manuscript and for being there through the journey

And hugs for:

Deepti Rebecca

Abira Nayesa

Amaarya

Laika

Loki

You have helped me stay grounded and sane all through!

Thank you.

Dinesh Prasad
London, 2023

About the Author

Dinesh is the best-selling author of *East of Love West of Desire,* a collection of novellas on the partition of India, published in 2015. He writes short stories, poetry and novels. His writing is lyrical and rooted in the experiments in Magical realism, Surrealism and Romanticism. He writes everywhere—at the airports, in the trains, in the cabs and the buses while commuting to work or over the weekends and holidays.

Dinesh is an avid traveller, an amateur sommelier, a cook, a photographer, and a passionate reader. He listens to music while writing, his preferences being rock, jazz, classical, fusion, Bollywood etc.

Dinesh is an Engineering graduate from Jabalpur, India, and a post-graduate in management from the Indian Institute of Management, Ahmedabad. He enjoys working in the Information Technology industry in Analytics and Artificial Intelligence. Dinesh is based in London where he lives with his wife Deepti, children Abira and Amaarya, and dogs Laika and Loki.

Contact Dinesh at:

Email: laikalokiprasad@gmail.com
Facebook: https://www.facebook.com/dinesh.prasad
Instagram: @dinographia

Readomania

Readomania exists to nurture, curate, and bring to you content you love. We are a publishing house that takes pride in encouraging talent, new or old, and provides a wonderful platform for awesome stories.

We make this possible in multiple ways.

The first as an independent publishing house. Readomania boasts of multiple imprints across various categories—fiction, nonfiction, children, to name a few. An eclectic mix of content for its readers, when you read a Readomania title, you enter a world that's yours, supported by unique and quality narratives.

The second, as an online publishing platform for writers—a place to share stories, poems, opinions, travelogues, a way to explore your creative talent. Available as premium, as well as free-to-read content across multiple genres, the reader is spoilt for choice.

Join us in this journey, as we explore, develop, and present stories to our readers and audiences. Welcome to the world of Readomania, get ready to craft stories that enrich lives.

You can visit us at: www.readomania.com